Fanny Kemble

Further Records 1848-1883

A Series of Letters

Fanny Kemble

Further Records 1848-1883
A Series of Letters

ISBN/EAN: 9783744765534

Printed in Europe, USA, Canada, Australia, Japan

Cover: Foto ©Andreas Hilbeck / pixelio.de

More available books at **www.hansebooks.com**

FURTHER RECORDS.

1848—1883.

A SERIES OF LETTERS

BY

FRANCES ANNE KEMBLE,

FORMING

A Sequel to Record of a Girlhood

AND

Records of Later Life.

WITH TWO PORTRAITS ENGRAVED BY J. G. STODART.

VOL. II.

LONDON:

RICHARD BENTLEY AND SON,

Publishers in Ordinary to Her Majesty the Queen.

1890.

CONTENTS OF VOL. II.

vi

CONTENTS.

CONTENTS.

FURTHER RECORDS.

Lenox, August 2nd, **1876.**

MY DEAREST H——,

. . . Mr. L—— intends returning with his
wife and child to his own country in January, and I
at present purpose to accompany them. . . . One of
the livings offered him lately was at Stratford-on-
Avon, and I cannot help thinking what a delight it
would have been to me to sit in that church and
hear him preach opposite Shakespeare's monument.
This is the merest childishness, however; and I feel
very sure that the place he has accepted, which is in
the potteries, among a poor, abundant, hard-working
population, is far fitter for him. He has a special gift
for dealing with what are called *rough* people. His
first charge was at a place called Bromsgrove, among
a parcel of nail-makers, and he was deeply interested in
his work. I think his great physical strength, activity,
and dauntlessness combined, with his sweet face and
voice, and the gentle tenderness of his manner, have
an especial charm for hard-working, rude, uneculti-
vated people. He may well seem a sort of angel to

them. . . . He has admirable common sense, excellent
moral sense, great liberality of thought and sensibility
of feeling, and true sympathy with the poor and hard-
working folk of his country. . . . Nobody endures
hardship and privation with such sweet-tempered
equanimity, but I hardly know anybody who has a
keener relish for, or nicer perception of all the
luxuries of the highest civilization—the civilization
of Stoneleigh for, instance. But he is extremely well
pleased with the prospect of the order of work his
Staffordshire living will give him, and I am sure that
he will work well, and do good wherever he is. He
writes me word it has been too hot, and he has been
too lazy to answer my letters, and that he has been
lying in the hammock under the trees, *except* when he
has been *playing cricket*, with the thermometer nearer
one hundred than ninety.

The food I get, dear H——, is fairly good, the
bread is occasionally heavy and sour, and the milk
and cream very apt to be turned, but the eggs, butter,
meat and vegetables are all good, and there is a most
kindly desire in the house, both on the part of masters
and servants, to make me comfortable, and I am so in
all essential respects, and very much better than when
first I came up here, though I have had occasional
attacks of dyspepsia. . . .

Harriet Martineau came to America, after I had
been married two years, and made our acquaintance
and visited us repeatedly at Butler Place. She came
up here to Lenox, too, and stayed with Catherine
Sedgwick, of whom she was very fond, and who had
an immense admiration and enthusiasm for her. . . .

For some time we were upon cordial and even affectionate terms, and she always began her letters to me with "Dearest friend," but we gradually ceased to see each other, she being in England and I in America, our correspondence died away, and I think that I was not as thorough-going an abolitionist as the rest of the friends in América with whom she kept up her intercourse.

Good-bye, and God bless you, my dearest H——.

I am ever, as ever, yours,

FANNY KEMBLE.

Lenox, August 7th, 1876.

MY DEAREST H——

Yesterday the thermometer here stood at a hundred and two, at a place forty miles from here at a hundred and ten; and I tremble to think what all my children and F——'s poor little baby must have been suffering in that hideous oven, Philadelphia and its neighbourhood. . . . The L——s thought the great heat over, and were to return to York Farm the day before yesterday. I trust with all my heart they have not done so, for the heat here, for the last few days, has been more oppressive than at any time yet this summer, and I cannot imagine how they are to support it there without being all made ill by it. . . .

In your last letter you said you thought I had found an easy and pleasant way of meeting the sudden failure of my income. Easy, certainly in this respect, that the matter I publish was already prepared in manuscript, and needs only copious omissions to make it transferable at once to the printer's hands; but it is not *pleasant* to me for several reasons, though occasionally I receive notices of and remarks about it that do give me pleasure. For instance, I yesterday received a letter from a lady I have known for many years, who lives near New York, and whom I do not often see, who writes me, after thanking me *heartily* for the pleasure she and her family have had in reading my "Gossip," thus: "A dear old English lady, a neighbour of mine, eighty-seven years of age, reads it with the greatest interest. She saw Mrs. Siddons play Belvidera, when she was a girl, and takes much delight in all you describe. She has but one eye, and she is too deaf to hear me read it aloud, so she works it all out for herself, and we all thank you heartily for it." This kind account of the pleasure so old and infirm a person had found in reading what I had written was pleasant to me, but the publication is profitable, and in that sense *only* pleasurable to me. . . .

I have had a letter from M——, who speaks with great enthusiasm of George Trevelyan's life of Lord Macaulay, to which she and her sister had contributed so many of Macaulay's letters to their father, who was his dearest friend. I thought the book delightful, and it has been read with general interest and satisfaction in America. As soon as the extreme heat is over I shall go back to Branchtown.

Ever, as ever, yours,

FANNY.

Lenox, Berkshire, Massachusetts, August 18th, 1876.

I am very tolerably well just now, my dearest Harriet; and as to moving to some other place where I could "procure eatable food," I am quite as well in that respect as I should be *anywhere*, except in a large city. **Sour** heavy bread, or bread made light with soda salaratus (whatever that may be), and a dozen other messes, intended to do the work of kneading and yeast, are the universal resource of American bakers, whether private or professional. Sugar and treacle are also common ingredients in country bread, the people having a great liking for what they call *sweetning* in everything, and making all the pies and puddings uneatable to me with quantities of sugar. The milk and cream are almost always **sour**; the meat, even when not tough, naturally **difficult of** mastication for my teeth, **that rattle in their sockets** when I shake my head, and when I talk give me a castanet accompaniment. I am as well off here, in every particular, as I could be anywhere, where I had as good air and as little (comparative) heat. The place and neighbourhood are full of my friends and acquaintances, and the master of the inn and his wife have known me for more than forty years—ever since I first came up to Lenox—and are extremely kind and obliging, and desirous to make me comfortable. As for travelling in any direction, with a view to bettering myself, that would be sheer madness, as the fatigue and horrible heat would inevitably make me ill; and I am at present tolerably well, and shall stay where I am and endeavour to remain so, for, says the Italian gravestone, "Stava bene, per star meglio sto qui." I do not think my dear J——'s liking for a Georgia plantation life so strange as it appears to you. *I* was fascinated by the wild singular beauty of those sea islands, and the solitary, half-savage freedom of the life on those southern rivers and sounds; and, *but for the slavery*, should have enjoyed my existence there extremely. S——, when she came back this winter from visiting her sister, after her illness, said that the place and the life and the climate were all like an enchanting dream.

By this time you have received my letter telling you that Mr. L—— has accepted a living in Staffordshire, offered by his brother-in-law, Sir Charles Adderly, and that, after Christmas, he, F——, their baby, and I shall recross the Atlantic and return to England; they to settle in his new field of duty and occupation, and I, I trust in God, to spend some weeks with you, my dearest Harriet. Amen.

Ever, as ever, yours,

FANNY.

Boston, September 3rd, 1876.

MY BELOVED HARRIET,

Your letters had better now be again directed to Branchtown, for, even when I am staying at Champlost, that is the best and quickest way of reaching me now that I have left Lenox.

My plans were all overturned, and I was compelled to give up my rooms there at a few days' notice, by a mistake in the arrangement when they were taken. The hotel-keeper understood me to have retained them only for two months, and immediately gave the pro-

spective reversion of them to other people, for whom
I was obliged to vacate them. This has occasioned
me a good deal of inconvenience and annoyance, especially in the inevitable uncertainty and confusion
of all my plans. Moreover, I am afraid you will be
without any letter from me a longer time than usual,
because packing **up and** departing suddenly in this
way, and travelling from place to place are, of course,
impediments to correspondence.

I left **Lenox last** Thursday in terrible heat. I looked
my last with very tender affection at the lovely country
we drive through for six miles, from the village **to the**
station, where I take the **railroad.** Of **course it** is
possible that I may live to return **to** see **it** again, but
very highly improbable, **and so I looked my** farewell
at it. I have enjoyed its improved beauty and **in-**
creased cultivation **and** agricultural prosperity extremely this summer. It will **become** more and more
attractive and charming **with time,** for the natural
features of the landscape cannot be spoiled, and will
admit of infinite improvement from tasteful cutting
and planting of trees and general cultivation.

The heat on the journey from Lenox to Boston was
terrible; and Friday, the day after our **arrival** here, **I**
suffered more than I have done on **any** day yet through
this whole dreadful summer.

Some time ago **I** commissioned **a** Boston friend of
mine to have a stone placed on my aunt's grave in the
Boston cemetery, at Mount Auburn, and **went** with
him to see that my instructions had been carried
out.

When first I came to Boston, forty years ago, Mount

Auburn was a wild and very picturesque piece of irregular ground, covered with the native forest, and where only here and there a monument glimmering through the woodland attested the purpose to which it was dedicated. When I was engaged to be married, —— and I used to ride out there and sit together under a group of trees on a pretty hillside, where the prospect over the country was very charming. I chose this spot for D——'s burial-place, and she was laid there; and I intended to put a memorial-stone over it, having it originally only turfed over and hedged around with sweetbrier. My unsettled, wandering life prevented my carrying out this purpose, till I gave the necessary directions last year, and the day before yesterday went to see how they had been fulfilled.

The whole place was a *marble wilderness* of tombstones and monuments and mausoleums—terrace upon terrace rising all over the hill, glaring with marble pillars, tablets, pyramids, columns, sarcophagi—a perfect stone labyrinth set in a flaming framework of the only flowers now in proper bloom here, scarlet geranium, scarlet salvia, and yellow calceolaria; and this, under the fiercest blaze of sunlight I ever endured, was really the most terribly suggestive place of *rest* for the dead that I ever saw.

The cutting up and dividing the cemetery for the occupation of its now immense population of sleeping inhabitants had so altered the aspect of the place, that I did not hope to recognize the precise spot I was seeking; but while, with map in hand and the number of the "lot" in his memorandum-book, our guide, one of the custodians of the place, was making out the

precise spot, I recognized the hillside and crest of trees
where I used to come, and walked through the perfect lanes of memorial-stones and *edifices* to my dear
D——'s grave.

The inevitable emotion occasioned by the associations of the place, and the oppression of the terrific
heat, quite knocked me up, and all day yesterday I
suffered from the fatigue and excitement of the expedition.

I really do not think that so trying a climate as
this exists in any other part of the world. Friday, as
I tell you, was hot enough literally to *kill* people; in
the evening it rained violently; the next day, yesterday, it blew a sort of furious hot hurricane, that all
but took the pedestrians in the streets off their feet,
last night it turned cold, and this morning the whole
ground was white snow and hoar-frost. One had need
have the strength of iron and the elasticity of gutta-
percha to endure it.

This afternoon I am going to see a very dear
friend of mine, whom I have known ever since she
was a schoolgirl, when I (myself little more) came
here to act with my father, when she used to hang
wreaths of flowers on the handle of the door of my
room, in the hotel where I lodged. . . .

I shall only be a day or two in Boston, and have
only time to see a few of my most intimate friends,
whom I do not expect to have a chance of taking
leave of before I return to England.

I should not, indeed, have remained here another
day, but that there is just a possibility of my grandson being able to stop and breakfast with me on his

way to his school at Concord, which lies beyond
Boston.   As soon as I have had this glimpse of him,
I shall turn towards my children and M. F——.   I
cannot go to any of them, because Champlost and
York Farm are both full; but I would rather be in
a hotel in Philadelphia, twenty minutes rail of them,
than anywhere else.   As for going to Butler Place,
poor S—— may be without servants, and without
food, for what I can tell; and I could not propose myself to her at the risk of doubling all her usual household tribulations by doing so. . . .

The whole country has been suffering dreadfully
from drought, and is burned to a cinder.   In Lenox
there has been no rain for six weeks, and even the
hillsides, fed with innumerable springs, were beginning to look baked and dried up.   People's wells were
giving out everywhere, and this frequently pre-
monitory symptom of earthquakes, combined with
the extraordinary heat of the weather, suggests some
violent paroxysm of the elements as the climax of
this abnormal atmospheric condition.

God bless you, my dear H——.   I must get ready
to go out.

Ever, as ever, yours,
FANNY KEMBLE.

Champlost, September 20th, 1876.

MY DEAR HARRIET,

Mr. L—— is gone to Boston to endeavour to
negotiate with some merchant there for the sale of
their rice crop, direct from the plantation, without the
intermediate expense and difficulty of agents and

factors; indeed, at present any such intermediate processes are entirely out of the question, as the Butler Island rice has always been sent for sale to agents in Savanah, and that unfortunate place is at present a prey to the yellow fever, and, of course, all communication between it and other places is entirely cut off. The rice crop on Butler's Island Plantation has been remarkably fine this year, and a large return may be expected from it. The orange crop has been injured by some of the strange vagaries of the weather, by which the trees received some damage, after they had put forth unusually abundant blossoms, and it is feared that the yield will be very much less than last year, which I am sorry for, both because it was a very profitable crop, and also because it is such magnificent fruit of its kind, that it is delightful to think of the splendid abundance of such a harvest of it as there was last season; nowhere here have I ever seen oranges comparable to them in size or flavour, they really were like fruits of paradise with their royal colour and delicious fragrance.

Of my dear M——, about whom you ask so many questions, I do not care to say much, only this much— her extraordinary power of *will* and indomitable determination of character, and her unwearied, incessant, generous, kindly interest in and thought and exertion for and about others, seem to me to supply the whole vital energy of her tiny, delicate, fragile frame. She is the bravest and the best little lady that ever lived, and one of the loftiest spirits withal. . . .

Dear H——, how infinitely blessed I have been in the *nobility* of my friends. To have been loved by such people seems to me almost enough to have made one good, alas! . . .

M—— is as light and quick in her movements as a bird, and while I sit *solidly* by the hour together stitching, reading, or writing, she flits and flutters in and out, and to and fro, now with a handful of fresh flowers, and now with a basket full of fresh fruit, finding endless errands all day long of courtesy, kindness, or charity, about her house and her gardens and her grounds.

Of myself I can give you a very good account. . . . I have nothing to complain of but the loss of one of my large front teeth, which fell out last night for sheer weariness of its existence, small blame to it. The departure of this *tusk* is really a great relief to me, for it had come down from its socket till I looked like one of the three fabled cabirü of Samothrace, who had got and kept possession of the solitary tooth they owned amongst them, and it shook and rattled in my mouth, so that I felt as if I was talking to a castanet accompaniment. I am very glad it is gone, and

I am ever, as ever, (not tooth),

FANNY.

Champlost, September 26th, **1876.**

MY DEAREST H——,

We are all in great distress about the outbreak of yellow fever in Savanah and Brunswick, Georgia. F—— and S—— have many acquaintances and some friends in both places, some of whom they know have been attacked by the malady, and about all of whom, of course, they feel the most painful anxiety. Brunswick is a miserably poor little seaport town, close to the rice plantation, and there the epidemic is raging in the most horrible manner; six hundred of the inhabitants, of whom there are not in all three thousand, being at present reported as attacked by the fever. F——, besides the distress of imagining so wretched a condition in the little place, with which she is so familiar, has been much troubled lest her agent and overseer should be among the unfortunate victims. This morning she luckily heard from one who was well, and reports his colleague as having also hitherto escaped the infection. Money and medicine, and physicians and nurses, have all been sent down to the succour of the poor pest-seized cities, but the only hope of any effectual check to the plague is in the arrival of cold weather—frost —and that seldom occurs in Georgia before the second week in November, and there is yet at least a month in which this luckless city may be liable to this terrible scourge. Of course, much apprehension is felt lest the dreadful malady should break out here, where at present the Centennial Exhibition is drawing such an immense concourse of people.

M—— and I are going to a party given by our old friends and neighbours, Mr. and Mrs. W——. They are both quite old people, and this is the fiftieth anniversary of their wedding-day, what is called here their golden wedding. As they are among the oldest friends I have in this country, and they have also been extremely kind and affectionate friends to my children ever since they were born, we are all going; but as they have asked four hundred people, a very considerable number of whom will certainly accept the invitation, we are rather in a state of trepidation as to the crowd we shall encounter, and how we shall get to and from the carriage, etc., the grounds of the house and approach to it not being very spacious or commodious for such an occasion, and every man in this country, and, what is more, every coachman, being his own policeman.

A curious direction was put on the cards of invitation issued for this festivity. At the bottom of the usual form of desiring the pleasure of So-and-So's company, etc., and specifying the hour at which guests would be expected, there were a couple of words printed in a line by themselves—" No presents." It seems that on the fiftieth anniversary, or golden wedding, of a married couple here, it has been a frequent custom for every friend invited to give them some token of regard *in gold*. Mr. and Mrs. W——, many of whose friends and relations could not well afford such a proof of their regard, have taken this method of preventing any such tribute from their guests. I think they are very right, and their manner of doing so, though looking rather strange on their invitation cards, very sensible.

Good-bye, my dearest friend, God bless you. How thankful I am that you can still find satisfaction in my letters.

Ever, as ever, yours,

FANNY.

York Farm, Branchtown, Philadelphia,
Monday, October 2nd, 1876.

M DEAREST H——,

I left Champlost and my dear friend, M—— F—— this morning, to come and take up my abode once more in this former little home of mine. I was grieved to take leave of Champlost, which is a charming place, of which I am very fond, where I shall, in all human probability, never *stay* again, though I shall constantly walk over there of a morning, and have promised M—— to keep up my practice of dining with her every Monday, as long as I remain in America. I left my dear friend, too, with profound regret, for though we shall meet constantly until I leave the country, we shall certainly have no such season of uninterrupted intercourse as we have had while I have been staying with her for the last three weeks. In spite of the regret with which I left Champlost, I am very glad to be here with my children, and am delighted to be under the same roof with my baby Alice. The little house looks cheerful and pleasant and homelike, and F—— had filled the rooms with charming flowers as a welcome home to me.

Mr. L—— has been very much interested in a cricket match between English and Americans. He played himself, and was very eager about the success of his countrymen. F—— drove over to the cricket-ground to see them play ; but I was too unwell to go, and spent the afternoon in the garden here, with my little grandchild, who, dragging a toy cart herself full of walnuts she had picked up, employed me to drag

another and a toy horse, neither of which performances
were quite as easy to me as to her. . . . The poor
little child is looking unusually pale and ghostlike,
and I am afraid to-morrow she will be very likely to
be quite ill, for this morning she got hold of a basket
of pears, set to ripen in the sun in the greenhouse,
and before any one was aware of what she was doing,
she had bitten *one mouthful* out of at least a dozen of
them.

S—— came in for a few minutes this morning, and
Dr. W—— this evening, when F—— and her husband
came home from the cricket-ground. They brought
news of the victory of the English over the American
players, with which they were both much pleased.
S—— had asked me to go to the International Exhibition, but I could not undergo the fatigue, which is
very great, of walking about and standing in such a
vast crowd of people, so she gave up going and came
over on horseback to the cricket-ground. . . .

Dear H——, this letter has been three days writing,
with constant interruptions to prevent my finishing
it. We are all quite unwell with violent colds—my
dear J—— with a sore chest, and I with a sore throat.
The sudden changes of the weather from heat to cold,
and now constant violent rains, are affecting the
general health very unfavourably, and there is a great
deal of sickness, pneumonia and diphtheria especially,
about. From the South the accounts of the ravages
of the yellow fever are terrible. Savanah, the capital
of Georgia, has had a frightful visitation of it, and so
has the little town of Brunswick, which is quite near
Butler's Island, and the only effectual stop to that

terrible pest is a sharp frost, and the setting in of cold weather, which cannot, unfortunately, be looked for in Georgia before the second week in November.

I went over this morning and sat an hour with S——, who, while she arranged flowers in her drawing-room vases, talked to me a great deal about the exhibition, which she visited constantly during all the heat of the summer with her boy, who was enchanted with it, and spent the greater part of his holidays there.

Good-bye, dearest H——. God bless you.

I am ever, as ever, yours,

FANNY.

York Farm, **Branchtown**, *Philadelphia*,
Tuesday, October 10th, **1876.**

MY BELOVED H——,

I have been a longer time than usual without writing to you, having been unwell and almost stupefied with a heavy influenza, in which half the world here is drowned. Dr. W—— says, and I am sure he is right, that it is really a form of the cattle plague. I remember perfectly when that prevailed in England, what a dreadful form of influenza, as it was called, was prevalent at the same time ; and I am sure what we have all been suffering from here is identical with that—such running in streams from the eyes and noses, such heavy headache and oppression in the breathing, such sore throats and chests, and shouting sneezes and shattering coughs, such pains in the back and loins and utter prostrations of strength, to which I added neuralgic pains in every one of my remaining teeth, dyspeptic **pain in my** breast whenever I ate or **drank,** and rheumatic **pain all over me** whenever I **moved. I am** happy to say **I am nearly** recovered now **from this** painful state, and am only **in the** disgusting **dregs** of the malady, coughing loudly **and** loosely at all'inopportune instances, and using only seven pockethandkerchiefs a day, so that I am quite convalescent. S——and **her husband, and** F—— and Mr. L—— have **all had their visitation;** and when I returned among **them were all still** suffering from it, and, of course, I **took it** directly. **To-day** E—— **has** begun to sniffle **and sneeze,** and **the poor dear little baby** appears to **have taken the infection too.** . . .

I look over, even as I write **to you, my dearest friend, to the** trees of Butler **Place, all glorious in their autumn** gold, and think of **my former hours there. I was** about **to call them evil, but withhold the word ;** and I feel an **impulse to** prostrate myself **in** thanksgiving **to God,** who has vouchsafed me such **a** blessed close **to my** struggling and tempestuous life. How **unutterably thankful** I feel for His great mercies !

I have been walking over to my dear M—— this morning, **but did not** find her at home. The walk itself is very charming—along **our farm** road, through fields cleared of their crops, **the** Indian corn alone **still** standing **in** yellow shocks in one of them, the apple trees now shedding their yellow leaves upon the **few** ruddy apples forgotten **at** their feet. At the end of this lane is a sloping **field, now cleared of** its crop, **which I cross** diagonally **to a passage,** left expressly for **me, in** the fence ; a few steps down another field, and then across the railroad, which here divides

Champlost from York Farm; then through a charming bit of oak woodland, with some noble trees, to a
tiny bright brook in the hollow of the wood; and up
a steepish footpath between the oaks to a small, heavy
swing-gate; down and up the steep side of a mimic
ravine, across the runlet of clear water; and then
through another gate on to the lawn, and under the
groups of charming tulip poplars which surround the
house to my friend's door. I do not think the distance
is a mile; and to-day, in beautiful, bright, breezy sunshine the walk was delightful. The colouring of the
woods is now in its autumnal magnificence; but the
glory and splendid loveliness of the sky is a thousand
times more wonderful. God bless you, my dearest
H——. Good-bye.

Ever, as ever, yours,

FANNY.

York Farm, Branchtown, Philadelphia,
Sunday, *October 15th,* **1876.**

MY DEAREST H——,

It is many days since I have seen E——'s
handwriting, and I am beginning to feel anxious lest
you should be ill again. I wrote to you a few days
ago, and was then without tidings from you. I hope
to-morrow will bring me a letter, for I am unhappy
about you, my dearest friend, and long to know how
you are faring. When last I wrote to you I had been
suffering for a week from a violent influenza, to which
every human being in this neighbourhood has been a
victim. I have not been able to throw it off; but, on
the contrary, seem to take fresh relays of it every few

days, and am now perfectly miserable with it. The
weather we are having now, however, is enough to
account for any amount of sickness; yesterday evening
the thermometer, which the evening before marked
forty degrees, rose suddenly to fifty-seven, with no
more than our usual fires. Our rooms were intolerably
hot, and we went to bed complaining of the oppres-
siveness of the weather. Before midnight we were
indulged with repeated peals of thunder; and then in
the morning when we got up the ground was white
with snow. Just imagine our dismay and astonishment! I do not think there is such another climate
in the world; and all this time the beauty and splendour
of the autumnal woods and skies are as indescribable as
the harsh capriciousness of the atmosphere. Of course,
no constitution can be subjected to such sudden violent
alternations of temperature without suffering from
them; and I begin to think that my cough and cold
will last me through the winter. I perceive the effect
of the southern climate on F—— and Mr. L——,
in their greater sensitiveness to the comparatively
moderate degree of cold which we have hitherto had.
They have already as many fires in the house as I had
all through the severest cold of the winter, and I really
wonder what they will do in December. The baby, at
present, does not seem to suffer from the change of
climate. . . .

S—— still continues her almost daily visits to the
International Exhibition. Her interest in it has been
so great, and her attendance there so constant, that I
really do not know what she will find to fill her time
and give her occupation and amusement when it closes.

The generally sober, orderly, decent, decorous, and good-tempered demeanour of the vast multitudes who visit the exhibition, and the intelligent interest and curiosity they exhibit, seem to me by far the most noteworthy features of the whole thing, and to speak more highly for the progress of civilization in this country than all their display of manufacturing skill and all their wonderfully beautiful and ingenious machinery. Of course you know that they have long had admirable sewing-machines; they have now invented a darning-machine, which surely will be the means of lightening many a poor woman's wearisome work over the stockings and socks of her husband and children. I think you will be amused when you hear what my latest occupation has been in the literary line—writing, or rather beginning to write, the libretto of an opera, at the request of my grandson, who is composing the music for it. He has chosen the subject himself—a pretty fairy story—and told me how he wishes it treated; and I am accordingly *working* at it *under* his directions, which I think is, at any rate, showing an amiable desire to please, in faculties grown stiff with nearly seventy years' wear and tear—used, disused, and misused.

God bless you. I hope I shall get a letter from you to-morrow.

Ever, as ever, yours,
FANNY.

York Farm, Branchtown, Philadelphia,
Tuesday, November 14th, 1876.

My dearest H——,

I am rejoicing extremely for S——'s sake in the recall of Sir Anthony M—— from his Australian government, and his appointment to Jamaica; which brings his wife, S——'s dear and charming friend, formerly Miss F——, within a few days' sail of the United States. I do not know whether you recollect a young lady who travelled in Switzerland with me one year, a person to whom S—— is extremely attached, who is full of admirable qualities, the possibility of personal intercourse with whom will be an immense pleasure and benefit to my dear S——, and will come most providentially to make up to her for the void occasioned by her sister's and my departure. I have not been so happy at any circumstance for a long time. Lady M—— is a particularly *wholesome* friend. She is very well informed, intelligent, and clever; and has a most equable, sweet, serene temper, and cheerful, happy temperament, and I am most thankful to think that S—— and she will be sure to meet before long and pass some time together. Lady M—— is a daughter of Mr. Dudley F——, of New York, and will come probably to visit her father and family, in the United States, on her way to Jamaica.

Good-bye, and God bless you, my dearest H——.

Ever, as ever, yours,

Fanny.

York Farm, Branchtown, Philadelphia,
Sunday, November 26th, 1876.

MY DEAREST H——,

Algernon Sartoris and his wife, after whom you inquire, came over to America a short time before my sister went abroad. They expect to stay here till the spring. Mrs. Algernon is to be confined some time in the winter. They had some thoughts of taking a house in Philadelphia for a few months, but I do not know whether they have determined to do so yet. Of course, in Washington, the young lady is at home in the President's house; but she has a great many friends here in Philadelphia, and I rather think Algernon himself does not particularly enjoy residing with the *famille* Grant.

Dr. Wister, like everybody else in this country, is intensely interested in its present political condition. I suppose that the course he has taken in this election will be that of a great many honest men, who have hitherto belonged to the republican party. Also, all through the war, his sympathies were entirely with the northern—that is, the republican party—and he has voted with them ever since the recent maladministration of the American Government; and the desperate rascality of many of the political republican leaders is such, that honest men of their own side prefer voting for the democratic candidate, Mr. Tilden, even to seeing the republican, Hayes, elected, because, although the latter is a perfectly honest, upright, worthy man, his coming into power might not displace the whole army of those who have filled all the public offices, and governed the government ever since

the inauguration of General Grant, because they are
the republican state machinery, and the republican
president may find it impossible to break up the
immensely strong organization which such a body of
office-holders spread all over the country and working
together to maintain themselves and each other in
place constitutes. Many honest republicans, therefore, like Dr. Wister, have voted for the democratic
president, Mr. Tilden, thinking him more likely to be
able to carry through immediate sweeping reforms,
such as are needed, than his opponent.

My dearest H——, you speak of your rapidly
diminishing brain power, and I suppose at your age,
and under your circumstances, the mental powers
must necessarily diminish in vigour and activity. . . .
So, by the time we meet, I shall perhaps be a match
for your own estimate of your own stupidity, and, if
so, my dear friend, it will be the first time in all our
long intercourse of many years that there has been an
approach to mental equality between us.

I suppose you know that as yet it is not publicly
proclaimed who really *is* the President elect. The
contest has been so close, and the returns from the
remoter parts of the Union so difficult to obtain, the
frauds and dishonest practices on both sides so patent,
that at this moment *one vote* will turn the scale.
Nothing positive can be ascertained how that vote (of
a state—Florida) has gone. There is no doubt that the
question will have to come before Congress, as to who
is really, legally, elected President; and I think the
great probability is that it will prove to be the
democrat, Mr. Tilden. The public excitement is

intense; and, in spite of the personal interest felt by every voter in the land, and the keen party spirit, the quiet, patient, temperate, good-humoured good sense and forbearance of the people is marvellous.

God bless you, **dear**.

Ever, as ever, yours,

FANNY.

York Farm, Branchtown, Philadelphia,
Sunday, December 17th, 1876.

MY DEAREST H——,

I have just had a fright and distress upon a small subject which, while it lasted, was poignant enough to wring the tears from my eyes. A little canary-bird, which my grandson Owen gave me a year ago last Christmas, escaped from his cage and flew out of window, and though the sun was shining brilliantly and I have no doubt the first rush into the open air was a delirium of ecstasy, the cold is intense, the thermometer standing at only eight degrees above zero, so the poor little wretch could not have failed to be frozen to death very soon. I was therefore much relieved when he was captured and brought back alive from Butler Place, whither he had flown, but so exhausted, either with its unaccustomed flight or numbed with the bitter cold, that he alighted on one of the gravel walks and allowed himself to be taken. You know I have always been fond of these little birds, and almost always had one. Their shrill, brilliant singing is not disagreeable to me, as it is to some people, and there is something cheerful to me in the wiry patter of their little claws on their perches;

and the volume of sound they pour forth from their tiny throats has never ceased to be a subject of astonishment and admiration to me. This particular bird is a particularly fine singer, having a sweeter and more mellow note than almost any canary I ever heard. Besides my value for him as Owen's gift, I have tended the little creature with my own hands for two years, and am greatly relieved to think that he is not to freeze to death in this pitiless cold. . . .

Mr. L—— writes cheerfully from the South. The rice crop has been the finest gathered on the estate for many years, and, that being the case, it is rather hard that the price of the grain itself has fallen lower than it ever has, under the combined unfavourable influence of general bad times and scarcity of money and the miserable political excitement of this presidential election, of which Charlestown, the principal rice market of the United States, is now a flaming focus.

York Farm, Branchtown, Philadelphia,
December 23rd, 1876.

My beloved H——,

Christmas is upon us, which must be made cheerful for our children and servants, and so the rooms are strewn with paper parcels, packages, presents, and all the indescribable confusions of the garniture of a Christmas-tree, a pretty piece of German Christmas joy which has taken root here and become quite an American institution, with all the profuse love of ornament, and bon-bons, and toys, and trinkets, and magnificent presents that Americans of all ages delight in. Yesterday evening Owen came home from school. He did **not** arrive until past nine, having travelled sixteen hours from **his** hyperborean seat of learning at Concord, in New Hampshire. **F—— and** I went over to sup with him. Coming away, I and Dr. W——, who was holding me, both slipped down the broad doorsteps of the piazza (Anglice, verandah), four of them, which were entirely coated with ice, **and sat ourselves down on the** gravel walk at the bottom of them, which **was** also one smooth sheet of **ice, and there we sat** laughing, so that **neither of us could get** up again **or** render the slightest assistance to the other, while S—— and F—— and young Owen **stood at the** top, afraid to set their feet on **the treacherous** steps, lest they should fall headlong **upon us,** crying out, "Oh, mother! oh, Owen! are **you hurt?"** and then shrieking with laughter **at our** absurd appearance as we sat opposite each other on the ice.

Between the Owens, father and son, **I was** got on my feet again at last and **led to** the carriage, and F——, with frightful slipping, sliding, sliddering, ejaculations and exclamations, was brought after me, **and we got** safely home, but anything so frightfully dangerous **as** the whole surface of the ground, paved with ice as hard and clear as crystal, and just powdered over with treacherous snow, you cannot imagine. It is as much as one's **life is** worth almost to walk a dozen steps in any direction. The trees, trunks, boughs, branches, every smallest stem and twig, are entirely coated with translucent ice, which glitters **like** silver with the **most** blinding brightness in the sun, and rattles **in** the wind as if they were made of metal, and is so heavy that the trees are bowed like great fountains by it, and every now and then some huge limb, weighed down by its beautiful heavy icy coating, breaks off, and strews the ground with perfect heaps of glittering icicles and a dazzling ruin as if a thousand chandeliers had been smashed in the road. It is magnificent!

God bless you, dear. I hope soon to hear from you; and I hope, oh, how I hope, soon to see you.

Ever, as ever, yours,

FANNY.

York Farm, Branchtown, Philadelphia,
Sunday, December 24th, 1876.

MY DEAREST H——,

I have just come back from church, whither I had intended walking; but the road is so frightfully dangerous—one sheet of glaring ice, with the thinnest sprinkling of snow over it—that I was warned by my family that I must not attempt to go even the short quarter of a mile distance; so S—— came in a sleigh for me, and F—— slipped, and slid, and skated, and scrambled, with the help of young Owen, who is now a stalwart man, nearly six feet high, and broad in proportion, and a cousin, a tall lad of the same age, of whom they are all very fond, and with this goodly escort she got safe to church. I am now sitting writing to you while mounting guard over a mocking-bird F—— has brought me from Georgia, which is out of his cage. I generally allow him a walk about my room on Sunday, while his cage is being cleaned; but he is never in any hurry to get back to it, and I sometimes sit more than an hour, waiting till it **suits** him to resume his captivity.

Our preparations **for** Christmas **are** rendered quite elaborate by the American passion for interchanging gifts. For a whole **week** before Christmas Day a stream **of** paper parcels, boxes full of bon-bons, baskets full **of** flowers, pour in and out of every house; and the **laborious** preparations **for** magnificent Christmas-trees make the enjoyment of the children a really severe labour to the parents and elders.

We are all unhappy at Mr. L——'s not being here to-morrow. He is away on the plantation, and will have a day of solitude, enlivened only by his church services and whatever festivities he may be able to give the negroes for the cheerful celebration of the day. He will not return till after the New Year.

God bless you, my dearest H——. In a month's time we sail for England. God grant me the happiness of embracing you once more.

Ever, as ever, yours,
FANNY.

York Farm, Branchtown, Philadelphia,
Christmas Day, 1876.

MY DEAREST H——,

You say you have not heard from me for a fortnight; and it is full a fortnight since I received your last letter. The winter weather is retarding the passage of the steamers across the Atlantic, and it is supposed the furious winds we have had here inland must have been felt at some distance along this coast, at any rate. I have been anxious about you, fearing

you were ill; but to-day's post brought tidings. To-day
has been a day of such confusion, as makes part of the
very enjoyment of children and young people, but it is
in itself a fatigue to older ones. At eight o'clock this
morning the interchange of presents between our houses
began; and I saw from my dressing-room window,
with dismay, the young man-servant, who was carrying
a dozen of wine over to Dr. Wister from me, slip on
the glare of ice, which literally sheets the gateways
of both our places. There is a slight descent from
each entrance to the main road that divides the two
properties, and they are literally like two inclined
planes of looking-glass. Luckily, though the lad who
was carrying the wine slipped, he did not quite fall or
let the basket drop, but my heart was in my mouth
for a moment, for I thought a dozen of precious
Château Yquem had gone to ice in an unprofitable
way. Our house is literally fragrant with roses and
heliotropes and carnations. The enormous sums of
money spent by people here in cut flowers, nosegays,
and baskets full of them is quite incredible. The
flowers are forced to such a degree, that they hardly
survive a single day, though put into water, and taken
the utmost care of, and the plants from which they are
cut are so ruined by this forced flowering, that they
are absolutely exhausted, and good for nothing when
the summer, their natural time for blossoming, comes.
I could not have believed it possible that flowers
could have been made vulgar, but the Americans
have contrived to do that with their profuse and
costly extravagance and ostentation in their use of
them, as one of their own women, the least vulgar

human being I have ever known, once said to me. F—— came home the other day from a dinner-party, (mind, close upon Christmas), with a nosegay of white rosebuds in one hand, and a wreath of pink roses in the other; another day she returned with two glass slippers (the pair of which Cinderella lost one, you remember), full of rare hothouse flowers which had been among the dinner-table ornaments. The luxury and display in the houses of rich people on a special "company occasion" is a curious contrast to the general discomfort in all the details of daily life. It is altogether anomalous and unpleasant.

My little granddaughter Alice had such a profusion of toys given to her, that one good-sized table was covered with them. In the afternoon, her mother had a very fine Christmas-tree for her, and all the little farmer's and gardener's children on the two places were invited to it; they were one and all Irish, and I must say did credit to their descent, for I never saw a stouter, finer, rosier dozen of children. . . .

To-morrow there is a Christmas-tree at Champlost, for M——'s servants and dependents, to which she has asked us and several of our household, and when that is over, every one's energies among us will have to be devoted to packing up and preparing for our departure, an event the near approach of which is becoming most depressing to me.

The presidential election, about which you ask me if I feel any interest, is a most extraordinary result of universal suffrage. The two candidates are so nearly in possession of the same number of votes, and on both sides such frauds and illegal practices have been resorted to, that it is really next to impossible to say who positively has the majority of votes. I heard a most curious story this evening upon the intimidation to which the negro voters had been subjected in some places in the South. Though very few of them indeed are African born, almost the entire black population of the States being native Americans, they retain, nevertheless, the traditions of the African Obi-worship in a great many curious forms of what they consider of evil omen, unlucky, *uncanny.* The white inhabitants of the southern states are well aware of these superstitious terrors of the blacks, and on the day of the election secured the absence of the negroes from the polls by sending grotesquely dressed-up men to tie various coloured ribbons round the liberty-masts erected at the booths, where the voting-tickets were taken. These incomprehensible, mysterious signals were considered by all the negroes what they called *Obi,* and they were effectually scared from voting by them.

Good-bye, dearest H——. My thoughts fly over the Atlantic to you, and, skipping my passage across it, land me once more in Ireland, and fill me with the hope of once more seeing you. God so grant it.

Ever, as ever, yours,
FANNY.

York Farm, Branchtown, Philadelphia,
December 31st, 1876.

MY BELOVED H——,

Here is the last day of the year, and to-morrow begins the month the end of which will see us on our way to England. It is no great wonder if our letters have been delayed in crossing the Atlantic, for the weather has been unusually tempestuous, and we hear of violent hurricanes encountered by the ships, and storms of unusual severity, and the steamers have made slower passages, and of course the mails are retarded and come irregularly.

The steamer in which our passages are taken, has, however, been a remarkable exception in this respect. *Britannic* is her name, and she crossed this way in seven days and sixteen hours, and went home the last time in seven days and thirteen hours. We shall be a large party returning, as we were coming out. Mr. L——, F——, myself, and the baby, Ellen, the child's nurse, our little English cook, who came out with us, and a young negro servant lad from the plantation. The man-servant who went home to visit his parents last summer is to come and meet me at Queenstown, and take charge of me and Ellen, as the L——s, of course, go straight on to Liverpool.

You ask me how I mean to carry on the publication of my articles in the *Atlantic Magazine* when I leave America ; but I do not intend to carry them on. The editor proposed to me to do so, but I thought it would entail so much trouble and uncertainty in the transmission of manuscript and proofs, that it would be better to break off when I came to Europe. The editor will have manuscript enough for the February, March, and April numbers when I come away, and with those I think the series must close. As there is no narrative or sequence of events involved in the publication, it can, of course, be stopped at any moment ; a

story without an end can end anywhere. I shall be
sorry to lose the very considerable addition it made to
my income, but living in England is much cheaper
than living in America, and I can much better spare
three hundred pounds from my yearly income there
than I could here, when that loss fell upon me.

We are all, of course, in much confusion with all
the first preparations for departure. . . . We are
expecting Mr. L—— back from the South in a few
days, and this chapter of my life is drawing very near
its close. I am thankful that my last hours in America
will be spent in the house that was my only married
home in this country, under whose roof my children
were born.

God bless you, dearest dear H——. It seems
wonderful to believe how soon I may see you again.

Ever, as ever, yours,
FANNY.

Butler Place, January 7th, 1877.

I trust in God we shall meet again before long, and
I look to many hours spent with you during my
month's stay in Dublin, in which I hope my voice will
reach you in reading and talking, and the consciousness of my proximity will be a comfort and pleasure
to you and some relief to your devoted nurse. I need
all the hope that my coming to you may be some
alleviation to the dreariness of your darkened life, to
help me to bear the heavy sadness of my parting with
the many good and kind friends I have in this country.

We are all pretty well, and all bent upon being
cheerful and courageous in view of our approaching

separation. . . . I am still lame from the effect of our overturn, from which, fortunately, S—— received no injury, but as I am merely badly bruised, outwardly and inwardly, and am gradually recovering from the effects of the accident, I feel only inclined to rejoice at the insignificant damage I have sustained from what might have been a serious disaster. . . .

An American woman's dress is never regulated by any consideration whatever but the money she can afford to spend on it; and, I am sorry to say, by no means always by that. My daughters, in common with all their countrywomen, think *no* articles of clothing can be obtained so good, so cheap, or so tasteful as those found in Paris; . . . and I dare say, as regards the elegance and cheapness, they are right. . . . I retained that result of my semi-French blood and education, that I do think French women the best dressers in the world, and while one is spending money in necessary clothes, I think it quite worth while to get them as elegant and agreeable to one's taste as can be managed for the price one gives.

I think you are mistaken in supposing that this country will split up into separate confederacies. In spite of its vast size and various populations, the feeling of national pride in the enormous extent and unlimited resources of the country will, I believe, hold its parts coherently together in a bond, the strength of which will, for many years to come, resist the strain of any merely sectional interest however strong. The whole attitude and temper of the *people* (not the *politicians*) from north to south and east to west of the Union, during these late troubled and difficult times, has been so admirably temperate, patient, reasonable and law abiding, that in this crucial test of a nation's moral capacity for self-government they have certainly come out triumphantly. In the process of altering and improving the machinery of their elective system, I have no doubt at all that they will give proof of sufficient wisdom in time. In the meantime, I feel sure that they will struggle out of their present imbroglio with less damage than any one who is not here to watch the course of events could believe possible.

Good-bye, my dearest H——, God bless you. I trust ere many days to see you once more, my best beloved friend.

Ever, as ever, yours,
FANNY KEMBLE.

P. S.—We sail on the 20th. God willing, we may reach Queenstown about the 28th. Please get some lodgings for me *near you.*

Butler Place, January 8th, 1877.

MY DEAREST H——,

It is very unlucky that just at this moment, when there are so many last things to do and to attend to, and when I wish to be as strong and well as possible for the inevitable wretchedness of my winter sea voyage, I have met with an accident, which for the present has made me lame. S—— and I were overturned in a sleigh the other day. She was not hurt, luckily, but I fell under her, and she is very heavy, upon the stones in the street, and I have remained crippled ever since, from some internal jar or contusion, which at first made me almost unable to move my legs at all. I am much better, however, and trust I shall be quite well before we sail. . . .

York Farm will henceforward be let for the summer, as it has often been before, at a rent which will just barely pay the land tax which the city levies upon it. This is all I have to tell you, except that several sales of quantities of the rice have been effected, so that the aspect of southern affairs is more satisfactory than when last I wrote.

Good-bye, and God bless you, my dearest H——. If your brains are really as much deteriorated as you think, we shall be more upon a mental equality, when we meet, than we have ever been in all our lives before.

Ever, as ever, yours,
FANNY.

Butler Place, January 13th, 1877.

My BELOVED H——,

We sail from New York this day week, and I have spent a sad day taking leave of some of my old country neighbours and friends here, for we are thinking of going to New York in a few days, and I do not expect to return here before we sail for Europe. . . .

Dear H——, you have fully prepared me for whatever alterations I may find in you, and I doubt if I shall think them as great as you describe them.

You will not see how greatly I am changed with the increased age visible in my face, my whole person, and all my movements. I am just now appearing

particularly old and infirm, as I am lame in consequence of having been overturned in a sleigh, and am
still unable to walk or move with any ease from the
violent jar and internal bruises I received. S——
was with me, and we were both thrown out; but
I fell on the pavement, and she, *fortunately*, on me, so
that there is every reason for thankfulness that we
escaped with so little injury.

The state of the roads and streets is really frightfully dangerous, and we hear daily of more or less
serious accidents happening to people, by falling on
the ice, with which the pavements are coated. The
winter has thus far been very severe, and began to
be so much earlier than usual. The vessels going
to Europe, however, have made remarkably quick
passages, and I think that generally, after the third
week in January, the neck of the winter is broken. . . .

The southern estate has been brought into the
most beautiful order by J——'s exertions or good
judgment. He has worked energetically and successfully as a clergyman among the people, and has been
mainly instrumental in having a decent church built
and consecrated, where it was greatly wanted. He has
devoted himself to the schools, and has done good in
every way among the inhabitants of the place and
the whole neighbourhood. Naturally enough he has
formed an attachment to and felt an interest in the
people he has thus been serving, which will survive
his residence among them. Then I think he has
enjoyed the life, full of manly activity and occupation,
of supervising this large property and all its opera-
tions. He likes the mild, soft winter climate, he is

a keen sportsman, and finds a great deal of game
in the woods and swamps of the Altamaha, and the
whole region has a wild, weird picturesque beauty to
which he is keenly alive.

He spent his Christmas and New Year's Day away
from us all and quite alone, as far as anything like
congenial companionship went; but he wrote us word
that on New Year's Day, after performing three full
church services for the people of the little town of
Darien, close to Butler's Island, he had rowed down,
by a beautiful moonlight night to St. Simon's, the
island at the mouth of the Altamaha, where the cotton
plantation used to be, and which, with its sea sands
and noble old groups of live oaks, is a beautiful place
which he delights in. . . .

My dearest friend, I have just come back from our
little village church. I could not walk, so my dear
S—— drove me in that same sleigh out of which she
spilt me ten days ago. The roads are one mass of ice
and snow, and the path from the entrance gate to the
church door a perfect looking-glass; but I was carefully
led and supported, and had my last holy church with
S—— and F——, and dear J——, and my young
Owen all round me, and lifted my heart in unspeakable thankfulness to God for the peace and happiness
of these my last days here.

I am called away to receive some friends, who
have come to take leave of me, and so shall close my
letter here. Good-bye, my dearest friend, I trust soon
to see you again. I *know* that you will never be
altered to me, and that I shall see you the same as
I have known you from the first. Those that we love

never alter, **unless we cease to love** them, and I am **ever,** *as* **ever,**

Your

FANNY KEMBLE,

as you **will be to the last, ever** *as* **ever, my Harriet** St. Leger.

23, *Portman Street, Portman* Square,
Friday, March, 23rd, **1877.**

MY DEAREST H——,

You will be glad, **I know, to** hear that Lady **M—— (who was that charming Jenny F——),** arrived **yesterday, with her husband and children, from their** Australian government **banishment.   She** came, poor **dear, directly to see me, and really I** was most delighted **to embrace her again.** She is excellent, very intelligent, **and one of the most** *agreeable* **persons I have** ever **known.   She brought two of her** boys to see me, fine little **fellows, looking fresh and rosy** and strong, in spite of **their eight weeks' voyage from the other side** of the **globe.   Sir Anthony M—— is now** made Governor of **Jamaica, and they will only have a** short breathing time **allowed them in** England **before they** have to go **thither. . . . She seemed overjoyed to be once more** **restored to life in habitable civilized** regions.

After lunch I drove her to Westminster, to call on Dean **Stanley.   Poor Lady Augusta and the** Dean **were great friends of hers.** The **Dean was not in** **town, however.**

After I had **put her down at** her **hotel I** returned **home, and was** pleasantly surprised by a **long** cordial visit **from the** Duke of Bedford. His **brother, Lord**

Arthur Russell, and his wife, had called on me as soon as they heard of my arrival, and the warmth of welcome which he and the duke expressed at seeing me again was very agreeable, and surprised me very much, for though I was well acquainted with their mother, and saw them often as young men, I should never have imagined that they remembered, much less that they cared enough for me to come and see me; and I was, therefore, pleased and touched with the almost affectionate tone in which they spoke to me of their former intercourse with my sister and myself.

Indeed, I have been gratified, and much surprised at the kind pleasure people have expressed to me at my return to England. I do not suppose it is really any excessive satisfaction to them, but I am astonished at the expression of *any* feeling on the subject by *any one.*

I should be very glad to have the companionship of a dog, but have an idea that women's dogs lead a dog's life, and are invariably stolen in London. The poor creatures I see led by a string by their mistresses in the Park do not appear to me to enjoy a very enviable existence; and as I am principled against paying dog-stealers for restoring my property, which they have stolen in the expectation of a bribe for returning it, my pet would infallibly, for want of ransom, go to the vivisectionists.

Of course, I cannot tell you anything of Fanny Cobbe at present, because, situated as we are, at the opposite poles of London, we shall probably see nothing or little of each other. . . .

I think Mary Lloyd really suffers from London;

nevertheless, not half so much as Fanny would from living out of it. They talk of going away, but there are impediments to their doing so; and I think they are likely to be here for some time yet.

I think you are mistaken in speaking of going with me formerly to the Temple Church. We used to go to Lincoln's Inn together to hear Morris preach; but I shall certainly not go thither now. Indeed, the amount of entoning, chanting, and singing, and general musical entertainment now introduced in all the churches is so distasteful to me, that I think I shall simply revert to the Unitarian chapel, because, if that beautiful Church of England Liturgy is to be *sung* instead of *said* to me, I would rather not hear it at all. . . .

Ever, as ever, yours,

FANNY KEMBLE.

23, *Portman Street, Portman Square,*
Tuesday, March 27th, 1877.

MY DEAREST H——,

You go so much faster in your imagination than events and circumstances with the friction of all the petty impediments and delays of daily life can go. You ask if I have finally concluded about the house in Connaught Square? No, indeed; for I have not yet received any report from the agent that was recommended to me by Mr. Ellis, whether the gas, drains, roof, etc., are in a condition to make it expedient for me to conclude the bargain.

I hear of such extraordinary adventures befalling unfortunate tenants who embark rashly in houses, that I am frightened to death about **my** own undertaking.

Mary Lloyd told me that after taking the house where they now are, she found all the gas pipes cut off, having very nearly set fire to the house in consequence of that fact before she discovered **it.**

Mr. Santley, **after** having taken a house, **was** obliged **to** spend between two **and** three hundred pounds in **repairing** the drains.

With regard to the house for which I am now **in** treaty, **it** is at present occupied **by** people who do not go out of **it,** I believe, till the second week in April; after which, **it** has to undergo **a** general purification from garret to cellar, **and sundry** superficial repairs, so that I have no hope or **expectation of** getting into it before **the third** week in **April,** *if even then,* for I cannot begin housekeeping **without servants, and** hitherto have **not** been able **to get one, and** I am seeking **four. . . . So** that you **see there is very little likelihood of** my taking possession of it soon; **and I dread the whole** operation **to a** degree **that** is making me miserably nervous and quite unable **to sleep.** Ellen's leaving me hang over me like a nightmare, and the idea **of being** left with **a** houseful **of entire** strangers is quite intolerable. **However, it will be** done like everything else that has to be done. . . .

You speak of my return to London **reviving my English** feeling **of** nationality. Have I appeared to **you to** have lost it? I am not conscious of having **done so ; and coming** in contact again with much that **I dislike** and disapprove of in my own country would not be apt to stimulate **my love** for it, which, how-

ever, I believe, does not need stimulating, as it lies a
great deal deeper than the disagreeables I dislike, and
the defects I disapprove of in our social system.

You know, my dearest H——, I do not in the least
share your retrospective affection for London. I
always, from my earliest girlhood, heartily disliked it,
and have no peculiarly pleasant or happy reminiscences
of early years to counterbalance the feeling of physical
oppression and mental depression which this huge
agglomeration of humanity always causes me, and
from which my mother and sister both suffered as I do.

I am staying at home this morning to see servant-
women, housemaids, and cooks, and am amazed alike
at their dress and address. The absence of all respecta-
bility in their attire, and of all respectfulness in their
demeanour takes my breath away. America has come,
and is coming over here with a vengeance, and I hear
nothing but universal complaints of the insolence and
want of principle of servants in the present day.

There is undoubtedly a great change in the household relation of the members of English families, but
it appears to me to exist quite as much on the side of
the employers as the employed.

I heard yesterday a piece of news which distressed
me very much, chiefly on my sister's account—the
death of Mrs. Nassau, senior, who was, I think, her
most intimate female friend. She was excellent and
charming, and Adelaide loved and esteemed her very
much, and will, I am sure, be deeply grieved by her
loss. God bless you, my dearest H——.

I am ever, as ever, yours,

FANNY.

23, *Portman Street, Portman Square,*
Tuesday, **April 10th, 1877.**

MY DEAREST H——,

My London existence just now is not agreeable. I am off this moment, ten o'clock, with my breakfast between my teeth (that is not true, I have no teeth; never mind!) to the co-operative stores in the Haymarket to get house linen, sheets, towels, napkins, etc., etc., of which I have absolute need. Here I am back again, having bought and paid for the same to to the tune of twenty pounds, and here I find waiting for me a note from my future landlady, desiring an interview with me, and leaving me in some doubt whether I shall have the house or not, which is rather more provoking than pleasant. Presently May Gordon rushes in, come up to London for a Bach concert, she being a member of the amateur chorus, who perform the same. Oh! I forgot to say that I had hardly taken off my bonnet on coming in, when Sir Frederick and Lady Gray came in from the country to see me. She was Barbarina Sulivan, granddaughter of my friend, Lady Dacre, and had written to me very affectionately to welcome me back and to beg me to go down and stay with them near Windsor. Well, they were no sooner gone, than in came May, and she was no sooner come, than in came Harry Kemble, and he had no sooner come, than in came Gertrude Santley, John's eldest daughter, with a daughter of hers, and they all stayed until I had to go out and see Lady Enfield, Lady Ellesmere's eldest daughter, who came to see me some time ago, and for whom I have an affectionate regard for her mother's and father's sake.

I also went to see old Lady Grey, not the countess, but the widow of General Sir Henry Grey, a woman of eighty-seven, living entirely alone, who is only just reluctantly putting aside her drawing and painting materials, with which, even up to last year, she was able to interest and amuse herself constantly, being really a first-rate amateur artist.

This evening I expect May Gordon and her husband to come and pay me another visit; and after the empty solitude of my American existence, this London life, absolutely quiet, as by comparison it would be called, takes my breath away. . . . I went yesterday to Leighton's studio, by his invitation, to see privately the pictures he is just going to send off to the Academy for this year's exhibition. I was very glad to see Leighton again, and he received me with an affectionate cordiality that quite touched me. I have known him ever since he was a mere youth, and he is so intimately associated in my mind with my sister, that I have a strong feeling of regard for him.

Now dear, I have told you my day's news. I am still without housemaid or kitchen-maid, and feel altogether as if I were standing on my head; but, upside down, or inside out, or wrong side before.

I am ever, as ever, yours,

FANNY KEMBLE.

23, *Portman Street, Portman Square,*
Wednesday, **April** 18*th,* 1877.

MY DEAREST H——,

My small troubles are swelled by the addition of poor F——'s, and hers are complicated with my own incessant and unsuccessful efforts to obtain two out of the four servants I require. I feel quite addled with a sort of cook, kitchen, and housemaid idiotcy, and as if I should address my friends and visitors with, "What wages do you expect?" or, "Why did you leave your last situation?" I do not quite understand who does the work in English houses now. I hire a cook, and she demands a kitchen-maid under her. I look for a kitchen-maid, and she asks for a scullery-maid under her; and I suppose the least the latter functionary would expect would be a turn-spit dog *under her*. Used this to be all so, or do I dream that it was otherwise? And how did my father and mother and four children contrive to exist upon their small income? and six servants—which we never had; a cook, a housemaid, and a footman forming our modest establishment. But to be sure that was a long time ago, for I was young then!

The manners and general demeanour, too, of the lady domestics are very novel and surprising to me. They stand close up to one, with their hands thrust into their jacket pockets, and before you can ask them a single question, inquire if your house is large or small, how many servants you keep, if you keep a man-servant; until I quite expect that the next thing I shall hear will be, and "how many back teeth have you left?"

Certainly things and people have greatly changed since I had anything to do with housekeeping in England. Not pleasantly, I think, for the employers. I hope the employed find it more agreeable.

Yesterday, directly after breakfast, I drove to the

Army and Navy Co-operative Stores, hoping at an early hour to find it empty, and so it was comparatively; but still there were some exemplary lords and ladies even then buying their own groceries. To come and make their own purchases in these dirty, crowded, most inconvenient, most troublesome, and most ill-mannered shops has become the high fashion and a daily amusement of the great and gay London folk; and the Haymarket in the afternoon is as full of fine carriages, opposite the co-operative store, as it used formerly to be on a gala night at the opera house, and friends and acquaintances make appointments for meeting at the co-op, as they vulgarly abbreviate it.

At my luncheon time, Harry Kemble came in and sat some time with me. I like him very much. . . . He is very affectionate and kind to me, and his Kemble face and voice, which are both very like his father's and my father's, are dear and pleasant to me.

After my luncheon, I took an American gentleman, an acquaintance of mine, and a friend of my dear S——'s, to call on my very old and kind friend, Mrs. Proctor. She is now, I believe, very near eighty, but has two days a week appointed for the reception of her friends, when she appears in a most becoming and elegant old lady's toilet, and does the honours of her afternoon tea, which her daughter pours out, with wonderful spriteliness and vivacity.

Here, my dearest H——, I was interrupted by a visit from Lady M——, who told me, that Sir Anthony's servants' wages alone in Australia cost him a thousand pounds a year. To be sure he is a governor! But Lord Mayo, remonstrating with a man who asked him a hundred pounds a year as his butler, to whom Lord Mayo said, "Why, my son and many other young gentlemen of his social position don't get more than that as curates!" "Poor young gentlemen," said the man, "I am really very sorry for them!"

I am going to see Fanny Cobbe this afternoon. She paid me a visit the other day, but my little old (eighty-eight years old), Dr. Wilson, who is as brisk as a bee, and runs up the stairs into my room before the servant can announce him, was here, so that I had but half the good of half her visit.

When he was gone we had free talk; and she told me, among other things, what did not surprise me at all—that her devotion to this vivisection cause had estranged many of her former acquaintances, and that she now saw comparatively few of her former pleasant intellectual associates: " *ainsi va le monde.*"

I go to see her at her office sometimes, and find the table strewed with *pictorial* appeals to the national humanity—portraits of dogs and horses, etc., by famous, masters, coarsely reproduced in common prints, with, "Is this the creature to torture?" printed above them. All this seems *small ;* but "despise not the day of small things," is the true motto for those who mean to achieve great ones; and "many a mickle makes a muckle" is a good saying, and hers are assuredly good doings.

God bless you, dear.

F. H. K.

23, *Portman Street*, Portman Square,
Tuesday, April 24th, 1877.

I am grieved, **my** dearest H——, at the terrible depression of the **letter** which **this** morning's post **brings me from you, and** sincerely **trust** that it may be **chiefly the result of** some temporary physical **derangement.**

My servants are all to be on board wages, which, **to my astonishment, I now find a** very general practice **here. My only reason for** adopting **it,** however, is **that I avoid by so doing the** question of furnishing **the young women in my house either** with beer or beer **money, a** custom that **I think so ill** of that I will **have nothing to** do with it **in any shape.** Of course, **if they choose** to allow **themselves beer out** of their **board** wages, I **cannot** interfere with their doing so, but **at any rate** wish **to** avoid giving my direct countenance to any such practice. Good night, dear.

Ever, as ever, yours,
Fanny Kemble.

23, *Portman Street*, Portman Square, Thursday.

My dearest H——,

My *settlement* in my new abode is sticking **fast** by the way for want of servants. I cannot either get housemaid **or** kitchen-maid. The **cook I** have engaged cannot **come to me** before **the 2nd** of May, and I **am altogether in a** state of semi-distraction, **which is** not decreased **by** poor F—— writing to me incessantly from **the country** to help in procuring her **a nurse** and lady's-maid, both **those** functionaries **leaving her** in the course **of next month.**

I think of going into my strange house with a
parcel of strange people with nervous horror. However, what has to be done always *is* **done**, somehow
or other, and if one does not die **of it, one** survives it,
which is good Irish.

Yesterday, my cousin, Cecilia Faulder (daughter **of**
Horace Wilson) of whom I am **very** fond, came and
spent **the** day with me. **In the** afternoon we had **a**
violent thunderstorm, the second within the last **ten**
days, which prevented **my** taking Lady **Musgrave's**
little boys to the Zoological Gardens, Lady Musgrave
and her husband, and her **son by a** first **marriage, a**
young Oxonian, having gone **to** Paris for **a** week,
during which time I promised **to look** after her three
little children, left in their London apartments with
their nurse. This I have done faithfully every other
day, and as they live in Westminster, the mere journey
there takes up more time than I **can well** spare.

Cecilia brought me some exquisite flowers, **from**
her own garden and greenhouse, **her** husband being a
devoted floriculturist, and as successful as his devotion
deserves to be.

In the evening I expected May and her **husband**
to come and get some supper, after **a great concert at**
the St. James's Hall, where amateurs perform **all the**
finest and most difficult music of Bach and **the great**
composers of **the severest** school. **This** chorus-singing
of sacred music is the high fashion, **and** all **the**
Cherubin and Seraphin **are** young women and men **of**
the best families "of such is the kingdom of heaven,"
who meet together once a **week** to rehearse this music
and then **perform it,** and very creditably too, in two

great concerts in the course of the season, to which the public in general is admitted, but the audience is a very fine one indeed, consisting (at all events in all the eligible parts of the room) of the noble and gentle parents and relations of the distinguished performers, royalty, in some shape or other, also generally lends its countenance to these occasions.

Otto Goldschmid and his wife Jenny Lind devote themselves to training these amateur vocalists, and the result is a really good performance, doing honour to the musical taste and skill of England in high places. May and her husband belong to this society, and sang at the great Bach concert last night, and at past eleven o'clock rushed into my room screaming for food, having been screaming for fun for three mortal hours; so I gave them some lobster-salad and sandwiches and tea, and sent them off to a friend in Harley Street, where they were to sleep. Their performance had been highly successful, and they were in great spirits, and it was very pleasant to me to have them come in so.

Now the carriage is come, and I must go and inquire the character of a kitchen-maid. I have written four answers to advertisements in the *Guardian* newspaper this morning. Good-bye, my dearest H——.

Ever, as ever, yours,

FANNY KEMBLE.

23, *Portman Street, Portman Square.*

MY DEAREST H——,

I did not send you the *Atlantic Magazine*, for I have not yet received it myself, and do not know where to procure it in London.

I have one difficulty to overcome in my determination to allow my servants neither beer nor beer money. I disapprove entirely of their practice of swilling malt liquor. The tea and coffee provided for them appear to me quite stimulus enough for young women, no harder worked than four maid-servants would be in my house, and if they choose to indulge in beer, they must procure it for themselves. I am persuaded that this habit, early acquired in our households, and bequeathed as an inheritance in the whole domestic class, produces part of the miserable drunken tendencies of after life in these women.

This makes the difficulty in my way; for the custom, though beginning to be resisted by some few persons who think about it as I do, is almost universal. I can meet the question by putting all my servants upon board wages, which, of course, enable them to live as they please. This, I find, has now become a very common practice in London. It is a saving of trouble, if not of expense, and perhaps, when I come back from Switzerland, I may adopt it.

All the relations of household life appear to me to have changed much for the worse in England, and the mutual *distrust* and absolute indifference of masters and servants towards each other strikes me very painfully in everything I hear from members of either class.

I believe my house will be ready for me about the fifteenth. I dread extremely finding myself there surrounded with strangers, and shall be thankful when the plunge is once over. Nobody can be of any use to me at all. In truth, there is no difficulty and nothing to do; and it is only my state of nervous depression that makes the thing appear formidable to me.

Poor dear Fanny Cobbe lives at the furthest extremity of London from me, and we waste time in calling at each other's houses and finding *us* not at home. . . . Mrs. St. Quintin and I have exchanged visits in vain, as is the wont of Londoners, who are always all out at the same hour of the day. Good-bye, dear.

Ever, as ever, yours,
FANNY KEMBLE.

15, Connaught Square, Wednesday.

MY BELOVED H——,

. . . My household is only by degrees getting into shape. I shall not get a cook or housemaid till next week, and must then tremblingly hope that they will not go away the same day they come as my last cook did. . . .

May wrote me a note a few days before the landing of General Grant, saying that she was going down to Warsash to meet Algernon and his wife, neé Miss Grant.

My complaint, my dearest H——, with regard to the apparent demoralization of the servant class in London, seems to me all but universal here, and the state of discontent, dissatisfaction, and restlessness in that whole class of society appears to be a general evil of quite recent and rapid growth.

I have just seen Lady Grey this afternoon, who has told me that her whole household are leaving her,

among the rest, a maid who has lived with her *twenty
years.* Poor F—— is struggling through the same
endless vexation and trouble; and I speak with no
one who does not say that the nuisance is intolerable,
and has been becoming so more and more within the
last two or three years.

F—— is looking forward with great satisfaction to
settling at Stratford. The house they have taken is
an old monastic edifice, a quondam sort of convalescent
hospital, belonging to the monks of Worcester Abbey,
and it retains a good many picturesque features of the
time of its fourteenth century foundation. I am in
great hopes, from all reports of it, that it will be a
pleasant residence for them. . . . Good-bye, dearest
H——.

Ever, as ever, yours,
FANNY KEMBLE.

15, *Connaught* Square.

MY DEAREST H——,

I have not been very well for the last few
days, . . . and thought it expedient to send for my
neighbour, Mrs. Garrett-Anderson, the lady doctor, who
has succeeded, you know, in making a considerable
reputation and acquiring a considerable practice in
the medical profession. She was at one time a great
friend of Fanny Cobbe's, but her thinking proper first
to marry and then to have a baby lowered her, I
suspect, a little in the estimation of her fellow
female *progresista*, and her refusing to join the anti-
vivisection movement caused, I believe, a coolness
between Fanny Cobbe and herself. . . . The lady

physicians that I have known have appeared to me clever and intelligent persons, but with something hard and dry in their manner, which would not have struck me disagreeably in a man, but made me wonder whether something especially and essentially womanly—tenderness, softness, refinement—must either be non-existent or sacrificed in the acquirement of a manly profession and the studies it demands. On the other hand, it occurred to me that this very peculiarity in these ladies might be a judicious assumption of the manly *unsentimental* " habit of business " tone and deportment. . . .

I attended on Saturday an anti-vivisection meeting to which Fanny Cobbe invited me, and was sorry, but not surprised, to find that there was a split among the advocates of this particular branch of philanthropy. They are quarrelling among themselves as to the best means of promoting their benevolent purposes, and have formed two distinct societies. That which Fanny Cobbe represents and upholds, called together its members and demanded of them a guaranteed subscription of two hundred and fifty pounds for the next two years to carry out their own peculiar views. I have given the very small *pecuniam* I can afford towards their support, but am afraid their obtaining such an income as they desire unlikely even for two years.

I have heard from S——, who is very well and very busy writing in magazines and newspapers upon the subject of college training and college examinations for women in America, a matter she is greatly interested in.

I must bid you good-bye now and go and walk, for

the day is fine and I take exercise whenever I can.
The mildness of the winter has been wonderful, and I
am almost afraid we shall have to pay **for** it presently.
Good-bye, my dearest **H——**.

Ever, as ever, yours,

FANNY KEMBLE.

15, *Connaught Square.*

MY DEAREST H——,

I have not much to tell you, except that **I**
am reading a French book, with which I am greatly
charmed, **the** letters of a certain **Monsieur Doudan,**
who was a sort of a tutor, **or private secretary, or** only
intimate friend and adviser in **the family of the Duc**
de Broglie, and whose correspondence **certainly gives**
me the impression of one of the most charming **persons**
I ever knew. F—— is living **just on** the other **side of**
the bridge which crosses the Avon, at the foot **of the**
main street of Stratford, **and within half a quarter of**
a mile of the famous little old country town inn of **the**
Red Horse, where I mean to take up my abode. I
have a *definite intention* that her baby shall **be** born
on the 23rd of April, Shakespeare's birthday; that it
shall be a boy, and christened William Francis Leigh,
all which **I amuse myself** with thinking, and none of
which will pretty certainly take place; but **it is an**
arrangement of circumstances that pleases my imagination.

I am going on Wednesday to **spend** a day or
two with my old friend, Lady —— ——, at that
palatial poorhouse, Hampton Court Palace, from
which she runs away as often and as much as she can,

and whence she sends me pressing invitations to come
and alleviate the state of chronic boredom, into which
she subsides the moment she returns to her royal residence, which I envy her, for its noble picturesqueness
and cheerful, blessed quiet. I think she would infinitely prefer this noisy corner of a London square, in
which I take such small delight.

I must go and get ready for church, where I have
the rare good fortune always to hear admirable matter,
delivered in an admirable manner, by the son of Sir
Henry Holland, who was an old friend of mine. God
bless you, dear, dear, dear old friend.

Ever, as ever, yours,

FANNY KEMBLE.

Alverston Manor House, Stratford-upon-Avon.

MY DEAREST H——,

I think you will like to hear of my arrival
here, . . . where Alice has a range of fourteen acres,
enclosed round the old house; and in the house itself,
which was an old *monkery*, belonging to the Chapter
of Worcester Cathedral, two rooms of most unusual
dimensions—a fine nursery and a noble room on the
ground floor; and she seems to enjoy her little life here
thoroughly.

I have just come back from church, the parish
church, where Shakespeare is buried, the lovely old
church in its lovely old churchyard, with the river
sweeping round it and the noble old elms still golden
leaved in the bright mellow autumnal sun.

The church was very full, and I hope the congregation were edified. I was rather unhappy, for the

whole service was intoned and chanted, and we had
to listen to the Athanasian Creed, all which are trials
to me, but **I could** only hope **they** were acceptable,
beneficial, and comfortable, in **some way or other, to**
my fellow-worshippers.

This house is **one of the most curious, quaint,**
picturesque old places **I ever saw; it** dates back to the
thirteenth century. **There is** not a room to enter
which you have not to go up or down two or more
steps, it is low and **irregular** looking from outside,
with pointed gables and clusters of queer chimney-
stacks, and a good deal of dark wood-carving. One
side of the house fronts the river Avon, **a** stretch of
lawn of about an acre lying between the lower windows
and the garden gate that opens on to the **road and**
river, running close by it, parallel **to each** other. A
very fine row of noble old elm trees borders this lawn
on either side, and beyond them **on one hand is** the
enclosure **wall** of the place, and on the other an
ancient grass walk, smooth and wide, with a high
heavy yew-tree hedge, evidently of great antiquity, a
perfect monk's meditation ground. Beyond this is an
orchard, bounded by an overarching avenue of large
old filbert **trees,** that **form** a perfect bower over
another wide grass walk. Beyond this is a **very**
large kitchen garden, with a **fine** fish pond at one
end **of it, the** monks' fish reservoir in the fishy
monkish days. **The whole** place **is most** curious and
picturesque, and though much out of repair and condition, might be made **in every** respect a delightful
residence.

Good-bye, my dearest H——, I am very tired

and sleepy, but thought **you** would like to hear of **my** first impressions of **this place.** God bless you, dear.

Ever, as ever, yours,
FANNY.

Alverston Manor House.

MY DEAREST H——,

I have **waited until the** day after Christmas, to **give** you some account of our holy tide here. I found F—— and **Alice** both **very well, the** former **rather** burdened, and **the latter much** excited, with **all the** Christmas preparations.

I came down on **Saturday. All the** trains were full, **all** the stations thronged, **all the arrivals late;** and I **did** not reach Stratford **till** almost an **hour** behind time, and missed seeing Mr. L—— at Leamington, who **was** not returning home that night, having **to perform early** duty next **morning,** but who came to the station, where I changed carriages **for** Stratford, just to shake hands with me, and missed me **and** shook hands with nobody, because **of** the unpunctuality **of** the train.

On Sunday the day was bad, and I was not well and did not leave the **house.** Monday, Mr. L—— came home from Leamington **in the** afternoon, and Henry James, the American **author, a** great friend of S——'s, whose acquaintance I made **in** Rome, arrived. . . .

Poor little Alice was in an ecstacy of delight and expectation as to what the next day **was** to bring **her. She had** learned **in America** the pretty German theory of the Christmas tree and **all** the Christmas gifts, referring them to the "Christ-kind" (Christ Child), and **how she** was to hang her stocking at the foot of **her** bed and **to find it** full of delight the next morning.

I went to kiss her in her crib, and her little eager face looked up from the pillow as she said, "Only one night more, and then to-morrow Christmas Day, and I have **been** *wethy good*." When she was disposed of, **her mother and I, the American** gentleman, and all the servants took possession of the nursery **and** dressed **it all up** with Christmas wreaths **of laurel** and holly, and trimmed her tree, which was a beautiful young fir, that was hung all over with toys and bon-bons, boxes and baskets, and really looked extremely **pretty,** as did **the** picture presented by **the** groups of operators.

The nursery itself is **a very fine** room, nearly twenty-five feet long and twenty **wide,** with an open arch roof of big oak rafters and **a** huge chimney-piece and a great heavy oak table **in the** middle, so that the **room,** when dressed up and **lighted by a bright brass** gas chandelier, looked really quite picturesque, **as did** our **band** of maidens, standing on steps, mounted **on** ladders, kneeling round the **tree, on the middle of** the table, the young negro man-servant **and our dark-** bearded, handsome American friend helping to make a series **of** pictures, which I (with my lap full of bon-bons, **with** which **I was** diligently filling small bags, boxes, and baskets to be tied to the tree), took great pleasure **in** observing.

At ten o'clock, Mr. L—— left us, still all busy at work, to drive his ten miles off to Leamington, where he had communion service the next morning at half-past eight.

Christmas Day itself was very delightful, Alice was **in absolute** ecstacies, the servants **all beaming** with delight at their various small gifts. **In the** afternoon **the** dear master came home, there was tea and plum cake **for a** table full of little children belonging to the coachman, gardener, **etc.**, and their mothers.

Our American friend seemed very well pleased with all the ceremonies of the day, including church service in Shakespeare's church, and though some of us went to bed very weary, it was **with** serving and pleasing and ministering to others, and **I** thought the fatigue not very deplorable.

I am not altogether **well, but very** contented and happy, and grateful beyond words for all the blessings of my present life. God bless you, my dearest H——.

I am ever, as ever, yours,

FANNY KEMBLE.

Alverston Manor House.

MY DEAREST H——,

. . . I heard yesterday of the death of my friend Sir Frederick Grey, an event not altogether to be deplored, as he was over seventy years of age, and would probably have endured much suffering had his life been prolonged. . . . His marriage had been **an** unusually happy one, **I** think, though he had **no** children.

A nursery is undoubtedly an immense bond of mutual affection, but, undoubtedly also, it necessarily prevents anything like the close and uninterrupted companionship **which** often exists between people who have no family.

I hope E—— is pleased by the new dignity conferred by Mr. Disraeli on **her** friend Mr. Gathorne Hardy. Sir Charles Adderly, **Mr. L——**'s brother-in-law, has received the new title **of** Lord Norton.

Ever, as ever, yours,

FANNY.

Alverston Manor House, Stratford-on-Avon.

. . . I have not been at all well since I **came** here, but I am, thank God, getting better and recovering my sleep. Of course I am most anxious to be strong and well just now. . . .

Mr. L—— has just gone off to the wedding of his niece, Miss C——, to Sir Ch. M——, whose unfortunate first **wife was divorced** and is now living, I believe, in a madhouse, circumstances **which, I should** think, would throw a gloom over the introduction of her successor **to the noble estate and fine house which was, not long** ago, the home **of that poor young woman.**

Miss C——, however, is, I believe, quite free from any misgiving on the score of being **haunted by any** such **sad** associations, and merely rejoices **in the splendour** and beauty **of her new residence.** So goes **the world.**

Shakespeare's birth and death day **yesterday** passed **off** very quietly **here. A** flag was hoisted on the bridge over the Avon, and a dinner given at the "Red Horse Inn," which prevented my taking possession of the rooms I **am** to occupy **there for the next two months,** but the celebration **went no further. Good-bye, my dearest H——.**

> **Ever,** as ever, yours,
> FANNY KEMBLE.

Red Horse Hotel, Stratford-on-Avon.

I went this morning to Malvern **to look for** some place of habitation for myself, **near the** small cottage which F—— **has taken there for** the next two months.

I give up my Swiss tour for so long, and shall only be able to make a very short pilgrimage to my dear mountains, if I cannot get abroad till September, which I do not expect now to do.

I do not know if you ever were at Malvern. It is a great many years since I visited it, and I was very much struck with its beauty and the singularity of the abrupt rise of its small group of hills, immediately out of the level plain at their feet, which reminded me a little of the position of the Alban Hills above the Roman Campania—I do not mean in beauty, indeed, but in their peculiar position and configuration. . . .

I have nothing to tell you of myself, dear H——, for F—— is just now the paramount object of my thoughts and care. She and the baby, thank Heaven, are both well. God bless you.

> I am ever, as ever, yours,
> FANNY KEMBLE.

15, Connaught Square.

MY DEAREST H——,

Here I am, back again in my London house, from which I shall probably not go away for any

length of time **again till** Christmas, **when I shall** go
down to the L——s **for a** week **or ten days.**

Next **week I have** promised **Lady** —— **to go and**
spend **a couple of days** with **her, at** Hampton Court,
but hardly call that **leaving** London.

I wrote **to you** just **before** leaving Stratford, and
therefore have nothing **to** tell **you. I have** already
been **out this morning doing** commissions **for F——,**
who is burdened with all sorts of demands upon **her**
time **and trouble and attention by her** American
friends, who **seem to me to think she** has **settled in**
England **solely for the purpose of being their unpaid**
agent and doing gratuitously **for them every species**
of troublesome commission in London and Paris. I
left Stratford with only a glimpse of Mr. L—— at
Leamington **station, as I was leaving the Stratford**
train **to take the London one, and he was taking the**
train **I** was leaving **to go to his home. He** had spent
the day and night away on Thursday, having had a
numerous confirmation to administer and lunch with
his Bishop to attend, and an evening **service to**
perform, **the church, as he told me,** being literally
crammed with **people. His duties take him to**
Leamington almost **every day, and** keep him there
almost all day **long, and** always from **Saturday to**
Monday; **and I think this** constant **running to and**
fro, **which is** rather more **than is** good **for him, and**
his consequent **incessant** absence **from home, wil**
help greatly **to reconcile them to leaving** Stratford
for a residence **in the** place where his **duties oblige**
him to be.

My week's **stay in the country has** done me good,

and the lovely weather, though one is sorry to spend
it in London, makes London itself more tolerable.

On Monday I am going to begin again at my task
of dictation.

Mr. Bentley, the publisher, has written to me about
publishing my " Gossip " here in London, but I do not
yet know what I shall determine about that.

Good-bye, dearest H——. Though I live in London,
I go nowhere and see nobody, and have not therefore
much to write about. I am reading Charles Kingsley's
life and letters. Oh ! how I wish I had known him,
or any such man ; but there are not many.

Ever, as ever, yours,
FANNY KEMBLE.

15, Connaught Square.

MY DEAREST H——,

I shall undoubtedly be more cheerful when
F—— and her child are here; but I am troubled beyond
reason at the idea of keeping house for such a much
larger family.

My state of health, I am sorry to say, is such as to
make the slightest things appear formidable, not to say
impossible. . . . I have been obliged to send for a
physician, and I think you will perhaps be surprised
and amused when I tell you that I have seen a *lady
doctor* recommended by Fanny Cobbe. I do not think
I should have done this, but that I believed that my
old medical adviser, Dr. Erasmus Wilson, had left off
practice. My lady physician calls herself Dr. Hogan. . . .

I have not been to the British Museum for many
years. I went not long ago to the South Kensington

Museum, **and** spent some time there delightfully, and thought I should return there frequently, but I have never been able **to** get there **since**. Much of my time is spent in returning people's visits, and the London distances are **so** enormous that, in point **of** fact, one's day goes literally travelling from one point to another of this preposterous city, **as** our delightful friend Dessauer used to **say,** *mais quelle idée folle que ce Londrès.*

My lady secretary comes to me every evening **and** interests me a **good** deal, poor thing. She has lost **her** mother since she has been writing for me.

Now I must go off to my dentist, and then **I** must go off again servant-hunting, having hitherto found it impossible to complete my household. **Good-bye, dear, God** bless you.

Ever, as ever, yours,
FANNY KEMBLE.

15, *Connaught Square.*

Mrs. St. Quintin **was good** enough to call here some little time ago, but I was not at home, and missed the pleasure of seeing her. Yesterday I drove to Chesham Place, and found her. **She** was, as usual, surrounded by young people, relations or connections, and looked placid and cheerful, and as well as she generally seems **now,** which **is not very** vigorous. I think, dearest **H——**, when you express satisfaction at my settling in a *home,* as you call it, that you **forget** that I have only taken this house for a year, and that I find it in many respects so undesirable as a *home,* that I would willingly leave it if I could. Moreover, two of the servants, who came to me a fortnight ago, my cook and housemaid, have already given me warning, and my time is literally passed in reading and answering advertisements, and seeing a string of miserable-looking women, candidates for my service, who seem to me utterly unfit for any employment in any decent family. I am miserably shaken and nervous, and am worried by all this to quite an unreasonable degree.

I should be most thankful to be able to go abroad and leave all this miserable mess—servants, house-keeping, etc., of which I now feel utterly incapable, but I do not know when it will be possible to do so, and I do not think I can look to my resuming my residence in this house under the cheerful aspect of returning to a *home*,—the *bugs*, at present, I am sorry to say, being my principal idea of Penates.

I refuse all invitations, and see hardly any one, for though my friends are very kind in asking me to their houses, and calling upon me, my disinclination and unfitness for society are quite insuperable, and in the matter of morning visiting, it is really a mere exchange of bits of pasteboard, as people are all abroad at precisely the same hour of the day, and everybody *finds everybody else out,* which, upon reflection, is rather an unpleasant social condition.

My old frend Mary Ann Thackeray has done me a real kindness in making me go with her to the fine weekly morning concerts given at St. James's Hall, which have been an immense refreshment to me. She has just now sent to ask me to go with her to the first flower show of the season, and I am thankful for anything that takes me out of this house; though I am entirely wanting in the courage and energy to go *alone* and seek recreation anywhere. . . .

I never did nor ever shall employ your bootmaker, though I think I recollect trying once to get a pair of footgloves (why not as well footgloves as handshoes, as the Germans say) made by him. I get my boots from Sparks Hall, and my shoes from Gundry, both royal furnishers, so I am shoed in good company.

I am going to-day to Mr. Sanders, her Majesty's dentist, to receive a set of new front teeth, which have been tried on (or rather in), and measured and fitted three or four times. I was determined upon the final extraction of my last shaky front tooth, and the replacing of the whole four, by the necessity I am under of going to my old friend Mr. Donne's daughter's wedding to-morrow. I had declined doing so, but both Valentia Donne and her father looked so annoyed at my not assisting at this solemnity, that I determined to pull out my last real front tooth, put in my four new false ones, and "haste to the wedding" as in friendly duty bound.

Mr. Sanders is an old-fashioned, conservative practitioner, who will not hear of teeth being kept in one's mouth after the new mode, by suction; and is filling my mouth (and his own purse) with the best of gold. God bless you, dear; I am off now to an intelligence office.

Ever, as ever, yours,
FANNY KEMBLE.

15, Connaught Square.

MY DEAREST H——,

I am going, as soon as I have finished this letter, to get some warm woollen socks, made expressly for night wear, to send down to little Alice, who has not been well. F—— talked of taking the child for a day or two to Malvern for change of air, but I am afraid that Malvern, at this early season, will be very bleak and not likely to do either of them good. . . .

Adelaide's account of Rome is simply that it is dull socially beyond all precedent, the death of the king and the death of the pope having thrown all parties alike into mourning, while building alterations and repairs at the English Embassy render all social gatherings there impossible at present. You will have felt for the position of Mario, reduced to poverty and blindness in his old age.

Ever, as ever, yours,

FANNY KEMBLE.

15, Connaught Square.

DEAREST H——,

It is a miracle of your love, my dear, that makes you still find pleasure in my letters (and your love was of a kind to work miracles). As for what you say about my Memoirs, I am not, you know, writing them, I am only copying and making extracts from my former journals and my early letters to you, and think, when I contemplate publishing them, that far from being lively or entertaining, they must appear monotonous and dull to almost as great a degree as they are egotistical. . . .

I am reading with the greatest delight and admiration, the life and letters of Charles Kingsley. What a fiery Christian soul he was, and what infinite good one such life must work upon every human life it comes in contact with.

I am particularly well off, as far as preaching privileges are concerned, for I am within a quarter of a mile of Lewellyn Davies's church and of Mr. Holland's chapel, and have made up my mind to go and call upon them both, and give myself a chance of occasional personal communication with two such excellent men, for which I shall be much the better, and they, I trust, none the worse.

I am going out to see my sister, who came here the other day to *beg* of me for Mario, the former great Italian singer, who, after having had money poured upon him in floods, is now in his old age literally *penniless*—a subscription being opened for him at Coutts's. Is not that deplorable? God bless you, dear.

Ever, as ever, yours,

FANNY KEMBLE.

15, *Connaught Square.*

. . . I for my sins am going to an afternoon representation of Othello by a German tragedian of some reputation, in whom a friend of mine is much interested, and with whom I have promised to go—a piece of considerable good nature on my part, for I confess that I do not expect the German tragedian to have enough genius to reconcile me to the very disagreeable **process of hearing Shakespeare pronounced** with a foreign accent.

For a London woman, **I** go out **so** little and see so **few** people, that I have almost as little to tell you as you can **have to** tell me. The prevailing fashion of having regular afternoon tea-parties would suit me, inasmuch as social gatherings at a reasonable **hour** are better than evening parties that begin in the middle **of** the night; but I have never given in to the practice of taking tea before my dinner, as I dine early, **and** prefer having my tea in the evening, so **I** do not **go to these** *kettle*-drums, to **which one is** now invited by special notes **of a particular form and** diminutive size, with a teapot and **" come early "** on the envelope **for a** device.

I have just received a missive **from a** lady who once asked me very urgently to go **to her house** to **meet some** *fag* *ends of gentility*, among whom she had the insolence **to** designate Sir Charles and Lady Trevelyan ! **I declined,** telling her I did **not** consider that I belonged *even* to the " fag end " **of** *such* gentility. Good-bye, **my dearest H——.** I have been quaking lest we should **go to war, and pray** God incessantly against it. . . .

Ever, as ever, yours,
FANNY KEMBLE.

15, *Connaught Square.*

MY DEAREST H——,

I have little to **tell** you, for though I am back again in this busy London, I go nowhere and see nobody, and **have** really **less** material for correspondence here than anywhere else. I have been driving about the dirty, muddy streets this morning, doing commissions for F——, with which she charged me when I left Stratford-on-Avon. Carrying the broken bits of a Venetian chandelier to Salviati's establishment in St. James's Street, where I had the pleasure of an Italian chat with the director, and we exchanged many admiring and affectionate ejaculations as he challenged me about my preferences for the various cities of his enchanting land—Rome, Naples, Florence, Venice, Milan, Turin, Genoa—with ahs! and ohs! of regretful reminiscence between each. I then went to Mudie's, and took a three months' subscription for F——, sending her down "Charles Kingsley's Life and Letters," and Captain Burnaby's "Ride Across Asia Minor." Of all the devices of our complex and complete civilization, I think this huge circulating library system one of the most convenient and agreeable; to be able for twenty-one shillings to have for a quarter of a year ten volumes of excellent literature for one's exclusive use, seems to me a real privilege, and capital return for one's money.

I am myself reading "Kingsley's Life and Letters," and wish regretfully that I had had the great good fortune of knowing him.

My lady amanuensis, who at one time was a member of the sisterhood at Clewer, has been spending part of her summer there again, and returns to me with a new semi (if *semi*) Catholic badge round her neck— a blue ribbon with a St. Andrew's cross suspended to it—the insignia of a new sisterhood, whose special *raison d'être* (as far as she would make it known to me) was that its members *were to be kind to one another.*

Is it not queer that **people should** find it necessary **to** band themselves together and tie themselves up like parcels, with **blue** ribbon, and **hang** themselves with crosses and badges and pledges, for the fulfilment of the first obvious duty of simple christianity? But this sort of thing has a wonderful attraction for numbers **of** people, especially women, and the **women** Catholics know perfectly well what they are about.

Your letters, my dearest **H——** (since you had **preserved those I wrote to you for** so many years), would infallibly, if not destroyed *en masse,* **have been** published somehow, **at some time or** other, by some**body.** It is the one **reflection that at all** reconciles **me** to having published them myself **in your** and my **own** lifetime. *All* the portions that **it was** most desirable **to save** from publicity have at any rate by **this** means been destroyed by myself, and I am still working at this task, which I hope not to leave to **anybody** else's discretion or judgment after my death.

Ever, as ever, yours,

FANNY.

15, *Connaught Square.*

My DEAREST H——,

I had thought **of** offering my **book to Murray,** but Mr. Bentley, without any application **on** my part to him, made me a very liberal offer.

I had a letter from F——, the day before yesterday, giving an account of **the** brilliant success of a fair **or** bazaar that has been got up to assist the **funds for the**

Sunday schools of Leamington, which were in a most neglected state, and moreover burdened with debt and insufficient and disgraceful, like everything else connected with the parish under the shameful reign of the late very good-for-nothing incumbent. They were anxious to raise two hundred pounds, and the result of the bazaar, thanks to Mr. L——'s zeal and great personal popularity, was six hundred. . . .

I give up my house on the 24th of April, but shall leave it on or about the 15th, to go down to Stratford, where I shall stay at the little country inn till the 1st of June, when, if all things are prosperous at the Manor House, I hope to go abroad for my three months to Switzerland.

When I return, I shall endeavour to find an apartment or lodging in London, as the constant small cares, troubles, and worries of housekeeping are irksome to me. It is almost time for me to get ready for church. I have the advantage of hearing most admirable preaching from a son of my old friend Sir Henry Holland, who officiates at old Quebec Street Chapel, close in this neighbourhood.

May Gordon and her husband dined with me yesterday, and went with me to the play. . . Goodbye, my dearest H——.

Ever, as ever, yours,

FANNY KEMBLE.

15, *Connaught Square,* **Sunday,** *17th.*

MY DEAREST H——,

I have just come back, that is, yesterday, from a three-days' visit to Hampton Court, to my friend

Lady ——, who absents herself from her royal residence, which she finds intolerably dull, as much as
she possibly can; but when she has exhausted all her
foreign resources, and is obliged to return home, she
cries aloud to all her friends to help her along with
her existence. And I, when I can, am glad to go to
her for a day or two, for " auld lang syne," and also
because, no not because at all, but also I think
Hampton Court beautiful, and am always glad to see
the grand old palace and the lovely, lordly, courtly,
old-fashioned gardens, which are now charming with
golden fringes of crocuses and silver heaps of blooming laurestinus. I have always the ill luck to find
Lady M. B—— absent. How I should rejoice in such
a residence as my friend Lady ——'s ! . . .

The weather has become suddenly bitterly cold, and
we are paying severely for the extraordinary mild
weather we have had hitherto. . . .

I am beginning my preparations for leaving this
house. . . . Good-bye, my dearest H——. God bless
you.

Ever, as ever, yours,

FANNY.

15, Connaught Square, Tuesday, 19th.

MY DEAREST H——,

I wrote to you to tell you of Fanny Cobbe
having succeeded in letting both their town house and
their Welsh cottage. She came here yesterday and
said she was very glad that they had done so, though she
regretted leaving her house in Cheyne Walk, and I am
sure she will regret more and more leaving London

. . . She certainly is eminently social in her tastes and tendencies. In the midst of all the confusion and worry and disorder of her affairs, preparing to leave her house, etc., etc., she invites people to tea-parties, and luncheon-parties, and goes out to dinner-parties. I have now lived so long, not only out of the London world, but out of every world in the world, that this desire and capacity for society perfectly amazes me. I go to a concert occasionally with a friend, and when it is over I go to bed thoroughly tired at eleven o'clock, when my friend has her hair powdered and pomatumed, dresses herself afresh, and goes off to a fancy ball, and my friend is sixty-five years old! I mentioned this incidently to another friend, who is *eighty* years old, and she tells me that she was at that very same fancy ball; and I had a headache the next morning with only two hours of the gas and bad air of the concert room and nervous excitement of the music!

God bless you, dear. I am much occupied in trying to find a nurse for F——, to succeed her monthly nurse after her confinement.

Ever, as ever, yours,
FANNY.

15, Connaught Square.

MY DEAREST H——,

I am in the midst of much business and confusion of mind, providing for everything, as well as I can remember to do so, connected with giving up this house.

It has been taken by a Mrs. E——, a widow lady with sons, who are to go to the London University.

She is a kinswoman of my old friendly acquaintance Sotheby, the poet, who was a great friend of Emily Fitz Hugh's, and whom Byron used impertinently to call Botherby.

It is odd in what curious small details family likeness reveals itself. This Mrs. E——'s brother, Vice Admiral Sir Edward Sotheby, wrote to me about the house, and his signature was exactly like old Sotheby's writing, from whom I had sundry notes and letters fifty years ago, about a play he had written called "Darnley," in which he wanted me to act Mary Stuart, which I declined, on the score of *personal plainness*, which I conceived unfitted me for the part though Mademoiselle Duchesnois, the ugliest woman in all France, was supposed to represent the beautiful Scotch Queen to perfection. . . .

I am going down to F—— on the 13th, to-morrow week, to stay with her till the 25th, after which I shall take up my abode at the little inn at Stratford-on Avon, where I cannot be received sooner, because, on the 24th, Shakespeare's birth and death day, every inn in the town is always crammed with visitors, who assemble to do honour for that occasion, by eating drinking, and speech making.

God bless you, dear.

Ever, as ever, yours,

FANNY.

DEAR E——,

You ought to be crowned with roses and lie on or in a bed of mignonette, which would not be comfortable. However, your friends do well, and their bounden **duty, to** succour you **with** flowers. To me they are always like good angels; may they be so to you.

Your friend—no!—Lady C—— is spouting **and** declaiming about the London gay world, like **an** actress in want of a situation, and a fine lady out **of** place. Good-bye, dear.

Affectionately yours,
F. A. K.

15, *Connaught Square.*

MY DEAREST H——,

I had a letter yesterday from my sister. **They** are settled **in** Rome, but by no means comfortably; **for,** out of a charitable desire to serve her old friend Mario, she **has** taken **his** apartment, **which is in the Corso,** instead of one of the higher **and sunnier situations. It** is dark, and small, and inconvenient; **and she is suffer-**ing much from cold in **it.** Mario, **who lives in the same** house, is constantly with them, and by all accounts his principal contribution to the general conversation is a set of stories, more improper and indecent, the one than the other. Fortunately, **young Mrs.** Algernon does not understand Italian, and **I** presume these anecdotes are not translated for her benefit. I have not much sympathy for Mario's **ruin. A man who** stood for years literally in a shower of gold has no right, in **my** opinion, to be much pitied for **not having** saved at least enough for a subsistence in his old age.

One thing I do pity him for, with **all my heart,** and was much shocked to hear it, that **he** has become blind. Moreover, his unmarried daughter is not comfortable to him; for these afflictions in his impoverished old age I have indeed infinite compassion. . . .

I went to the play with F—— yesterday evening.

I have *finished* my Memoirs, I am thankful to say. It was a very great relief to me to come to the end of them, and throw into the fire the last of my letters to you, detailing all the misery and anguish of that whole year. It is all done, I am thankful to say, and I have kept nothing of the record of my unhappy life but what I trust can give pain to nobody.

Our weather here is almost *warm*, and very wet, muddy, and disagreeable. God bless you, dearest H——.

Ever, as ever, yours,
FANNY KEMBLE.

15, *Connaught Square.*

My DEAREST H——,

I think you may like to hear of a visit I had from Fanny Cobbe on Sunday, because, though she was coughing very much, and did not look well, she was able to be out; and how full of active benevolent energy you may judge from this note I have just received from her. The Bill she refers to is one she wants to bring into Parliament for preventing or punishing men's cruelty to those animals, their wives.

"I did get a capital half hour with Lord Coleridge, and obtained his full approval of my Bill, and most useful advice about it and on the whole subject. Then I went off to the M.P. who is getting up our deputation, and settled a great deal of business with him, and other business with his wife about amalgamating two women's suffrage societies; so, altogether, I broke the sabbath in a frightful manner."

Now you see, H——, this sort of perpetual movement and interest seems to me absolutely indispensable to Fanny Cobbe's existence; and I really do not think she could endure a life in Wales, or indeed anywhere but in the midst of all this excitement and occupation to which she is now accustomed. It made me sad to hear of her squabbles and struggles and contentions with American booksellers; and altogether I feel sorry for the constant effort which she seems to me to be making. . . .

Ever, as ever, yours,
FANNY KEMBLE.

15, Connaught Square.

MY DEAREST H——,

Fanny Cobbe and Miss Lloyd were to have dined and gone to the play with me this evening, but the day before yesterday Fanny came here to cancel the engagement, poor Mary having been seized with an acute attack of lumbago, which obliged her to keep her bed. Yesterday morning I went down to Chelsea to see them. Mary was still confined to her bed, and Fanny busy writing for dear life. . . .

From there I went on to Carlyle, who lives in their neighbourhood, and who is now considerably over eighty years old, and has lately been ill. He is pleased to be visited by his friends and acquaintances, and I sat with him an hour, and sang him the Scotch ballad of Lizzie Lindsay. He was very eloquent, and very severe in his denunciations of our present government, and far from cheerful in his prognostications of the future of England.

When I came home, I had a visit from one of Mr. Mitchell's, of Bond Street, clerks upon a very sad errand, to collect subscriptions for my poor old caretaker, Mitchell's most trusted travelling agent, Mr. Chapman, whom you may perhaps remember, whom Mitchell used to send everywhere with me to take charge of the business arrangements of my readings. He has become helpless and speechless from paralysis, and I was requested to give something towards his assistance. This is sad enough. He was an extremely intelligent man, and most considerate and courteous in his attendance upon and attention to me; and he went up and down through the whole breadth and length of Great Britain, managing the business of my readings for several years. . . .

I am expecting F—— and her husband and baby on Monday, with three servants, so that I shall have a house full. God bless you, dearest H——.

Ever, as ever, yours,
FANNY KEMBLE.

15, Connaught Square.

MY DEAREST H——,

I have just returned from Hampton Court, where I have been spending a couple of days with my old friend, Lady ——, who at seventy-six is as upright as a Maypole, walks and trots about with the lightness and activity of seventeen, is neither deaf nor blind, works crochet work without spectacles, dresses in the height of the fashion, with blonde caps and wreaths of artificial flowers, is perpetually running about from one pleasant country house to another, has a charming, comfortable, commodious and elegant apartment in Hampton Court Palace, and incessantly deplores her condition and position, and the intolerable dulness of her life, so that in many respects she is a subject of regretful astonishment to me, that so many good fortunes should result in so little satisfaction. She is a good and rational woman too in a great many respects, a lady of the old school in her ideas, feelings, and manners, and I have a regard for her that dates back almost to my girlhood; and so, when she implores me to come and relieve her lonely dulness with my society, I am very glad to do so, though I can hardly forebear from that unwise and often very unjust feeling, that if one was in one's neighbour's place, one would value their blessings more than they appear to do. Certainly her early life in the house of her very distinguished father, and in the midst of the society which frequented it, was not a good preparation for a secluded and solitary old age.

Your sleeplessness, my dearest H——, seems to me a thing to be much regretted, as several discreet naps, even in the day, would, I think, give you a sense of rest and relief; and, since you do not sleep at night, would not injure you in that respect. As for me, I never take up a book at any hour of the day, even for a quarter of an hour, without nodding over it. Of course this sort of doze is not a prolonged slumber, but it is the invariable effect of any attempt at reading, so that I really get exceedingly little profit from my literary studies, be they what they may, in spite of which tendency to somnolence, I am contriving between my naps and while my maid is brushing my hair, to read the "Life and Letters of Charles Kingsley," with which I am profoundly interested and touched. What a spring of vitality is such a life as that! and to how many more than he could himself know in this world he must have imparted saving influence for good, to last and spread from soul to soul beyond possible reckoning. It seems to me that some perception of the spiritual good they have accomplished in their lives here must be among the future rewards of such servants of God hereafter.

I began this letter yesterday, immediately on my return from Hampton Court, and in the afternoon was interrupted by a visit from my old and intimate friendly acquaintance, Mrs. Procter, who is another wonderful woman, close upon eighty, full of life and spirit and animation, and still as she always was, a most amusing, sparkling, and delightful talker.

Our weather is just now very deplorable, and I am afraid will cause widespread disease as well as distress in all the flat and low parts of the country, which are becoming flooded. Good-bye, my dearest H——.

Ever, as ever, yours,
FANNY KEMBLE.

Connaught Square.

Thank you, dear E——, for the kind pains you have taken for me about F——'s poplin. My experience

of orders given to London shopkeepers of the present
day is all of the same description as this result of
dealing with Dublin ones; they either take or fulfil
the directions with such careless indifference, that the
consequence of the most painstaking effort in giving
them is failure, that would be ludicrous if it was not
so very provoking. I am very sorry for the trouble
you have had, and even more obliged than if you had
succeeded, because I know you must have been
annoyed at not doing so.

Your affectionate,

F. A. Ḳ.

MY DEAREST H——,

It is pouring with rain, and the sky is the
colour of pea soup (yellow pea soup, not green), and
the streets are thick with mud, and London looks its
very *beastliest*. Natheless, I am going to drive down
to the middle of Kensington to try and find my sister,
whose hours and mine agree so ill, that she will
probably leave London for Italy without our having
met half-a-dozen times. I *am* always at home at
certain hours, and she has found me twice; but she is
never to be found, even when at some inconvenience
I go down to her at the hours she herself appoints, and
neither is May Gordon, who has taken a house close to
her mother in Kensington, and at whose door I leave
fruitless cards, merely to show that I have been to see
her.

After that visit in Kensington, I must drive
through *four miles* of this huge town to pay another
visit to the second daughter of my friend Theodore

Sedgwick, who is about to settle in England, marrying Mr. William Darwin, son of the eminent naturalist, who is a banker in Southampton, and lives a few miles out of that dear old pleasant town.

Yesterday evening I had a great pleasure, I went to Exeter Hall with my friend Miss Thackeray, to hear Mendelssohn's Oratorio of St. Paul, all the fine music was given very finely, and that of Paul himself was admirably sung by my nephew-in-law, Charles Santley, who has a noble voice and is a first-rate artist.

At the same time that I have extreme pleasure in hearing these beautiful sacred compositions, I never can become reconciled to listening to the most solemn thoughts and holy words and awful incidents of the New Testament history set to music and sung. Thus our Saviour's call to Saul, "Saul, Saul, why persecutest thou me?" and His awful answer to Saul's question: "Who art Thou, Lord?" and Paul's own most solemn words, "Know ye not that ye are the temple of the living God?" shock me with a feeling of absolute desecration, when I hear them sung instead of spoken; and of course this interferes greatly with my pleasure in listening to such a performance as that of St. Paul. . . .

Friday, Fanny Cobbe dines with me. I have been out of town, and so has she; and I have seen nothing of her since the day she lunched here, more than a month ago. Good-bye, my dearest H——; God bless you.

Ever, as ever, yours,
FANNY KEMBLE.

15, *Connaught Square.*

MY DEAREST H——,

I have just received a note from my old friend Mrs. Procter, whom I dare say you remember, which has really filled me with astonishment. She is close upon eighty years old, and from her home in Queen Anne's Mansions, near Westminster Abbey, she *walked* to my lodging in Portman Street, to call upon me, three days ago. I really was amazed at such a vigorous proceeding in a person of her age, for the distance must be over two miles, and I could no more *walk* than I could fly it. Very unfortunately, too, I was out, and missed her, which was very hard, when so old a woman had made such an effort to see me. . . .

I went at extreme inconvenience to myself, but at her own special desire, to hear Fanny Cobbe speak at her anti-vivisection meeting, and was very much pleased, both with what she said, and *how* she said it. It was a thoroughly *womanly* speech, putting the whole question upon moral grounds, and appealing to the sense of humanity in the hearts of those who heard her. I was delighted with her moderation, both in what she said and what she forebore to say. I think her speech was calculated both to touch and convince people. The meeting was quite a large one, and I do not think the dying away of the public interest in the question need be apprehended. . . .

As for forming any idea when I may set out for Switzerland, that indeed I cannot. I often think I should give it up altogether, I feel so worried and uncertain about the propriety and safety of leaving my young servant-women alone in this house in

London for three months; . . . and I am miserable with an unmade-up mind. I gave up my evening dictation of my Memoirs while F—— was with me, of course, and have hitherto been too busy to resume it, but expect to do so next week, as I am extremely anxious to get it finished.

The weather here is really quite too disgraceful— incessant east wind or bitter cold, with which one is literally *parched*.

Oh, my dearest H——, it makes me smile, a sorrowful smile enough, to think of my taking any part in what you call the social dissipations of the London season. People are very kind in coming to see me, and asking me to their houses; but I have and always had an absolute distaste for and shrinking from society, and have refused every invitation I have received, among others, one to meet the *Princess Louise at dinner*, which made me wonder very much whether that royal lady chose her own company or whether it was chosen for her, in which case, in my case, I should say it was ill chosen.

I see a great deal of my nephew Harry, and am growing very fond of him. Adelaide is expected back on the tenth of this month, but if I were she, I'd stay where I was.

Fanny Cobbe and Mary Lloyd are coming to lunch with me on Monday; it is the only way of seeing anything of them. Good-bye, dearest H——.

I am ever, as ever, yours,
FANNY KEMBLE.

15, *Connaught Square, April* 28*th*, 1877.

MY DEAREST H——,

You must be thinking me dead and buried in my new house, that it is now so long since I have given you any sign of life; but F—— has only this moment left me after being here since last Thursday. I was very glad to have her; the sight of her was a pleasure and a comfort to me, and her spirits are bright and buoyant, and she cheered me very much, though she could not help me much in my difficulties, which have been manifold and are not yet over, I am sorry to say, by any means.

I was informed by my landlady's agent that I was expected to take possession of the house last Wednesday. I came accordingly, was shown into a room in good order, and, supposing the rest of the house to be in a state of readiness for my reception, I paid my rent and signed my agreement; and, having done so, had the pleasure of discovering that the stair carpet was not down, that one of the rooms, which was to be thoroughly cleaned, recarpeted, and refurnished, had not been touched, and that the inventory had never been delivered to my agent. Having signed my year's lease, and paid my first quarter's rent, I had of course no redress and so here I am. The stair carpet has made its appearance reluctantly, bit by bit, the untouched bedroom remains sacredly untouched, and the inventory cannot be obtained by any means under heaven. I have told all this to Mr. Ellis, who says there is undoubtedly a remedy for these matters, but that it will be worse than the disease, *i.e.* going to law; and I need not assure you that remedy does not

enter into my contemplation for a moment. I took
the house, such as it is (and it is a sufficiently nice
and convenient one in several respects), with a view
to being able to have Mr. L—— and F—— with me
whenever they wish to come to town. I took it now,
instead of at the end of my summer abroad, because
their unsettled condition made it desirable that I
should be able to offer them that accommodation at
once, and it has been a great satisfaction to have F——
avail herself of it, as she has done for the last few
days, though of course, having no cook yet and no housemaid, my material embarrassments have been rather
increased, not so much really at all by her being with
me, as by the vexation and annoyance of feeling that
the house was upside down, and that I could not make
her decently comfortable. However, as I said before,
she is very bright and cheerful, and it was an immense
comfort to me to have her.

She, poor thing, has been overwhelmed with commissions for things to get and send to America.
Umbrellas, parasols, shoes, stockings, body-linen, and
all with such minute and inconceivably particular
directions as to shades and shapes and materials, that
poor F—— has been half distracted, and exhausted
herself in fruitless endeavours to obtain the identical
things sent for. With all this, visits to receive and
return, yesterday was a real rush from one thing to
another. In the morning to the co-operative store
for shopping, in the afternoon to the opening of a
new picture gallery, the Grosvenor, in Bond Street,
an enthusiastic artistic enterprise for the relief of
painters, whose feelings have been wounded by the

Academy, and opened by Sir Coutts Lindsay, where I really did not know which to admire most—the beauty of the women, their wild extravagant dresses (I mean *the live* women), who *exhibited themselves,* or the fantastic affectation and at the same time great cleverness of the pictures exhibited.

In the evening we were to have gone to the theatre, but were both of us too *dead beat* for that effort at amusement, and stayed at home. To-day my nerves are all shattered and shaken, and since F—— went away, I have spent my time in alternate crying and sleeping, a despicable condition of mind and body, out of which, I trust, I shall emerge by degrees. God bless you, dear.

Ever, as ever, yours,
Fanny Kemble.

15, *Connaught Square.*

My dearest H——,

I have just come up from Windsor, where I have been spending a few days with our old and attached friend Miss Thackeray. My cousin Cecilia Faulder, of whom I am very fond, spent the day with us, while I was there, and came back to town with me this afternoon. I found a pile of letters waiting for me, and among them one from Fanny Cobbe, saying she should be in town next Wednesday for some days, and hope to see me. I, however, leave London again on Friday, the 26th, so that Thursday will be the only day on which I should have a chance of seeing her.

Miss Lloyd does not come up with her, being

detained in Wales by the serious illness of her sister. . . .

My F—— writes me that the late gale has blown down a fine chestnut tree in their grounds, and torn up by the roots quite a number of the splendid trees in Stoneleigh Park, which is a dreadful pity.

We had very fine weather while I was at Windsor. On Wednesday we were out rowing on the Thames for a couple of hours, and it was really quite delightful.

I drove over from old Windsor on Wednesday afternoon, all through that splendid and lovely Windsor Park, to the opposite side of it, near Staines, where my friends, the Grays, live, and was much shocked to find Sir Frederic confined to his sofa. . . .

I had a visit just after I reached home from my dear old friend, Mr. Donne. . . . His son, who married my brother's daughter Mildred, and was left a widower by her death, has just married again, and my dear William Donne seemed pleased with the marriage, and with his son's new wife, and I hope his poor little children by Mildred will fare the better, and not the worse, for having some one in their mother's vacant place to take some care of them.

Good night, dearest H——; I have many letters to write, and must make up for lost time.

Ever, as ever, yours,

FANNY KEMBLE.

15, *Connaught Square.*

My DEAREST H——,

I am having rather a hard week, which began on Sunday by a sharp attack of indisposition, . . .

which obliged me to take to my bed and send for
a doctor. . . . This has not only deprived me of
several pleasures that I had anticipated—my Monday
evening concert, to hear Joachim play on the violin, the
private view of Leighton's pictures, to which he had
kindly invited me, and a visit that Mrs. Tom Taylor
and her sisters were to have paid me,—but by losing
the beginning of the week, these last days have, of
course, had more than enough to do crammed into
them, and I am very busy, and a good deal tired
and worried and confused, my attack having shaken
me, and made me very nervous.

Ever, as ever, yours,

FANNY KEMBLE.

15, *Connaught Square.*

MY DEAREST H——,

It is just eleven o'clock, and I am writing to
you by gaslight. The atmosphere without is literally
black with one of our London fogs, and I am obliged to
give up my purpose of driving to return some visits
I owe, for not only is the outer air unfit to breathe,
but I should think the extreme thick darkness must
make going about in a carriage really dangerous.

I want very much to go and see Fanny Cobbe,
who is suffering from a bad attack of bronchitis, to
which this terrible choking atmosphere must be most
pernicious. She wrote to me a few days ago, telling me
not to come to her, as *she could not speak at all.* . . .

I am happy to say Mary Lloyd, who has remained
in Wales until quite lately, is now with her. I do
not think she, Miss Lloyd, will rejoice much in London,

which she always detests. My nephew Harry Kemble
is to dine with me to-day, and was to have taken me
to a new piece, in which he is interested, because it is
given at the Prince of Wales's Theatre, to which he
belongs; but unless the fog disperses I do not think it
will be possible for us to go.

I have not seen a newspaper this morning or
heard a word of what was done in Parliament yesterday; but I have no idea that we shall go to war for
the Turks, *even* to spite the Russians. I sincerely
hope the time has come for Mahomed to evacuate
Europe? I should like the Greeks to have Constanti-
nople, and that it should become Byzantium again;
but my politics, you know, are very womanly and
sentimental. God bless you, dear H——.

Ever, as ever, yours,
FANNY KEMBLE.

Guildford Cottage, Godalming.

MY DEAREST H——,

I am out of my well-detested London, and
to-day, when the sun shines, the sky is heavenly,
purely clear, and the earth fresh as the garden of Eden
after the late rain. It seemed to me an exquisite
enjoyment merely to walk round and round the gravel
walk that surrounds the acre and a half of lawn and
wintry flower-beds that constitute the pleasure-ground
of this small domain.

The climate here must always be very mild, for
there are two fine magnolias growing against the
house. The yellow Mezéreum is in full blossom, and
a long low bed of violets sent forth a delicious breath

of fragrance as I passed to and fro beside it. I do not
know whether you retain any recollection of having
seen or heard of my hostess, a Mrs. R——d G——e,
who was a Miss S—— T——, and who has made
herself conspicuous in London society by her passion
for reciting poetry. She is an *actress manquée*. Her
social position and connections would have made her
going on the stage quite inexpedient, but I think she
has *hankered* after it all her life, and has consoled
her defeated aspirations by reciting and declaiming
whenever and wherever she could. She is rather
ambitious in her attempts, and not long ago, for a
charity, an entertainment part musical part decla-
matory, being given in London, she undertook to
recite *Queen Constance!* and earnestly begged *me*
to go and hear her, which I did. She has a good
deal of dramatic feeling, and is not without dramatic
talent, but she has an inexpressive face, and a bad
voice, in spite of which she makes certain recitations
of some of Tennyson's poems very effective.

You know this semi-theatrical passion is not
a thing for which I have much sympathy, but
Mrs. G——e fancies that she has an enthusiastic
affection for me (I am bound to say she has fancied
it now for a good many years), and is always im-
ploring me to come and see her; and though I do
not profess an enthusiastic affection for her, I do
not like to refuse pertinaciously to come and see her,
having no better reason to give for my refusal than
that I do not particularly wish to do so. Her mother,
a most beautiful old lady of seventy, who is neither
dramatic nor theatrical, but a very devout and rather

peculiar religionist, is much more to my taste. Her spirit is ever so much better than her opinions, and her soul than her mind; and though she talks *her* religion to me to try and convert me, and makes my blood run cold with her appeals to ideas and beliefs and symbols and sacred things wholly alike to both of us, only in so different way, I like her and her exaltation, better than her daughter and her recitation.

My coming here was an effort to me, and I shall be glad to go back to town to-morrow, though I have had a walk this morning, every minute of which was a hymn of praise in my grateful enjoyment of it.

F—— and her baby come to me next week, to my great delight.

I have met here the editor of the *Nineteenth Century*, the last new periodical, a remarkable publication for its ability and its illustration of the intellectual temper of the times. God bless you, dear.

Ever, as ever, yours,
FANNY KEMBLE.

Grosvenor Hotel, Victoria Station.

MY DEAR E——,

Talking to Mr. L—— about the strange disappearance of poor Louisa's husband, he asked me if it was likely that the man was out of work, and dispirited, as he knew of many instances in which, under those circumstances, workmen left their wives, some only temporarily, some taking themselves off to America or the colonies. Had Louisa a child? A great many women who have left service to marry, are compelled to return to it again, being deserted by their husbands.

Mr. L—— told me a very strange story of that kind the other day. A poor young woman came to him to beg him to find her husband for her. She was the daughter of tolerably well-to-do farming people, and was in service in London, where she married a milkman. The man was intelligent and ambitious, and got her parents to advance him money to educate himself; went to King's College, in London, completed the necessary course of studies, took orders, and was ordained by the Bishop of London, and got appointed to some position in a church at Wigan. Soon after this he separated himself from his wife upon the pretext that she was too ignorant and uncultivated to be a proper companion for him in his altered circumstances. The poor woman acquiesced in this sentence, and he agreed if she left him to give her a certain sum annually for her maintenance. This, however, he had left off doing, and she remained quite destitute. On seeking him at Wigan, she found he had left that place, and gone to a curacy elsewhere. With infinite searchings and trouble, Mr. L—— at length found the *gentleman* filling a clerical position not far from Stratford, Mr. L—— himself having had some slight personal knowledge of him, though not of his circumstances. Is not that a curious story, and like a thing in a novel ?

Westminster Hotel, **West Malvern.**

MY DEAREST H——,

I was sure, if you had any recollection of my dear and faithful servant Ellen, that you would be glad to hear of her safety, and the birth of her child. . . .

I cannot remain with any great comfort or pleasure in the Swiss *mountains* (I do not haunt the towns and fashionable lake shores hotels) after September, and think of going for the month of October to the Lago Maggiore, where I shall be able to pay Ellen a visit in her own home, which lies in the Varese Highland, half way between the Lake of Como, and the Lago Maggiore.

F—— and her little girl continue to thrive in this hilly region, and I hope to find myself the better for it, after I have left it, as one often does with mountains and seaside and watering places, and as I undoubtedly did last year for the Engadine, after I had left it. At present either the air itself or the water (the qualities of both elements have strong peculiarities here) affect my skin and my eyes uncomfortably, and F—— complains of a similar affection in her eyes here, from which she was certainly free for two days lately, when she went down to Leamington to see the American bishops, whom her husband had invited to come there, one of whom, the Bishop of Louisiana, was an old friend of hers, having been for many years clergyman of a church in Philadelphia that she used to attend. He is an excellent old gentleman, whom she was very glad to see again.

Mr. L—— has been very busy organizing and opening a workmen's club and coffee-house, one of those excellent enterprises by which it is hoped something may be done to diminish the attraction of the vile gin palaces and public houses, and counteract the habits of drinking of the poor working men. At present it is promising to be very successful, and my

dear son-in-law may, I think, congratulate himself on
having done a worthy work among his parishioners.
They have just made him rural dean, which adds
responsibility and labour to that of his position as
vicar, but does not increase his emoluments, which
I regret, as the living of Leamington is not a very
good one, and he has no vicarage house and is
obliged to keep two curates.

God bless you, my dearest H——. I was *delighted*
to get your few words of dictation.

Ever, as ever, yours,

FANNY KEMBLE.

MY DEAREST H——,

My life here at Malvern is very quiet and
pleasant, and no doubt salubrious for soul and body.
On Sunday a very dear American friend of mine,
sister to one of the bishops who have come over from
the United States to attend the episcopal council,
turned aside from her way from Liverpool to London
to spend a day with me here. She and her daughter
are among my most intimate and oldest Boston
friends. The mother I knew before either she or
I were married. They had seen S—— just before
they sailed for Europe, and so brought me the latest
personal tidings of my child. To-day they have gone
on their way to London.

Yesterday afternoon Mr. L—— arrived from
Leamington, bringing with him F——'s pony-carriage
and pony, little Alice's donkey and Spanish saddle, and
a beautiful dog of his, who is a great favourite with
us all, all which *articles* will be additions to the

comfort and pleasure of F—— and their child's summer residence here.

I crawl up and down the hilly roads in the morning, enjoying the fine air and beautiful views, and in the afternoon inhale the one and contemplate the other from my sitting-room window, which is admirably situated for both purposes. Of course I regret my beloved Alps, but am nevertheless quite alive to all the loveliness, and healthiness, and peace, and quiet, and comfort of this place, and am abundantly thankful for it all.

I see F—— and my little Alice every day, and hope they will both benefit by this place as much as they seem to enjoy it.

We had some fearful hot weather when first I came up here, but since that the climate has reverted to its usual agreeable temperature at midsummer, *i.e.* that of a *mild winter*, which I, who do not like heat, find very pleasant. God bless you, dearest H——.

Ever, as ever, yours,
FANNY KEMBLE.

Westminster Hotel, West Malvern.

DEAR E——,

Please give my dear love to my dear H——, and tell her we have been much cheered, since the death of Alice's deeply lamented donkey, by sundry small festivities, in which she has participated.

Three days ago Mr. L—— brought up all his little choir boys, twenty of them, from Leamington, to spend the day on the Worcestershire Beacon, the high grassy hill that rises behind this house. They had an excellent dinner at this house, and spent the whole afternoon running about the grassy slopes. Mr. L—— walked up, and F—— went up on a pony, and Alice and a little American girl, a friend of hers, on donkeys ; and they had a most delightful time, running races for halfpence, jumping over pocket-handkerchiefs, in all which the " Vicar " joined, to the great ecstasy of all the children. Yesterday there was a school-feast and distribution of prizes for the village children here, to which little Alice and her American friend went, and the child was in a perfect frenzy of delight at the cheering with which the school children wound up their feast in honour of their clergyman and teachers, insomuch that after Alice was put to bed, and had gone, as was supposed, to sleep, her mother, who was in the room beneath her, heard her calling, as she thought, and running up to see what she wanted, the little thing said, half asleep, " No, mamma, I did not call, but I was saying ' Hip, hip, hip, hurrah ! ' " Wasn't that funny and pretty ? Good-bye, my dearest, dearest H——.

I am ever, as ever, yours,
FANNY KEMBLE.

Westminster Hotel, West Malvern.

Thank you, my dear E——, for your account of Mr. Thompson's adventures. I agree with you in thinking his long endurance of his perilous position singular, to say the least of it. Perhaps his further account of the circumstances will make it less extraordinary. It is frightfully dangerous for people to go straying about in those Alpine precipices without guides.

I remember an account of a gentleman and his wife who got into a *mal passe* on the Kirchet, from which he, being an experienced mountaineer, was able to effect their escape, but only by leading his wife with *her eyes shut*, lest her fear at the danger of their position should paralyze her.

Though I do not read any newspapers, I did know of the various items of public news which you are good enough to give me. I wish Sir Garnet Wolseley would black his face, now that he is "Governor of Cyprus." Is he married? and is his wife's name anything like Desdemona? It would seem more Othello like and natural if it was.

Surely no "curiosity of literature" of the elder Disraeli was ever half so curious as his son's career. By-the-bye, do you know why Jacob was commanded to take the name of Israel?—because it would never do to have had the whole chosen nation called *Jacobites*. If that jest appears to you in any degree irreverent or unseemly—I beg to inform you that it is a quotation from an eighteenth-century sermon.

I wonder if my dear H—— retains any recollection of my excellent and devoted maid Ellen. You, I have no doubt, remember her. To my great joy, I had a letter yesterday from her worthy husband Luigi, informing me of her safe delivery of a boy baby, a circumstance of great rejoicing to me, as I was very anxious about her. . . . Luigi's Italian paraphrases are very droll. "*Il mio figlio, venne a la luce!*" Imagine an

English butler or footman telling you at what hour his son first " saw the light"!

We have had rain and storms at last, and the great heat is somewhat moderated, for which I am very thankful.   Our accounts of the heat in America are terrible.   God bless you, my dearest H——.

I am ever, as ever, your

FANNY KEMBLE.

Stuttgart.

MY DEAREST H——,

I am detained here, very bitterly against my will, by the non-arrival of my luggage, which is *supposed to be* reposing in the Cologne custom house. Harry Kemble got me my tickets, and had my luggage registered for me to this place, Stuttgart, without however being aware that it would have to be *examined* at Cologne, so on I came, nothing doubting, and here, where I expected to embrace my trunks, am told that they are waiting, poor things, to be rummaged at Cologne.   This is very vexatious, as I am eager to get to my mountains, and have no particular liking for Stuttgart, which is a funny little German imitation of Versailles, a huge palace with a tiny town tied to its tail.   There are, however, very pretty gardens and park, and these are rather a comfort, especially as, in addition to the detention for my luggage, a mistake was made about the hotel to which I was taken, and I spent Saturday and yesterday in a second-class German hotel, where people smoked in the eating-room, where none of the modern decencies of life were known, and which was on the noisiest street of the

town, immediately opposite the railroad station, so
that the racket was incessant and intolerable.   This
morning I have changed my residence to a better
hotel, and a less noisy neighbourhood, and am preparing
my mind to wait with patience for the clothes of my
body.   I suppose such pieces of carelessness or ill
fortune are not infrequent with travellers, as all the
hotel people and railroad officials seem to take our
case very much more philosophically than we do ourselves.   We were assured that, by sending a telegram
to Cologne, the things would certainly be forwarded
here by yesterday evening.   They did not make their
appearance then, however, and we were comfortably
assured that they would come to-night.   I do not,
however, much expect to see them, as I was also
informed by one of the clerks that I might be thankful if they arrived to-morrow, and so I will; in short,
when I see them, I shall leave off expecting them.   My
poor maid-servants are worse off, than I am myself;
for I had a few changes of linen with me, while they
literally have nothing but what they stand in.   On
the other hand, the novelty of the place, the pretty
Versailles like gardens, the fountains and statues, etc.,
divert and console them more than they do me.

This place has only one valuable association for
me.   Close to it, at the other end of the park, is
Koenigstadt, a charming village often resorted to by
Dr. Norman Macleod, when as a youth he studied at
Stuttgart.   He speaks of it more than once in his
letters and memoirs, and as his life, which I have
been reading lately, has impressed and *exhorted* me
more than any book I have read for a long time,

I was glad **to make** a pilgrimage thither for his sake, and that **of** my friend Thackeray, with **whom it** was also much-frequented ground.

Good-bye, dear. I wrote to you yesterday, but as there will be many days when I shall not **be able** to do so, I write again to-day. When I begin climbing the mountains, my writing and sending letters will be a little less frequent. **God bless** you.

Ever, as ever, yours,

FANNY KEMBLE.

Bagni di Leprese.

MY VERY DEAR H——,

I found your letters, among **others, waiting for me** here on my arrival yesterday, **but I had had a** carriage journey of eight hours, in great heat, and was too tired to write to anybody but F——, from whom I also found a letter. I was grieved to **hear how ill** you had **been,** my dearest H——, and shall **be most** anxious to know of your entire recovery, and **how you** are able to tolerate a new person attending upon you, . . . to serve a person well and conscientiously seems to me almost as **certain to** make one love them, as to be so served naturally would, especially when the assistance rendered is personal, **and** such as you, my dearest H——, require.

I can give you a very good account of myself thus **far; the** distressing nervous symptoms, **the** constant tendency to hysterical crying, and **the** intolerable trembling feeling of apprehension, as **of some impend**ing catastrophe, have entirely left me, **and I have had no** unpleasant sensations except those consequent upon a slight sunstroke, which both Ellen and I experienced after a long drive under a broiling sun, in an open carriage up the Finster Munz ; nausea, and such dizziness as absolutely to stagger about at the end of a long day's journey, in which we had suffered extremely from the heat, and eaten scarcely anything. It was a mere effect of exhaustion and fatigue, by which I was never so affected before in travelling,—to be sure, I never was sixty-eight years old before in travelling.

I have now gone over the only one of the great Alpine passes with which I was hitherto unacquainted, the Stelvio, and am inclined to think that it is the grandest of them all. The summit is nine thousand feet above the sea, and the ascent on the Swiss side beautiful as well as sublime in the highest degree. Strangely enough, on the Swiss side, splendid forests of large trees, and the innumerable variety of lovely mountain Swiss wild flowers accompanied us almost up to the very top, while on the Italian side great fields of snow extended far down the grizzly chasms and abysses, and snow was falling as we came down. Certainly the bare horror of that precipitous descent was anything but Italian.

The summer has been rainy hitherto, I am told, and perhaps it is one of those rainy seasons, two of which are said, by observers of such phenomena, to alternate in Switzerland with every third and dry season.

The place from which I now write to you is on the edge of a small mountain lake in a valley at the foot of the Bernina Pass in the Engadine. The lake has undoubtedly been a volcano ; it has the unmistakable features of an **extinct** crater, **and the** place moreover is celebrated for **its hot** sulphur baths, which are another indication **of the former** volcanic condition of the neighbourhood. I expect **to rest here for a** week.

I have left myself but little room, dearest H——, to tell you of the new prospect which is just opened **to the L——s. The vicar of** Leamington, **an old** and sickly man, is recently dead, and his living **has** been offered to **Mr. L——.** In many respects it seems to me an advantageous and **desirable** thing for **him,** but poor **F——,** who has just settled herself in her new home **at** Stratford-on-Avon, **and is** enchanted with it, is in despair at the idea of having immediately to give it up, and go and live in Leamington, which she dislikes. "Will fortune never come with **both** hands full?" Certainly it seems to me a piece **of** unusual good luck, attended by sharp disappointment. I **wish F——** could think **less** of the latter **than she** does.

God bless **you, my** dearest H——. Good-bye; you **shall hear from me as soon as** possible again.

Ever, as ever, yours,

FANNY.

Hotel Rosegg, Pontressina.

MY DEAREST H——,

I have only just **arrived at this place over** the **Bernina** Pass, from Leprese, whence **I last wrote** to you. After my five days consecutive travelling over the Foralberg, the Finstermunz, and the Stelvio passes, I was very glad of the quiet of the little Italian (for though in Switzerland its whole character is southern) watering-place by the side of an extinct volcano, now filled with a pretty lake abounding in trout, and with hot sulphur springs coming up on its shores to prove its former fiery character.

I wrote to you immediately on my arrival there. I hoped to have found some tidings of you here, but have not done so, and now I fear I must wait for my letters till I get to Samaden, which will not be for several days. My week at Leprese was not without some excitement, for we were in daily expectation of the arrival of Luigi to claim Ellen, . . . and I, starting at eight o'clock this morning to cross the Bernina Pass to this place, left them standing at the inn door, whence they were to go down to the Lake of Como in the afternoon. . . .

Our journey to-day was a very tedious one, for the Pass of the Bernina is not comparable to many that I have traversed. The weather was dreadful, pouring with rain all day, and the step by step crawl of five hours up a steep mountain pass, in torrents of rain with snow lying over all the mountain tops and turbid, furious torrents springing from every gap in them, and threatening at every moment to tear the road away under the horses' feet, is not cheerful.

This place, however, Pontressina, as far as I am able to see from the windows of my rooms, is really very beautiful, and deserves all the praises of its enthusiastic admirers.

I have a magnificent snow mountain and glacier immediately opposite to me here, and very noble ranges of Alpine peaks rising in every direction above the lower rocks and cliffs and pine-covered slopes of the valley.

If the weather would only clear a little, I am sure it would be splendidly beautiful, but the summer hitherto has been unusually wet and cold, and I am sorry to say, after a few transient gleams of sunshine, the clouds have gathered all over the valley again.

Dearest H——, I am tired with my journey, but very fairly well; to-morrow, I have no doubt I shall be quite "jolly." How are you, my dear? I am very anxious to hear that you have thrown off all remains of your late cold, and to know how Louisa's successor discharges her duties to you? God bless you, dear.

I am ever, as ever, yours,

FANNY KEMBLE.

Silvaplana.

My dearest H——,

Never come to Silvaplana, which is a charmingly pretty place in the Engadine, because it has a climate worse than anything I ever experienced anywhere of the worst kind of March weather. The roads are blinding white and deep with burning dust, the tops of all the mountains are blinding white and cold with never-melting snow, and a piercing wind blows through this narrow alpine corridor, which flays the skin off your face, at least, whatever skin the sun does not broil off it at the same time.

Having said this, I will return to the more agreeable characteristics of the place. It is charmingly situated on two pretty little lakes, which just in front

of the village are joined together by a channel not
wider than the Liffey at Dublin. In short, they are like
a pair of spectacles, on a large scale, laid down in the
middle of smooth green meadows of such grass as
Switzerland only owns. The water is of a curiously
beautiful green colour, suggesting the idea that the
lake bottoms are lined with copper. Pine and larch
woods frame in these pretty mountain meres, and
above them tower the crags, and cliffs, and rocks, and
snow, and glaciers, of the Engadine Alps; and if the
sun did not fry, and the wind scorch, and the dust
suffocate one, I think it might be a pleasant, as it
undoubtedly is, a pretty place.

To-morrow I go back over the Juliar Pass to
a place called Thusis, at the entrance of the Via Mala,
at the northern foot of the Splügen Pass, and shall
probably stay there a week, in the course of which
I expect H—— will join me, and I shall send Mac
Farland home to take care of my house till I return to
London.

S—— has made no mention whatever in her
letters of the railroad strikes and riots in the United
States, nor have any other of my American corres-
pondents alluded to them.

As F—— very much prefers her one year's residence
at Stratford-on-Avon, in her picturesque manor house,
to leaving it directly, I am of course very glad that
the Bishop of Worcester allows her that indulgence.
She does not fancy Leamington, which I regret,
because Mr. L—— has accepted that position, and it
appears to me, in many respects, a fitting and appropriate one for him.

A poor gentleman, a certain archdeacon, arrived here a few days ago, to fill the English chaplaincy at this place for five weeks, and I really am concerned for the worthy gentleman, who yesterday read the prayers admirably, and preached an excellent sermon to his wife and two children, myself and my two servants—a large congregation, which will be half as large next Sunday, when I shall not be here. No English people ever stop here. It is only three miles from St. Moritz, and a few more from Pontresina, to which two places all English travellers in the Engadine betake themselves, and where there are already resident chaplains provided for them. I am really very sorry for the archdeacon. I have told you all my story, my dearest H——. I am well, though I have a slight touch of erysipelas in my face and neck, from the effect of the sun and wind. It causes me some annoyance, but does not signify much.

God bless you, my dearest friend; I am thankful that my letters have still the power to cheer and interest you.

Ever, as ever, yours,
FANNY KEMBLE.

Thusis.

MY DEAREST H——,

My nephew joined me yesterday evening, a day sooner than expected, and as every place in this house, and indeed in the whole village, I believe, is crammed with travellers, he was obliged to put up with a *shake down* in the billiard-room for the night, for which he was not otherwise than thankful, not having stopped a night on his way from London here.

He is very glad to get rid of his theatre work, which was beginning to be oppressively hot and trying, and to have a month's holiday of fresh air, and change of scene before he resumes it again. I am very glad to have him with me; he is very kind and affectionate to me. He is like his own father and my father, but likest of all to a water-colour drawing I have of my uncle, Stephen Kemble. I remember, when he was a little child, his great resemblance to a portrait I had of Stephen Kemble's daughter, my cousin Mrs. Arkwright. Before leaving England, he had been staying several days at Warsash, and brought me a very good account of my sister and her family, who are all assembled there. . . .

By-the-bye, I have just had an interview, in the garden of this place, with ex-president General Grant and his family. . . . I heard they were expected to pass through this place, and having promised a poor man to do him a service, which I thought General Grant could help me to do, I went down to the garden where he was sitting smoking. . . .

I laid my case before him, that of a poor Swiss man, porter of one of the Engadine hotels, who had lived sixteen years in America, and served in the Northern Army, and been pensioned by the United States Government, having lost an eye in the war; but he could only draw his pension by the means of certain vouchers, which I thought General Grant could possibly give him. My application, however, proved fruitless, for the General was not going into the

Engadine, but the other way, and so my poor Swiss man will not get his pension through that venture of mine.

It is Sunday, and I am going to church; not without some painful misgiving as to the amount of edification I am likely to derive from that ceremony. Anything more extraordinary than some of the so-called English church services I have attended since I have been in the Engadine cannot well be imagined. At one place the clergyman intoned the whole liturgy, at the top of his voice and the top of his speed, only varying this wonderful chant by dropping every three minutes into an inaudible whisper, from which he emerged like a subterranean river, and went on again at the top of his voice and the top of his speed. Another day, the officiating clergyman spent half his time kneeling, apparently in silent adoration, before a cross, which was in the middle of the communion table, with his back to the congregation; then intoned the Litany, at the end of which the service was understood to be over and everybody departed. Many of the persons crossed themselves, with an inclination towards the communion table on entering the church. In short, anything less like the Protestant Church of England than all these performances cannot well be described.

You asked me if S——, in her last letter, had said anything about the trade riots in America, and I told you she had not; but F—— in her last letter, and M. F—— in hers, speak of them as having been very serious indeed, and having required the intervention of the armed force everywhere to put them down.

I am upon the whole rather glad than sorry that

this question of the relations between labour and capital, the one vital material question of modern civilized society, should have come to a crucial debate and trial in America, where the whole matter will be reduced to its simplest fundamental elements, and no side issues and complications, such as would attend dealing with them in Europe, exist to obscure the understanding of the people or trammel legislative action upon the matter. Nowhere else are the circumstances equally favourable for arriving at a sound and permanent result with regard to the rights of employers and employed, and the two great forces, which in truth are but one, of modern commercial industrial and financial civilized existence, capital and labour, and the settling once for all their respective claims and powers, as in America, where the conditions of society are most favourable for so doing, and will simplify the process, even for older countries and more complex communities, where the difficulties are greater and the *elbow* room for all experiments less. Now I must go to church.

God bless you, dearest H——. I leave this place on Tuesday, and shall probably not have time to write to you again before that.

Ever, as ever, yours,
FANNY.

St. Moritz, Engadine.

MY DEAREST H——,

I remember many years ago your telling me that you thought the most beautiful thing in all your travelling experience was the descent of the Splügen

to Chiavenna, on **the** Italian side, **so I** thought much
of you three days ago, **as I came down** that same
beautiful mountain staircase.

I have not, however, changed my opinion or altered
in my preference of the Swiss over the Italian side of
the Alps. Thus I think the Swiss side of the Splügen
not only grander and more sublime, but more beautiful and charming **than** the Italian side. This has
something to do with my delight **in** the exquisite
flora of the Alps, in the gems with which **the green**
mantles of the huge mountains are embroidered, **the**
tiny blessed blossoms that creep to the very feet of the
terrible glaciers, and the trembling sprays **of tender**
vivid colour that hang tearful and decked with diamonds
over the black chasms of **the** roaring cataracts. The
incomparable bright soft verdure **of the high** Alpine
meadows is far lovelier to me than all the vines of the
South. The one seem **almost too** immaculate, in their
close-cropped velvet freshness, to harbour the smallest
unclean creeping thing; the other, with their untrimmed,
flaunting, **luxuriant** garlands, **trailing** over white walls
alive with lizards, suggest earwigs, and spiders, and
scorpions in every corner and crevice of their crum-
bling terraces. The *unpaintable* huge mountain heads
and shoulders, and dark large woods and rushing
torrents, which have **never** found, and **never will find,**
adequate representation in art, are far more fascinating
to me than those exquisite, ready-made pictures that
meet one at every quarter of a mile in Italy; with the
ruined, tumble-down houses and degraded-looking
population, forming always to me painful features in
the landscape.

But the wild flowers alone in Switzerland are such a delight to me, that I know nothing of the sort comparable to it anywhere else. The preference these exquisite creatures themselves show for the highest parts of the mountains, where just earth enough clings to support them, the masses of rhododendron, the sheaves of blue bells of every shade, from almost white, to deepest purple, and every size, from the clumps of tiny blossoms that shiver in the spray of the waterfalls, to the large single deep bell vibrating on its hairlike stem in the keen mountain breeze, and those lovely things the rose veronica, the deep blue dwarf gentian, and the ermine edelweiss that are never found but where the everlasting snow is their neighbour, these are an enchantment to me, which nothing in all the glorious, glowing, untidy dishevelment of a southern landscape compensates for. The fact is, the moral of the two aspects of nature is absolutely dissimilar, and the one is congenial in its severity, and the other not in its softness, to *my* human nature.

The Swiss people, I think, the most disagreeable people in both worlds; but their country is my earthly paradise.

My diary records thus of our journey from Splügen to Chiavenna: "Lordly, lovely, wonderful mountain-pass; Italy at the bottom, cypresses, vines, chestnuts; every quarter of a mile a perfect picture, wretched population, hideous human dwellings, fit only for cattle; at the hotel, lofty rooms, scaliola floors, marble, mirrors, magnificence, bad smells, and—bed-bugs."

We have just arrived at this place this morning,

and I think we shall stay here a week, though such is the tyranny the innkeepers of this region exercise over unfortunate travellers, that it is rather difficult to be sure of what one will be allowed to do. I hear of people who are turned out of their rooms, neck and crop, under pretext that they were already bespoken, and that the unlucky occupants were only received without being aware of it *pro tem.*

As soon as you arrive you are challenged as to the length of your stay, about which perhaps you have not even made up your own mind, in order that your rooms may be let to other people the very hour before you leave them. It is really curious to see the fervent zeal of money-making by which every class of the community here and every individual of every class is animated. Their season is but of two months, which is their sole reply to every remonstrance against the exorbitance of their charges; and certainly they cannot be accused of not making hay while the sun shines.

Harry and I get on very pleasantly together; he seems an amiable, well-disposed person, is very quiet and well bred, and is kind and affectionate to me. I hope he enjoys his holiday travelling, and though I am afraid he finds me rather a dull companion, our fellowship upon the whole is, I think, satisfactory to both of us. He remembers very gratefully your kindness to him when he was in Dublin, and was speaking of it with great warmth the other day.

I ought to have told you, while I was on the chapter of my travels, of how we came out of Italy here, that is from Chiavenna by the Maloya Pass into the Engadine. The Italian, the lower part of the pass, is extremely beautiful, and the upper part very fine, but it is not to my thinking one of the most beautiful or finest of the Alpine passes. The final ascent from the southern side to the summit is peculiar, and unlike any other I have gone over. Generally zigzags that take one up the last stage of these portentous climbs are conducted over the necks and shoulders of the mountain crest, but in this instance our last approach to the summit seem to be made up the inside walls of a huge well in the earth, the sides of which were clothed with enormous larches, that made it look from the top like a great thousand-feet-deep *hole* cut in a forest growing perpendicularly up to the sky. Round this gigantic ball the road wound in spiral curves like the bore of a rifle till it got to the top, and then there was no descent on the other side, for the valley of the Upper Engadine is a mere strip of meadowland, with a chain of charming lakes, formed by the course of the Inn, running through the middle of it, and the mountain tops hemming it in on both sides, and its lowest level is five thousand feet above the sea. So here we are. It is all very fine and very charming; but the air is too sharp and bracing for me, and with all due respect to the Princess de Metternich, and the gentlemen of the Alpine Club, who set the fashion of the rage for the Engadine, it is by no means the most beautiful part of Switzerland. Good-bye, my dearest H——. God bless you.

I am ever, as ever, yours,

FANNY KEMBLE.

Samaden.

MY DEAREST H——,

What you say in your letter about my nephew's enthusiastic juvenile impressions of Switzerland made me laugh, and him, to whom I imparted it, smile.

He has already seen more than once the most beautiful parts of Switzerland, and under far pleasanter circumstances than those of his present journeys with me.

Charles Santley, the singer, who married **Gertrude Kemble**, has **been always a very kind** friend of Harry's, and has two or three times brought him **to** Switzerland, during the theatrical recess, and **in** those tours he had not only Santley's companionship, walking **over** some beautiful passes, but the **cheerful company** of his family, young girls, and Gertrude **herself, who is, I** should think, endowed with good **animal spirits,** and what **is called** nowadays "jolly," **which I, my dear** H——, am decidedly not.

I dare say **Harry may** like coming abroad, and travelling with **a certain** amount of **luxury,** but I doubt **very much if** his holiday **will upon the** whole have been **half as pleasant as** those he has spent in Switzerland before.

He **is peculiarly amiable in** his manner, **and** gentle and **courteous and kind to me.** His **temper** appears perfectly even **and sweet,** and the reasonableness and sound common sense **of all his** views and appreciations of life and people, though **not** perhaps **an** attractive quality in so **young a** man, is a very unusual and valuable **one.** He has a great deal of character, but is

very reticent and as guarded and courteous in express-
ing his own thoughts and feelings, as he is quick
and keen sighted in observing those of other people.
Our intercourse is pleasant to me, because of his
gentle and affectionate manner, and his occasional
great likeness to his father and grandfather. Mine, I
suspect, is not altogether pleasant to him, because of
my abrupt and brusque manner and quick, sudden
strong transitions of feeling; but we get on very well
together. I am very glad to have him with me, and
he, I have no doubt, gets some enjoyment out of our
journey together.

We are both rejoicing to-day at having left St.
Moritz, which we had neither of us liked at all. The
place itself is less attractive than any other where we
have stopped in the Engadine, and its essentially
watering-place character, crowded with over-dressed
dandies and equivocal or unequivocal ladies, with a
perfect fair of booths filled with rubbish, at extortionate
prices, incessant *braying* of bands and ringing of bells,
the eternal inrushing and outrushing of arriving and
departing travellers, made it altogether an unpleasant
residence. I am stopping here only for one day,
to-morrow, Sunday; and on Monday leave the Upper
Engadine for the baths of Tarasp, another but much
quieter bathing-place, at the lower end of the lower
valley, which I shall leave by the pass of the
Fintzermunz, by which I made my first approach to it
over the Stelvio.

To revert to the question of enthusiasm, my
remains of that quality, and ready capacity of
excitement are, I take it, a matter of no small surprise

and amusement to Harry. . . . Good-bye, God bless you, my dearest H——.

I am ever, as ever, yours,

FANNY KEMBLE.

Tarasp, Lower Engadine.

MY DEAREST **H——,**

Your new maid's comment upon your bodily infirmities and your spiritual graces enchants me. Louisa never, till the day of judgment, would have found out, or at any rate expressed that your patient fortitude and warm benevolence of heart could be put into the scale against the sad deprivation with which you are afflicted. She must be a good and wise creature, so to interpret your trial and your character, and it comforts me to think you have such a person about you.

I came to this place the day before yesterday, leaving Samaden and driving down the Upper Engadine and into the lower valley, a journey of about thirty-two miles, which was in itself very delightful, for the weather was perfect, and the scenery lovely the whole way.

I do not endorse the general enthusiasm for the Upper Engadine, to which it is now the fashion for tourists to flock in thousands.

The scenery, though fine, is hard in its character, the climate, though invigorating, harsh, and too sharply stimulating; and the great height of the valley above the sea-level forbids all vegetation but the grass of the meadows, and larches, and pines of the lower mountain slopes, above which shine the cold splendours of the glaciers and everlasting snows.

But the rage for this *superior* region is something wonderful. Every hotel in every village is crammed with people, sleeping two, three, and four in a room. The hotel-keepers are the direct descendants and representatives of the robber knights of old; fleecing the wretched wayfarers, and adding insult to injury by telling you in the most pathetic way, if you complain of their extortions, that *their season only lasts two months.* Poor ephemeræ! . . .

The Lower Engadine, though infinitely less be-praised and crowded with illustrious tourists than the Upper, seems to me quite charming. The snow peaks and glaciers, it is true, are lost sight of, but mountain ranges and rocky cliffs, from five to ten thousand feet high, with dolomite colouring, are not despicable boundaries to one's horizon in every direction. The valley of the Inn itself, which one follows all the way to the Tyrol, is a succession of fine deep gorges, with precipices for their walls, and the level basins, which alternate with these, are not only soft with the perfect grass meadows of the Alps, but varied with warmer tints of ripening grainfields, and the larch woods are rendered less monotonous and gloomy by the ad-mixture of the forest growth of a milder climate.

The friendly (as the Germans say) aspect of the landscape suggest human industry and cultivation; the villagers are really perfect studies for a painter, with their quaint old houses, all covered with friezes, arabesques, and ornaments, the fine mahogany colour of their woodwork, their highly wrought antique iron balconies, and the profuse fringes of exquisite flowers, especially carnations, blooming all over and streaming like garlands from them, they are really surprisingly curious, picturesque, and charming.

I am very much pleased with this place itself, where I expect to stay until next Monday, and then to leave the Engadine by the Finstermünz Pass, recrossing it in the opposite direction from that in which I traversed it at the beginning of my tour.

Good-bye, my dearest H——. It is most delightful to me to be able, by my letters, to give you ever so small a share in the pleasure of my journey. God bless you, dear.

Ever, as ever, yours,
FANNY.

Ragatz.

MY DEAREST H——,

Here we are out of the mountains, at least so far as to be once more travelling by railroad. We took our last drive through the lovely Foralberg on Wednesday, and are now in the nook of the mountains, opening out on the broad Rhine valley, and on the railroad to Zürich.

My departure from the Engadine was celebrated on my part, precisely as my entrance to it had been, by a severe bilious attack, which sent me here staggering with sick headache and far from happy.

I have enjoyed my whole summer very much, though the Engadine has not agreed with me, and I am sure that unless people require and are able to bear the climate, it is not a good residence for them.

I have just had a visit from Mrs. Storey, the American sculptor's wife, who tells me that her husband was quite unable to endure the sharpness of the air at St. Moritz, was obliged to sit up, gasping for breath, half the night, and was altogether so depressed and miserable (in that atmosphere to so many people exhilarating) that he was obliged to leave it and come down to find air that he could breathe. I was able to *endure* it, and to pass four weeks at different places in the Engadine, but I felt unwell and very uncomfortable the whole time, and especially so at Pontresina, and at St. Moritz, the very favourite places of resort of English enthusiasts.

I have stayed at this place before, but not at this house, and when I left it, it was to start immediately for England and America; that was when you brought me, at the Euston Square Hotel, those splendid red roses and myrtle branches, that lived across the Atlantic, and are now flourishing plants in my dear Mary Fox's greenhouse.

We shall only stay here a week, and then go straight to Paris, where Harry will leave me, and I shall remain to shop, and then go on to Brussels.

I do not expect to get to England much before the first of October, or to Wales much before the fifteenth, which will, I am afraid, be later than they would like me to come; but I shall not be able to manage it earlier.

I shall have no more pretty places and pleasant journeys to write you about, my dearest H——, and I am sorry for it, nothing but the old unchanging story, then.

I am ever, as ever, yours,

FANNY.

Ragatz.

I wrote to you, my dearest H——, on my arrival at this place, but yesterday's post brought me two short letters from you, and I cannot leave your dear words unacknowledged, although my present circumstances of quiet stay here do not afford me much matter for letter-writing.

Nothing can be more unlike than my nephew Harry's disposition and mine. . . .

His face is handsome, though rather heavy for so young a man; his figure is bad, short and thickset; altogether he reminds me of Charles Mason, and by times of my father and his own, by strong likenesses of countenance and expression. We get on very well together, but are very decidedly unlike each other in every respect.

The season of this place is nearly over, and the house comparatively empty. Several of the remaining guests are American, and among them is Mrs. Storey, the wife of the sculptor, whom I knew in Rome, and who, failing the smallest scrap of English or foreign nobility or even gentry, whose society is the daily bread of her life, when she can get it, has fallen, in her utter destitution of better things, upon me, and assures me I am to her a perfect "oasis in the desert."

The poor woman has been ordered here to take the baths, and I think will die no other death than the dulness of her cure.

By-the-bye, if Mrs. St. Quintin can travel so far as north of Aberdeen, she ought to come here next summer, and take a course of these waters, which are really wonderful for all rheumatic and gouty-rheumatic

affections.   A short stay would probably be sufficient
for her, and the place is so pretty and pleasant, that
it would really repay her for coming so far to do
herself good.

The hotel is, after the fashion of modern hotels, a
perfect palace—spacious, luxurious, magnificent, and
comfortable.   The baths are in the house, and are
quite delightful, both in the temperature of the water
itself, which is warm and soft, and in their arrangement,
the baths being square wells about four feet deep, sunk
in the floor of a dressing-room, lined with white china
tiles, cleaner looking even than marble, and always
full of this pellucid water, which runs through them
the whole time.

The house is surrounded with a most charming
garden laid out in terraces, with fountains and flower-
beds, and magnificent oleander and pomegranate
bushes, in large green cases, adding a stately smiling
formality and dignity to the bloomy flowering
fragrance, and less artificial beauty of great masses of
roses and geraniums and variegated beds of coloured
leaves.

My principal delight, however, is the kitchen-
garden, a fine space of level ground of about three
acres, lying below the terrace and fountains of the
flower-garden, admirably laid out and kept, and full
of the finest fruit I almost ever saw—pears, apples, and
grapes, trained with the utmost care and considerable
taste over espaliers—a really beautiful sight, and
peculiarly charming as one looks over the low wall of
enclosure from this space of cultivation, perfect of its
kind, to the sharp and splintered spikes and cliffs of

barren rock, and the **huge** shoulders of wood-mantled mountains rising into the sky in every direction, and sheltering this beautiful bit of human industry.

I wonder whether **the soil** here derives heat and consequent prolific power from the subterranean fires, by which I suppose these natural hot springs are sent boiling to the earth's surface ?

If you never were here, it would be worth your while to get dear **E——** to look out an account **of it** in Murray's "Swiss **Handbook**" and read **it** to you, for it is very curious and interesting.

God bless you, **dear H——**. I think you had now better send your letters to Coutts, **as** I leave this place for Paris **on Thursday next.**

Ever, as ever, yours,

FANNY KEMBLE.

Brunnen, Schwytz.

MY DEAREST H——,

I travelled all last week, and arrived here the day before yesterday. My desire to avoid Paris took me round through a part of Belgium I had never seen before, and through the forest of Ardennes (I suppose Rosalind was the daughter of a dispossessed Duke of Brabant), and the Grand Duchy of Luxembourg. This region of the Ardennes is wild and wooded, and much more picturesque than I supposed anything in Belgium to be. I also traversed the scene of much of the late war between France and Prussia, passing through both the poor siege-wrecked towns of Metz and Strasbourg, and coming into Switzerland, through a defile of the Vosges, all which was new to

me, as I have hitherto come to my beloved Alps either
straight through Paris or by the Rhine.

The weather is very unfavourable for travelling,
being hot and stormy and very wet, and the complaints
about it are universal. It does not seem, however, to
daunt or deter tourists much. The day of my arrival
at Lucerne, three hundred people were seated at the
table d'hôte, and the boats that touch at this place
three or four times a day, going up and down the
lake, are crowded with passengers. I have very
often passed by this Brunnen on my way to and from
the St. Gotthard, but never disembarked. I am now,
however, here for a week, and find it in every respect
a most excellent halting-station. It is immediately in
the *Elbow* of the Lake of Lucerne. The upper half of
the arm stretching to Lucerne and the lower to
Fluelen. The position of the hotel is beautiful, commanding both the reaches of the lake, and all the fine
mountains of this part of it.

On Saturday I am going to a place called
Axenstein, which is a very fine hotel some way up
the mountain, immediately behind this place, which
from its greater elevation has more extent of view,
but loses the advantage of being immediately on the
shore of the lovely lake.

When I leave this neighbourhood, I am going to
stay on the Lake of Geneva, in order to let my new
maid pay a visit to her friends and family. They live
near Montreux, mother and grandmother and brothers
and sisters, and she has seen none of them for five
years, having been in service in Scotland all that time.

I do not like staying at those crowded places on

the Lake of Geneva, full of full-dressed American and French tourists, but I hope by doing so to make my poor little Swiss girl and her family very happy.

Good-bye, my dearest H——; the beautiful lake and mountains are vanishing behind a thick curtain of rain and it is quite cold, as well as wet. It is pleasant to know that when the sun shines again, the beautiful lake and mountains will be there. God bless you, dear.

Ever, as ever, yours,

FANNY KEMBLE.

Do think of people going up the Righi by railroad! I think that must have been an American idea.

Axenstein, above **Brunnen.**

I do not think that the exertions I make in travelling deserve your admiration. The beautiful scenery, I am still, thank God, able to visit, lies within easy reach of travellers by railroad and steamboat, and demands but little effort of any sort.

This morning, however, I have performed something of a feat, for I have gone down to Brunnen *on foot* and by what may be called the back staircase on the mountain, literally the dry bed of an Alpine torrent, *fifteen hundred feet* down the steepest possible hillside, by the irregular broken rocky steps of the mountain nymphs—leaps and plunges. Before I got to the bottom, I thought I should become as *liquid* as herself. The pretty creature can have no *knees.* How my old rheumatic ones did shake under me and my fourteen stone weight! She has feet, however, and with them has worn her rocky steps so round and smooth that my heavy mortal boots slipped and slid over them, threatening to make my descent headlong more than once. Arrived at the bottom, I took a carriage at Brunnen, and returned by the main road, resolving, until I became a centipede, nothing should tempt me to walk down fifteen hundred feet of perpendicular mountain side again.

The present mode of travelling detracts much from its pleasure, in consequence of the vast crowds of people one meets in every direction. The inns or hotels, begging their pardons, are all like palaces (gin palaces, I think I ought to say), magnificent, flaring, glaring, showy, luxurious, in all their public apartments, but noisy, disorderly, dirty and quite deficient in comfortable *private* accommodation. There are hardly any private sitting-rooms to be had any longer anywhere. Every room, except the great public sitting-room, is a bedroom, with two, three, and four beds in it; and if you insist, as I do, upon having a place of my own to inhabit, the unnecessary bed or beds are abstracted from it, one left for my occupancy, together with toilet table, washhand-stand, and all etcs. A sofa or armchair and extra table are then introduced, and you are told, "Voilà, madame, voilà votre salon," and made to pay for it as if it really were a first-class sitting-room, being assured, if you remonstrate, that you are occupying the bedroom of two or more persons to the great injury of the house, since you can only eat for one, and probably drink no wine.

To the attractions of these huge houses of entertainment are added musical bands, illuminations, fireworks, fire-balloons, and spectacles of every kind, *besides* that of the sweet, solemn, and sublime natural features of the beautiful scenery—all **which** seems to me very *vulgar*,—bread and butter, and pâté de foie gras, and marmalade and jam, **and** caviare, one **on top** of the other; but I am thankful for what I have enjoyed, and do still enjoy, though under such different conditions.

God bless you, **my** dearest H——. I wish **I** had ever travelled in Switzerland with you in former days. How much I should have enjoyed both that and the remembrance **of it.**

Ever, as ever, yours,

FANNY.

Axenstein, above Brunnen.

MY DEAREST H——,

I am sitting in **the midst of** clouds and darkness, thunder, lightning, and down-pouring rain. The mountains **are** all packed in cotton wool, and the whole aspect of the sky and earth and water is most lugubrious.

After ten days of brilliantly beautiful weather, we have this very unpleasant change, and as to-night the moon is **at** her full, **I am** afraid we may have a succession of storms for some **days now;** the whole season has been most unpropitious for travellers this year, and **the** summer seems **inclined** to end **as** it began.

I left the borders of the Lake **of** Lucerne on Saturday to climb **up to** this place, which is more than a thousand feet above it, and where on level ground, surrounded by charming woods and meadows, a magnificent hotel has been built, commanding views up both the arms of the lake and its mountain walls. The position is really magnificent, and the house a sort of an Aladdin Palace, with flower-gardens, terraces, and fountains. The immense amount of travelling now could of course alone meet the expenses of such establishments as these, which are literally springing up in every direction all over Switzerland, and are emptied and filled literally by a *tide* of travellers every four and twenty hours, who cover the whole surface of the country, rushing in and rushing out at each place for one night, or even perhaps for only half a day, and then tearing off somewhere else.

Of course, since you and I first travelled in Switzerland, the whole mode and manner of so doing has changed. An enormous mass of restless humanity rolls about in every direction, and the provision for the accommodation of such multitudes is very different from what travellers formerly required. These splendid houses, with their huge public dining and drawing-rooms, and *table d'hôte* at which people sit down and feed by the three and four hundred at a time, are neither clean, quiet, nor comfortable, but they meet the wishes of the *pilgrims* of the present day, and I, to whom they are simply abominable, in their noisy, vulgar luxury, *endeavour* to rejoice in the increase of the pleasure of "travelling for the million," while I do really rejoice that my travelling was done under far other conditions.

Next week I spend on the lake of Geneva, to enable my new maid to visit her family, whom she has not seen for five years, and after that I go to the

Lago Maggiore to see, I hope, my dear Ellen and her baby, so that in point of fact I am making what may be called a domestic tour through Switzerland.

I am ever, as ever, yours,

FANNY KEMBLE.

Territet Montreux.

MY DEAREST H——,

I wrote to you last from the Lake of Lucerne, and am now looking over the Lake of Geneva, at its lower end, where the Dent du Midi and the mountains of the Rhone Valley form such a splendid group above and beyond Villeneuve. I think you must have stopped at Villeneuve, some time or other, going over the Simplon into Italy. There used to be a charming house there, the Hôtel Byron, standing alone in its own grounds, quite at the end of the lake, and just above the Château Chillon.

I used always to stay there on my way up and down the Rhone valley. It was kept by two brothers of the name of Wolff, who were proprietors also of the good old-fashioned hotel L'écu de Genève in Geneva. They having failed, and the person who took the Hôtel Byron after them failed also, the pleasant house is now shut up, and I do not suppose it will ever be opened as an hotel again. The railroad now runs all the way from Geneva to the foot of the Simplon, an easy journey of less than eight hours, and nobody wants to stop half way at Villeneuve. Then, too, there is really almost a continuous terrace all along the shore of the lake from Lausanne to Villeneuve of hotels like palaces, one more magnificent than another, with terraces and gardens, **and** fountains and bands of music, and **such** luxurious **public** apartments, and *table d'hôte,* **that it is absolutely** impossible that some **if not several proprietors of such costly** establishments **should fail to** make **them answer, especially** as **in travelling, as well as everything else, fashion** directs **the movements of the great** majority **of** people, and **for the last few years** there has been **a** perfectly **insane rush of the whole tourist world to the** valley of **the Upper Engadine, to the** almost **utter** forsaking of **the** formerly popular **parts** of Switzerland.

The house where **I** am, **the** Hôtel **des** Alps, is **a** magnificent establishment, **but there** are very few people **in it, and** the manager **seemed** to me rather depressed in giving **me the account of** the failure of **the** proprietors of the Hôtel Byron, and said that there **was** not **a corner** of Switzerland **now** without a huge **hotel, and that** every year half **a** dozen **hotel** keepers became **bankrupt.** . . .

The week after next I expect to **be** at Stresa, on **the** Lago Maggiore. . . . My incidents of travel are **of a** strictly *domestic* character, **but** very pleasant **withal, and the weather is** perfectly beautiful.

I am enjoying this lovely paradise to the utmost, though **I** now *rail* **along the base of** the mountains, over **whose tops I** formerly used always **to** take my **way. God bless you,** dearest H——.

I am ever, as ever, yours,
Fanny Kemble.

Territet Montreux.

MY DEAREST H——,

Though I did get down the back stairs of the mountain at Axenstein, I get up the front stairs of my hotel here, which are broad and by no means steep, with no little trouble, not that there are many of them, for I am on the first floor; but I am acquiring a very considerable difficulty in the art (or nature) of breathing, and think that I may yet, before I die, develop the accomplishment of decided asthma.

I always had a tendency that way, for even as a girl going up-hill was a difficulty to my respiratory organs, and both sides of my family may have bequeathed me confirmed asthma. My Uncle John, as you know, suffered from it, and my mother's mother, old Madame de Camp, was a grievous martyr to it. Fanny Twiss, too, had very severe attacks of it, so that I feel rather entitled to be asthmatic. As for my descent of the Axenstein, I do not think I should have attempted it, if I had known what it was; but I had no conception of its depth and steepness, until I had gone so far down that I felt any amount of descent would be easier to me than the ascent of even a quarter of the way back, so I persevered to the bottom. My man-servant told me it was the roughest and steepest path he had ever gone down, but he is neither a very good mountaineer nor a vigorous person, and I thought that if he had achieved it I could; but I certainly had no idea what it was, until I was too far engaged in it to give it up, and having to go up *or* down, as I could not remain in the mountain

nymph's bed till she returned to occupy it herself,
I chose the least of two evils. It was extremely
beautiful, for the whole course of the torrent was
through the forest that clothes the mountain side, of
splendid pines, and larches and beeches, their great feet
sunk deep in brown moss, and the golden sunshine
sending its shafts of light through their branches.
If the water had been there it would have been
enchanting; but if the water had been there, *I* should
not.

I shall finish my week at Montreux on Monday,
and then go to a place only an hour further on by rail
in the Rhone Valley, called Bex, where I also mean to
stay a week before I go over the Simplon. I am not
here at Montreux itself, but about a mile further on,
nearer the end of the lake, at a place called Territet
at the Hôtel des Alps, which, now that the Hôtel
Byron is closed, is about the best of these fine establishments on the lake shore.

My purpose in taking up my abode here was to be
as near as possible to the home of my maid's friends
and family, that she might get to them every day as
easily and stay with them as long as possible. . . .
There are two or three huge pensions and hotels at
Glion and the Righi Vaudois and half way over the
Col de Jaman. It is all very beautiful, but swarming
in every direction with this invading population of
travellers and tourists. I sometimes think what an
amazement the present aspect of these shores would
cause Rousseau, if he could see them now! I have felt
half inclined to get the " La nouvelle Heloise " and
re-read it here, but am too lazy to go to the library for

it. **One** ought really **to** read **it here. God** bless you, my dearest **H——**.

I am ever, as ever, yours,
·**FANNY** KEMBLE.

Bex, Rhone Valley.

I have this moment received, dearest **H——**, **your** letter in answer **to my own** from Montreux. **It** rejoices **my** heart whenever **I** now get **a few** lines of your own dictation, **as** I regard your having the power to make that exertion **a** favourable indication of **your** whole condition. **How** thankful **I** am, my beloved friend, that you still can "eat and drink **and sleep**," and that you are mercifully **exempt from** physical suffering, **beyond that**, which **I fear is**, however, an almost equal trial, the **weary sense of** weakness, which in itself must be a grievous burden.

I write you **from a** place that **you have not for**-gotten, **for I do not** imagine you were never in **it**, half way **between** the lower end **of** the Lake of Geneva and Martigny, and directly **on the line** of the railroad, which is now finished all the **way** from Geneva to the foot of **the** Simplon at Brigne—a small **town or** large village called Bex, which I suppose owes its creation and continued existence to the salt mines immediately behind **it**, and in the mountain. This supply of salt is the only one in Switzerland, and the works are very considerable, **and** employ a great many people, **and I** imagine really support the town.

The **hotel**, a large and fine establishment, is about **two miles from Bex, and three from** the railroad and main valley of the **Rhone. It is** near the salt works,

and calls itself "le Grand Hôtel des Salines," and is a
large bathing establishment, supplied with a copious
stream of almost ice-cold water by the mountain
torrent that dashes down the ravine close by it.   The
house stands in a complete *cul de sac* of the mountain,
opening between fine sweeping lines of wood and rock
in the direction by which it is approached to the
valley of the Rhone.

There is level ground enough about it for charming
gardens, and pleasant grounds and winding paths cut
in every direction through the chestnut and walnut
woods, with which the lower slopes of its encircling
mountain walls are clothed, and a most beautiful
fountain, one of the highest water jets I ever saw,
springs from the midst of the flower-beds immediately
opposite my window.

It is a very charming place, and is very much
frequented by foreigners, French and German people,
but not much, I think, by English or Americans, to
which I attribute the circumstance, particularly
agreeable to me, that the cookery is French and good,
and that I am not exasperated with daily offers of
tough raw flesh, calling itself *rosbif* and underdone
vegetables a "l'anglaise," that is to say, not even boiled
through, and accompanied with a white fluid simula-
ting melted butter. . . .

Ellen and her baby are to come down from her perch
in the Varese to Stresa, on the Lago Maggiore, and
pay me a visit of a week there.   This arrangement is
better in many respects than my going to her, for
their home is a farm in a *piccolo paese*, and she would
have worried and exerted herself to make me comfort-

able, English fashion, and the effort would have been very bad for her.

God bless you, dear. I am *squeezed* for room on my paper, but

Ever, as ever, yours,
FANNY KEMBLE.

Bex, Rhone Valley.

MY DEAREST H——,

I write you one more line from this place, because to-morrow I shall leave it, and as I expect to travel for the next four days, I may not find it so easy to write to you again till I get to Stresa.

I have been quite charmed with this place, where I never made any stay before, though I have twice passed a night here on my way down from the mountains, but have always given it the go-by in passing up and down the Rhone Valley.

It is very much frequented by foreigners, French and German, who come here in the spring and autumn for the benefit of the fresh salt water bath.

English travellers do not often visit it, and as a rule know nothing whatever of the medicinal properties of its waters; but the place itself is very beautiful, and in spring, when all the orchards, with which the valley is covered, are in blossom, it must really be exquisite, and worth coming from England, I should think, to see. The valley is a horseshoe of gently undulating meadows and orchards, rising gradually to the mountains, the lower half of which is clothed with beautiful chestnut and walnut woods, above which the rocky walls and spires and summits peer down upon the green Eden at their feet. The valley opens down to the great main river road of the Rhone, on the other side of which, immediately in front of my windows, towers the huge Dent du Midi, with its snow slopes and glaciers and pyramidal rocky peaks piercing the sky.

There is no water view from the house, but a lovely fountain, eighty feet high, the daughter of the mountain stream, which seems to be leaping up to her cradle in the high rocks above the house, immediately faces my room, and a rushing foaming torrent is seen from several parts of the well-laid-out pleasure grounds that surround the house, but we have no lovely lake expanse in our view. The place is very charming to me, the weather is just now beautiful, and I have hopes that we shall cross the Simplon in sunshine. My next letter to you will be from Italy, where I hope to be on Thursday. God bless you, my dearest H——.

Ever, as ever, yours,
FANNY KEMBLE.

A gentleman who sat by me at dinner to-day told me what I was very sorry to hear, that the wine-making vines in France had been attacked by a destructive insect come over from America, which it was apprehended might destroy the crop; that the price of wine had risen already in France in consequence, and that great alarm was felt on the subject throughout all the grape-growing districts of Switzerland. It is quite as bad a plague, he says, as the Colorado beetle.

MY DEAR E——,

I should find it impossible to tell you how very very sad your letter made me, not for my beloved friend, whose growing infirmity of mind and partial unconsciousness are merciful alleviations of the heavy tedium of her prolonged trial, but for you, my poor E——, whose burden seems to me indeed one of the heaviest I can imagine. It is vain wishing that things were other than they are. They are as God wills, and our best resource, even when He allows us others, is still our absolute resignation to His will. He will surely support you, under the task He has appointed you, and to be what you are to H—— must reward you in some measure with the consciousness of your admirable devotion to the duty you have accepted.

God bless you and sustain you to the end. The time cannot be far off when she and you will alike be set free, and you will only have to rejoice that you have been so faithful and so good.

You will be sorry to hear that my last letter from F—— brought me the bad news of a furious hurricane having swept over the coast of Georgia, terribly injuring all the estates, the plantations, and absolutely devastating their property at Butler's Island. The whole rice crop is destroyed, the fields submerged under from three to four feet of water. The rice had been harvested—that is, cut—but only stacked in the fields, where the portion of it that has not been swept down to the sea by the flood is lying rotting.

This is not only the loss of the year's income,

which depends upon the crop, but also the loss of the means of planting for the next year, unless money is borrowed for the purpose. Altogether it is a most distressing occurrence.

I am just going off to church now to be present at the baptism of Ellen's baby. Luigi has very kindly, and I think wisely, consented to allow the child to be christened in the Protestant church.

I want you to get your "Peerage," and look out for me who is the Countess of ——. There comes to the *table d'hôte* here such an extraordinary woman calling herself by that name, that I really would give something to know who and what she is. She is quite old and extremely handsome—must have been a rare beauty in her youth. She is now exactly like a wax figure in a barber's shop. Her complexion, the fairest blush rose; her eyebrows pencilled, like the Empress Eugenie's; a perfect turban of auburn plaits all round her head, without a shred of cap or lace on it, and her ears hung with large rubies, set in diamonds; her collar fastened with a huge opal, set in diamonds, and her fingers covered with more precious stones, of every sort, shape, and size, than I ever saw on any human hands before. She has with her a young Spanish duke, but whether by way of husband or son, I do not know; and she is Countess of ——, and who and what is she?

I have just come from church, where Ellen's big boy has been baptized. The poor little fellow will not, I trust, prove a "fair-weather" Christian, for it is pouring torrents of rain, the sky is as black as London, the lake as black as the sky, all broken up

into angry foam, and the beautiful opposite shores
blurred, dark, dirty, and dreary-looking.

Good-bye, my dearest H——.   Good-bye, my dear
E——.   God bless and comfort and support you both.

Ever, as ever, yours,

FANNY KEMBLE.

MY DEAR E——,

I shall not see Como, or indeed go any
further south than I am now. From here I go to
Mentone, on the Riviera, for a couple of weeks, and
then turn northwards, and expect to meet F—— in
Paris, and go with her to Leamington. Apart from
any associations that may make the Lake of Como
interesting or dear to you, it is undoubtedly considered, and I suppose is really, the most beautiful of
the four Italian lakes; but the Lago Maggiore is my
special favourite. I think it grander, more serious
and severe, in fact, less southern in character than
the others, really more Swiss than Italian in some of
its aspects, and yet having all the perfect picturesqueness in every town, village, church, convent, villa,
palace and hovel on its shores, which belong exclusively to this side of the Alps. . . .

I had a talk with Luigi on the subject of his boy's
christening before it took place. He appears to me
to be as little of a real Roman Catholic as I am myself,
though—or perhaps I ought to say *because*—he was
originally intended for a priest, and partly trained for
that purpose.

He said, which I thought great good sense and
good feeling, that Ellen would have been made miser-

able if her boy had not been christened in her own church, that she would have the bringing up and religious instructing of the child, and that she could certainly only educate him according to her own belief, and that when he grew up, it would always be perfectly in his power to become a Roman Catholic if he wished to do so, all which seemed to me very wise, as well as kind, but not very Roman Catholic, and so he stood by the font, Macfarland (who had been Ellen's fellow-servant in my house for two years in America), who was the child's godfather, proxy for one of Ellen's brothers, by his side, and at every response Macfarland made, Luigi nodded assent, and so the baby was christened.

I do not know whether I wrote you word that F——'s last letter said that hope was entertained that half the rice crop, which was an unusually fine one at Butler's Island, might perhaps be saved.

S——'s last letter informed me of her boy's installation at college, and of a most interesting visit she had had from Dean Stanley, who spoke unreservedly to her of his admirable wife, who had been very kind to her, and for whom S—— has the most affectionate admiration.

Good-bye, dear E——. This is, of course, for my dearest H—— as well as for you. Give her my tenderest love.

I am ever, as ever, hers,

FANNY KEMBLE.

Mentone.

MY DEAR E——,

After the miserable letter in which you told me not to expect any more words dictated by my dearest friend, it was a most unexpected and vivid joy to receive those she sent me through you. I cannot tell you how dark a curtain seemed to have fallen at last between me and my beloved H——, nor how great the relief has been to see it once more lifted.

There are some losses for which no length of preparation seems to avail; the blow that has threatened one so long loses none of its heaviness when it falls, in spite of prolonged anticipation. Thank God for these words of *hers*, which I thought were never to reach me any more.

My beloved H——, it was a great, great joy to me yesterday evening to get your letter. I imagine, my dearest friend, that your thinking powers, which appear to you so miserably deteriorated, are now not at all below the average of those of most of your fellow females, to whom what you call *cogitating* is a process unknown, and whose brains, like a child's kaleidoscope, filled with odds and ends, more or less rubbishy, by dint of shaking, and the simplest possible adjustment of means producing accidental arrangement, keep them amused and *lively*, by a succession of tolerably pretty and symmetrical patterns, without any real value, connection, or significance.

I have often thought this represented very fairly my own thinking machinery and results, for you know I have always deliberately eschewed deliberate *cogitation*, as altogether too hard work, and certainly not (what the lazy Italian peasant *men* call all extra hard and heavy manual labour) "lavoro di donna."

For rheumatic complaints I do not think these southern residences, with all their external brightness, by any means as good as our closer or more comfortable northern abodes. Thus I am writing to you in a room about sixteen feet square, with three doors and two windows (which are, in fact, glass doors) opening upon a terrace, and where to put myself to escape only one or two of the draughts (the rest are hopelessly unavoidable) I cannot with all my ingenuity devise.

It is raining, and is cold and damp. I have a small fireplace about two feet square, and it is expected to keep me warm, but it does not, with a small supply of small knots and chunks of some incombustible wood, intended only to ignite and burn in small stoves. (I think they might take a patent out with it, for building houses warranted *never to take fire or burn*.) There is a carpet in the room, but the floor beneath that carpet is brick, and the cold comes through very fearfully. I do not find the climate of Mentone exempt, which I supposed it was, from the scourging winds that are the atmospheric pest of the Mediterranean seaboard, as far round as Marseilles; and Merimée, describing Cannes, whither he betook himself every winter, describes all these places, when he says, "Au soleil vous êtes roti, et puis de l'autre côté vous avez un vent comme un rasoir qui vous coupe en deux."

The great advantage of most places over my dear native land is in their supply of *light*, and that I do think an immense superiority, that France and Italy and America have over England.

The absence of sufficient provision against cold in all southern countries makes such cold as one does have rather worse than the home article. We have had furious winds here, and rain-storms, and hail-storms with stones as big as nuts, and thunder and lightning. The sea looks dirty, and bilious, and *sick of itself,* and is raking and rasping the shore in a manner that must be most aggravating to the sand and shingles, and a palm tree lifting its forlorn oriental head against the dingy sky, looks as much out of place as if it was growing at Wandsworth.

I keep thinking of my dear Mr. L——, who is on that hideous Atlantic, with its flinty mountainous waves, and I pray God for his safety.

I leave Mentone on Monday morning, and expect to join F—— in Paris on Thursday. It is a long journey, and I shall be thankful when it is over, and not sorry to be quietly housed at Leamington with her and the dear little girl.

God bless you, my dear, dear, dear H——. Your words are very precious to me.

Ever, as ever, yours,
FANNY KEMBLE.

Mentone.

MY DEAREST H——,

I have just come in from walking and sitting on the road along the seaside, that answers to the parade at St. Leonards, where you and I have so often walked together. The Mediterranean, it is true, with its blue *countenance*, and many-coloured *expressions*, is a different creature from the leaden or silvery pale-coloured expanse of water that divides England from France on the Sussex coast. On the other hand, there is no tide, that retires and returns here sufficiently to reveal stretches of smooth golden sand, or reefs of rock, or wreaths of brown and amber seaweed, and there is an almost total absence of the delicious fresh salt smell, that is so exquisite a quality in the air of our northern coasts and shores.

Instead of the modest turf-crowned red-brown wall of rock that rises behind St. Leonards, this place (which perhaps you know) is guarded landwards by a magnificent range of rocky pinnacles, that glitter in the sunshine like battlements of oxidized silver.

At St. Leonards, as the spring came on, I used to have cowslips, and primroses, and crimson daisies, and cinnamon-coloured wallflowers in my room. Here at the opening of winter I have on my table a bowl full of heliotrope and monthly and tea-roses, out of a small garden belonging to this house, which opens directly upon the sea.

I have nothing to tell you, dear, except a piece of information I obtained from a journeyman glazier yesterday, who was mending a window I had broken in my sitting-room. I was admiring the rapid dexterity with which he worked, and asked him what length of apprenticeship was necessary to acquire it. He said that depended, of course, much upon natural qualifications, the first of all requisites being *courage* —courage to handle the glass without timidity or nervous apprehension of breaking it. " Enfin, madame, il faut **savoir manier** cela comme si cela n'etait ni plus ni moins **que du papier.** Avoir la main sûre et légère et surtout *ne pas avoir peur* et si cela se casse, eh bien alors, tant pis." I thought there was rather a fine moral in that.

Good-bye, my dearest H——. God bless you. **The** sea unfurling on the shore sings **of you** to me. God bless you.

Ever, as ever, yours,

FANNY KEMBLE.

The **friend to whom the** above letters **were** addressed died **before I reached** England.

Adelphi Hotel, **Liverpool,** *May 12th*, 1848.

MY DEAR ARTHUR,

I sail for America on Saturday **the 13th—** to-morrow. I fully purposed to **have written a line to** you and dear Mary Anne to **bid you good-**bye and remember **me.** My sister will reach England exactly two days after I have left it, and only for **the** next six weeks I have engagements made to read that would have paid me upwards of six hundred pounds, which I must now forego, and accept instead grief, vexation, **and loss.** . . . and all is utter uncertainty before me; **but** you know I have good courage, and **faith and hope,** the foundations **of** which cannot **be** shaken by **human** hands, **so** that **nothing can go desperately** ill with **me.**

I have thought much and **anxiously of your affairs,** and have vainly endeavoured, for your sakes, to understand **the statements of this** Indian business * that

* The failure of a bank.

I read in the papers, and I hope all will be for the best with you, but know very well that neither you nor Mary Anne depend for your happiness upon mere accidents. Give my affectionate love to her, my respectful love to your dear mother, and believe that I am, and shall always remain,

Your very gratefully attached

FANNY.

Lenox, Sunday, October 29th, 1848.

MY DEAR ARTHUR,

It gave me great pleasure to receive your kind letter, and to find that hitherto, at any rate, out of sight has not been out of mind from you to me.

I never shall forget a certain visit I paid your wife, or the calm and cheerful composure with which she was awaiting what might prove the news of your ruin. I do trust most sincerely that matters will adjust themselves for you less disastrously than for poor Lady Malkin, though I am afraid you will think me horribly stupid, when I tell you that I do not understand what you yourself have written me about this wretched money catastrophe in India.

I am dreadfully troubled at W. G——'s implications in these failures. He married my cousin, a very sweet person of whom I am very fond, daughter of my dear Mrs. Harry Siddons, and sister of that Mrs. Mair at whose house you visited me in Edinburgh, and who, I fear, will be terribly distressed by her brother-in-law's position. . . .

What a frightful condition all Europe, except

England, is in! the excesses in Sicily and Frankfort really almost make one doubt the theory of the earth's motion, since Christianity and civilization, and the progress of time have yet brought human beings no further out of their pristine state of barbarity ; or will the wild beast, which a friend of mine once assured me was at the bottom of every man's heart, never be eradicated, but manifest itself, and take the ascendancy during certain periods of the world as long as it lasts ? God protect our blessed little England. This great country is safe enough from some evils by its enormous extent, and the very slackness, so to speak, of all social ties, the almost insensible pressure of a form of government in some respects extremely simple, and the absence of all that complicated intertwining of interests, which belongs to countries that have only grown out of barbarism and feudalism by slow degrees through the lapse of centuries.

I wish, dear Arthur, you would remember me very affectionately to Mary Anne. The more intimate intercourse I had with you both, during my last stay in England, has much fortified the friendly attachment I had entertained for you for many years. I hope to renew it next year, when I return home, and beg in the meantime that you will neither of you forget me.

I see my brother John has advertised a " History of the Saxons." He and I, without having quarrelled, never correspond, so that I know nothing whatever about him. If you write to me again, tell me something of his book, and, if you can, of himself. I wish, if you ever write to Donne, you would give my kind

regards to him. I am only waiting for some decided
turn in my affairs to answer a most amiable letter of
his. Remember me to Miss Cottin and the Horace
Wilsons, and the Ellises, and all our common friends,
who *do* remember and feel an interest in me, and
believe me

Very sincerely and affectionately yours,

FANNY.

Rochester, **New York, February 4th,** 1850.

MY DEAR ARTHUR,

If I write to you upon ruled paper it is
because in these remote parts of the globe none else
is to be obtained. I have just read over your kind
letter of the 4th of June last, with a sort of remorseful
twinge at the date. It should not have remained so
long unacknowledged, I confess, but I have had much
to suffer and much to do since I received it, and I
am growing lazy and cowardly about the effort of
writing of my affairs; in short, I do not think I
have any real apology for not having answered you
sooner, but that the spirit did not move me to do so.
If you are half as much my friend and half as wise as
I suppose you to be, you will forgive me, and, what's
more, you won't care. . . .

I think I shall certainly be in England in the
autumn. I have not yet quite finished making my
fortune, in spite of the magnificent accounts of my
wealth with which the newspapers abound, and I
think I shall come and put the finishing stroke to it
among my own people.

With regard to the American law of divorce, about

which you inquire, it is different in **different** parts of the country; the several States have each their own independent government, jurisdiction, and institutions, and deal with matters matrimonial as with **various** others, according to their own peculiar laws. Pennsylvania, you know, is greatly peopled by Germans, **and the** divorce law there follows that of Germany, which itself is **founded** on the French Code Napoléon; it **admits** divorce on the plea **of** desertion (non-cohabitation) on the part of husband or wife for **a space** of **two** consecutive years. I believe a joint appeal may procure a separation from the legislature upon the ground of absolute incompatibility of temper and character, and also that a legal separation of person and property is sometimes allowed for other reasons. None of these processes of relief from the bonds of matrimony are available to Roman Catholics in America any more than elsewhere. Marriage is one of the sacraments of their church, to be annulled only by the authority of the Pope. The greater facility of obtaining divorce in the State of Pennsylvania occasionally induces citizens of other States to appeal to the Philadelphia tribunals. In Massachusetts, where **the** English law prevails, divorce is granted only for cause of adultery.

Good bye, my dear Arthur. I beg you and Mary Anne to be very glad to see me again, **as** I certainly shall **be to see** you, being yours and hers very affectionately,

FANNY KEMBLE.

Norwich, Friday, October 31st, 1851.

My dear Arthur,

I received your kind note two days ago at Bury, but I determined to wait until I had left our friend Donne before I answered it, and indeed, had I determined otherwise, should have done no otherwise, for he really plunged me into such a sea of social "distractions," as the French say when they mean something eminently agreeable, that I really had not a moment's leisure. Of his kindness to me it is impossible that I should say enough; it really was— like your own and Mary Anne's, my dear Arthur— so cordial and so generous that, like the regard and affection you and your wife have shown me, it absolutely and very seriously puzzles me to account for it. I cannot tell you how much I have been struck with my own good fortune, in retaining, as it were, possession of the *roots* of so much valuable friendship, and seeing them put forth such pleasant blossoms, when it would have been more reasonable to expect that time, absence, and distance would have dried up the kindly sap in them, and left them mere withered sticks, remains of an early planting that had early died, for want of the cherishing habit of intercourse and proximity, by which poor human love is for the most part sustained, and indeed not seldom withers, even with all such ministry. However, perhaps the more rational conclusion is that it is no wonder, since you all remembered me, that you have liked me all the better for seeing nothing of me for several years.

I wish I could write you as good an account of

Donne himself, as of his dealings towards me. I think
he is looking very unwell, worn and feeble, and I fear
his anxious desire to discharge his duty to his family
induces him to tax himself far more heavily and
constantly with labour than is good for him. I really
was almost glad of all the running about and trouble
and fuss, which my stay at his house and my reading
in Bury occasioned him, as I thought almost anything
interposed between him and the incessant grinding
round and round in his mental mill would be wholesome, if not agreeable to him. He has sworn to come
up to the Highlands with me and pay you a visit
next summer, and I am sure that something of the
sort is really indispensable to him. He certainly is a
very charming person. It was a matter of some
regret to me, as well as of surprise, to perceive, however, upon the more intimate acquaintance of our
late intercourse, a vein of deep and black malignity,
running through his character, for which I confess I
was not prepared; you, from long observation, probably
are aware of this, which to me seems a curious and
lamentable anomaly in this otherwise uncommonly
amiable man.

I enclose you, my dear Arthur, half a five-pound
note for your "auld brigg," which please to acknowledge, and when you have duly done so, I will enclose
its better half for the "new brigg." I make you this
munificent donation out of my love for Corrybrough,
and a little, too, out of a mere consideration of my
own accommodation, for I shall certainly go very
frequently across the new brigg, and you know I do
not think lightly of myself, and wish the modern

bridge to be solid enough for my repeated passage in safety over it.

Donne did the honours of Bury excellently, and showed me the beautiful church and gates, and the school.

Perhaps it was as well that Dr. Donaldson, who was extremely civil and kind in showing me over the latter, was not sympathico (as the Italians say) to me, otherwise I think I might have been quite overcome at the sight of the soil where such a human harvest was raised as that of which your good father was the husbandman.* When I thought of all that goodly grain (some tares, too, no doubt ; but the devil knows his own, and what's more, will have it, too, some day, as I shudder to think)—when, I say, I thought of you all, my schoolfellows, and how far we all are already from those days, I think I might have fallen very sentimental, but for the tonic effect Dr. Donaldson had upon me—a sort of stringent influence, which quite acted as an antidote to all softness. He seems to me hard all over, from the brass sound of his voice to the steel-spring jerk of his body. He certainly is very unlike the last head master of Bury School—my master.

Your grouse were pronounced capital by an assembly of friendly feeders Donne gathered together yesterday, and he has given me a brace to carry to Adelaide. (He is very indiscreet, too ; can't keep anything to himself.)

Edward's lease of Kunston Hall is up next summer, and unless they go abroad, I think it really possible

* Dr. Malkin was the Master of Bury School.

that he may take a fancy to coming up to the Highlands. Good gracious, how charmed I should be!— always supposing that I am still in England next year, and could go with them to Scotland.

Thank you, my dear Arthur, for the offer of the Corrybrough homespun, which I should like to wear if it were possible to make it less thick; but I fear that any garment made of the material of which you sent me a sample would be too heavy for me to wear with much comfort. Could not a thinner texture of the same sort of thing be woven, that would not be so massive? If this were practicable, I would give you an order for as much as would make me a whole suit for the moors next year. The sample you sent me is, I think, too thick for my wear.

I shall be in Edinburgh about the second or third week in December. What could be more acceptable (to all parties, I trust) than your being there at the same time? Donne said he should write to you to-day. I don't wish to make mischief, but are you at all aware how very much Donne likes your wife? Don't mention it to Mary Anne, it might shock her; and, indeed, it were every way best forgotten, or, at any rate, taken in connection with a due remembrance of that singular vein of quiet depravity which I told you I had lighted upon in my late season of intercourse with him. Rather curious, I think, that two of our friends, Donne and dear "Monsieur Jem," * should resemble each other in so remarkable a respect.

I am glad you have found out a picturesque *lion* in your neighbourhood for the sake of yourselves and

* Mr. James Spedding.

friends, if you have any who are minded to go far
afield for *sitch*. For my own part, I desire, if ever I
should visit Corrybrough again, to see no lions or wild
beasts more sublime or beautiful than decent-behaved
grouse, **rising within** shot from the **black** side of a
hag, or a salmon in Mr. W——'s landing-net on a
shingly reach of the Findhorn. Give my most friendly
pats to all the dogs; my respects to Campbell, Fraser,
and Jessie; * my very affectionate regards **to** dear
Mary Anne, and believe me always, my **dear Arthur,
yours and** hers most truly and gratefully,

FANNY KEMBLE.

[William Bodham Donne, **of** Mattishall, **Norfolk,
was** the school and college mate, and lifelong friend of
my elder brother; good, amiable, handsome; an elegant
writer, an accomplished scholar, **a** perfect gentleman.

"Monsieur Jem" was the rather disrespectful title
by which, in the immediate circle of his intimate
friends, we designated a person for **whom** we **all** entertained a very sincere admiration and profound respect.
Mr. **James** Spedding, **whose** name recalls **to** all who
knew **him** the gentle, wise philosopher and man of
letters, **whose** habitual silence was silver, whose seldom
speech **was gold,** whose **lifelong labour of** love on the
character, career, and writings of Bacon, was the most
appropriate task that sympathy and competency **ever**
devoted themselves to, and whose intimate knowledge
of the text (letter and spirit) of Shakespeare made his
intercourse most interesting and valuable to **me.**

A small incident **of our** life at Corrybrough will

* **People on the farm at** Corrybrough.

give one instance of his habitual self-forgetfulness and consideration for others. By some unlucky accident one day, when the gentlemen were out shooting, part of the charge of one of the guns struck Mr. Spedding in the leg. He was obliged to return home, and did so with some pain and difficulty, leaning on Mr. Malkin. As they approached the house, he straightened himself up and withdrew his arm from his friend's support, saying **as he passed the** drawing-room windows, " Don't let me lean **on you** as we **go** by ; the women will be frightened, and think something serious has happened." He was not altogether merciful to me, for one day that I went to pay **him a** visit, while **he** was still confined to his room by his accident, he had Milton in his hand, and asked me to read **to** him the terrible string of " ancient names " which occur **in** " Paradise Lost."

My musical instinct kept my delivery of them right by the harmony of the noble measure, in spite of my absolute ignorance of the classical value of the biographical, historical, and geographical names of the whole formidable catalogue and nomenclature.

Corrybrough, my friend's pleasant home in the Highlands, was a moorland sheep-farm and grouse-shooting property. The house stood within its own grounds, **at a** distance from any other dwelling, entirely isolated, with no habitations in its neighbourhood but those of the people employed on the land, which circumstances **I mention as** rendering curious in some degree the **incident I am about** to **relate,** of the singular **character of which I** can give no plausible rational **explanation.**

I was expected on a visit there, on a certain day, of a certain month and week (the precise date I have now forgotten). The persons staying in the house were friends and acquaintances of mine, as well as of the "laird's," and had all been looking for my arrival in the course of the day. When, however, the usual hour for retiring for the night had been somewhat overpassed, in the protracted hope of my still-possible advent, and that everybody had given me up and betaken themselves to their bedrooms, a sudden sound of wheels on the gravel drive, the loud opening of a carriage door and letting down of steps, with a sudden violent ringing of the door-bell drew every one forth again to their doors with exclamations of, "Oh, there she is; she's come at last." My friend and host ran down to open his door to me himself, which he did, to find before him only the emptiness, stillness, and darkness of the night—neither carriage nor arriving guest—nothing and nobody, so he retired to his room and went to bed. The next day I arrived, but though able to account satisfactorily for my delay in doing so, was quite unable to account for my sham arrival of the previous night, with sound of wheels, horses' hoofs, opening of carriage door, letting down of steps, and loud ringing of the house-bell, all which pre-monitory symptoms were heard by half-a-dozen different people in their respective rooms in different parts of the house, which makes an unsatisfactory sort of ghost-story.]

Canterbury, Sunday, September 26th, 1852.

I do sympathize, or did at the proper time, my dear Arthur, with you, because you had the lumbago, and because I have had the lumbago, and am perfectly competent to sympathize to the fullest extent with you, and if my sympathy had "had a body in it," and could it have availed anything in the world towards your alleviation, I should not have delayed so long my expression of it; as it is, this tardy expression of it is but a cold poultice, fit for no use. You are doubtless long enough ago lithe and lissom as is your wont, but I was sorry for you at the proper time.

How exceedingly little you know of the gastronomic resources of that most capital hotel, the Royal, at Lowestoft, if you imagine that grouse were not there among our commendable delicacies! Except the Bedford at Brighton, the said Royal Hotel at Lowestoft is the most luxurious establishment in her Majesty's dominions, and assuredly in the work I mean to publish by-and-by upon the hotels and inns of England, of which my peregrinations through all parts of the land have afforded me a vast and various experience, I shall certainly award it a distinguished and honourable position. Of course we could have had grouse there if we had pleased, or I believe peacocks' tongues, and therefore hold yours upon the subject of our marine fare, for though we had just as many shrimps, herrings, and lobsters as we wished (which you cannot), we also had mutton and game, and were thus incomparably your superiors; after which bragging, let me add that, though I have no doubt we might have had caper—what the deuce is their name? the

wonderful wildfowl that Lord Breadalbane preserves
with such tender solicitude, eight *hens* of which
precious bird Mr. Gordon Cumming shot through carelessness the first day he went out at Taymouth—if
we had pleased. We never did have any game on
that north sea-coast, but a certain red-legged Frenchman of a partridge, which my friend and then companion, Lady Monson, very nearly threw into the
waiter's **face,** so indignant was she at the interlope-
ment (that's the reverse of elopement, isn't it ?) of the
parlez-vousing biped in our preserves, which she said
would consequently amalgamate with and deteriorate
and degenerate the English birds. I wish I had had
some grouse to stop her mouth with ; but if any come
while I am at Bury next week **I will** bless you first
and immediately after stop my own mouth therewith.

My dear Arthur, if I had (as I and Marie both
supposed I did) shown you my " George," the jewel
I have lost, I am very sure you would not have forgotten it ; it was the exact counterpart of the ornament worn by our Knights of the Garter, except that
instead of being made **of** or with brilliants, it was of
plain and solid gold, most beautifully wrought. It
would have more than covered the palm of your hand,
and was so heavy that I never could wear it suspended
round my neck, but was always obliged to support it
on my breast with a large pin or brooch. The only
thing in which it differed from the ornament worn by
the Queen was in the motto, the royal device of "Honi
soi **qui** mal y pense " being replaced by that of the
New York St. George's Society, "Let mercy be our
boast, and shame our only fear." It was presented to

me in consequence of some successful readings which
I gave in aid of the funds of the society, and bore on
the reverse an honourable inscription to that effect.
I valued it extremely; it was very precious to me.
But of course all attempt to recover such a thing was
as useless as an endeavour to recover a sovereign once
tossed into the melting-pot. It was a mere lump of
gold, no more to be identified as what it had been
than the last shapeless lump picked out of the
Australian diggings. It is gone, and a great, great
vexation to me it is.

You bid me recommend any good servants that I
know to your use. I do not know any; my sister's
household were so good that they have all found
places, to which they will go immediately on her
departure, and several of them with the understanding
that when she returns they are to resume their situations in her house. If you and Mary Anne finally
determine to go abroad for the winter, you will surely
go to Rome, and then you and Adelaide will foregather, for which I shall envy you all round. How
much I am tempted to leave my laborious money-
making and go with them towards the sun! God
knows, when they are gone abroad, I shall be exceedingly forlorn here, and if you and Mary Anne depart
too, my sources of consolation for Adelaide's loss will
be grievously curtailed. " Coraggio, Bully Monster,
corraggio!" God knows, it's the one thing needful
in this "cruelty world," as a little girl once called it.
The same mean underbred cause that keeps me from
Italy, viz. impecuniosity, prevents Donne from getting
up to the Highlands. It's really disgraceful to be so

poor, and I wonder he isn't ashamed of it; I am, I know. We are despicable paupers, and only fit company for each other, and therefore I am going down to Bury next week to add my beggary to *his'n* for a few days (perhaps the addition will make something of both of us). I shall make sixty pounds by that same, he of course not sixty pence; but, at any rate, one of us will have mended our estate by so much.

Adelaide says she is coming down with me, but I don't believe her; I wish I did, for their departure is fixed for the twenty-first of next month, and I shall see very little of her, I fear, before they go.

There is some talk of my going to Woodbridge, which I only rejoice at for the chance it will give me of seeing Edward Fitzgerald once more. That amiable hermit deserves to be better forgotten by his friends than he is.

I write this to you from the old city of pilgrimage, where I shall abide till Wednesday, when I go for a couple of days to Dover; after that I return to town for one day, previous to going to Bury.

I shall be all the sadder, my dear Arthur, if you do determine to go abroad, for the loss of your and Mary Anne's kind intercourse will be a very great one to me; but I wish to go so much myself that I cannot help thinking it must be the pleasantest thing in the world for everybody to do.

I am reading your "Motherwell," and, what is more, marking it. Will you mind that?—or, as my friendship and vanity together have whispered to me, will you value the book a little the more for my hieroglyphics therein ? I think so, and therefore have put them where the text tempted me.

Give my kindest love to Mary Anne, and remember me to Hugh, and Donald, and Campbell, and Jessie. How sorry they will all be if you do not return next summer. I wish you were in your old home * and school next week, when I shall be there ; but neither you nor your father and mother. Give my respects to her when you write to her.

Good-bye, dear Arthur. Believe me ever yours very affectionately,

FANNY KEMBLE.

[Mr. Edward Fitzgerald was an eccentric gentleman and man of genius, who shunned notoriety and fame as sedulously as most people seek them. His parents and mine were intimate friends, and he, during the whole of his life, my brother's and mine. He printed (but I do not know whether he ever published) two small volumes of capital English prose, " Euphranor " and " Polonius," and translated, or rather paraphrased (for he never would admit that they had what he called the merit of translations) the fine Persian poem of " Omar Kayyam," the " Wonderful Magician," and " Life is a Dream," from the Spanish of Calderon, and the " Agamemnon " and "Œdipus " of Æschylus and Sophocles, which he rendered in such admirable English blank verse as to deserve the name of noble original works.

For many years before his death he made his home at Woodbridge, and when I did read there his friendly

* His father, Dr. Malkin's house.

devotion to me and my family was an occasion of
some embarrassment to me, for when I came on the
platform and curtseyed to my audience, Mr. Fitzgerald
got up and bowed to me, and his example being immediately followed by the whole room, I was not a
little surprised, amused, and confused by this general
courtesy on the part of my hearers, who, I suppose,
supposed I was accustomed to be received standing by
my listeners.   Mr. Aldis Wright, Edward Fitzgerald's
intimate friend, has long promised the reading public
his memoirs, in which, if justice is done to him, he
will appear not only as one of the ripest of English
scholars, but as a fine critic of musical and pictorial
art, as well as literature.]

99, *Eaton Place, Belgrave Square,*
Sunday, October 17th, 1852.

MY DEAR ARTHUR,

Let me first tell you that my Order of
Knighthood is happily recovered, and I shall again be
the only woman besides our gracious lady, the Queen,
who will wear St. George and the Dragon upon my
breast.

It was discovered in a crack of a very old and
curious carved oak wardrobe which stood in the bedroom I occupied at Carolside, and in which my personal attire was deposited.   Marie put it therein with
the rest of my gear; but the piece of furniture, being
antique in the extreme, had sundry secret gaps and
crevices, into one of which my knightly insignia
slipped, and was only discovered there last week by
the merest chance by a housemaid, who carried it to

Lady **Monson** (joint occupier of Carolside with her and my friend Mrs. Mitchell), and asked her "*whatever* she thought it could be meant for." Doubtless the **worthy** Dustabella thought it some *auld warld* relic, which had lain in the cracked epidermis of the old wardrobe for any number of hundreds of years, and for my part, though I am extremely glad to be again in possession of my patron saint (the dragon ?), I am half inclined to deplore its coming to life before 1973, when it would have occasioned such pretty speculations and such wise disquisitions as to the who, and the how, and the why, and the where, and the when, and what women were, or were not entitled **to** belong to orders of knighthood, etc.

Talking of the dragon, did Adelaide ever tell you her application of the vulgar favourite nursery rhyme to me, her sister ?

> "The Dragon **of** Wantley, round as a butt,
>   Full of fire from top to toe,
>   Cock of the walk, to the village I strut,
>   And scare them all wherever I go."

My week at Bury was very pleasant, and could only have been more so if you and Mary Anne had been there to see, and if dear Donne had not so mistrusted his own value and my value for him as to give me more of almost anybody's company than his own ; but he is a modest man, God help him ! and the consequence is, he asked people to meet me, as it is called (oh ! how gladly would I shun those meetings for the most part), and shared me with his friends, whereupon I can only conclude that he found me a great deal too much for himself.

On returning to town last Monday I was a good deal alarmed to find my father in the worst stage of one of his lumbar attacks; the malady has, however, passed the crisis very successfully, and he is now again so far recovered as to be able to walk out every day.

Adelaide is in all the discomfort and confusion of preparation for departure, and I in all the sorrow of looking on. They start on Monday week, and I shall certainly be very forlorn until the middle of January, when I think I shall take flight sunward myself, and pursue them to Rome. Perhaps about that time you and Mary Anne may have made up your minds thitherward too, and we may all foregather among the great ruins within sight of Soracte and the Sabine sisterhood of hills, a different mountain group and under a different sky from that which we last contemplated together.

Thanks for all the domestic accounts of fish, flesh, fowl, and *apple*. Do you think of making cider? You asked after my plans as regards residence. While I remain in London I have many reading engagements, which will keep me pretty constantly on the move till January; my headquarters, however, will be London, and as long as this house remains unlet I shall make it my home while I am in town. After it is let (which I make no doubt it will be after Christmas) I shall betake myself to a very comfortable lodging-house in King Street, St. James's, kept by some old servants of the last Lord Essex, respectable people, whom I have known for a long while, and with whom I have found very comfortable accommodation on various occasions.

Your old friend Mr. Dalton dined with Donne one day while I was at Bury, and I sat beside him at dinner. I did my very best to be conversible with him, but did not find it very easy, and after dinner he was appropriated and retained by a lady of the party, and did not address me again except to bid me good night.

I do not know whether I shall be in Edinburgh at all this winter. I have had certain overtures, "there have been motions made," **but as at** present the arrangements are all floating vaguely in a very indefinite Scotch **mist, I** can speak to no precise time for my being in Scotland, though I suppose I shall **be** there some time in the winter.

My providences (now that I have cast off Mitchell) are all local, that is to say, I go only to those **places** to which I receive a special invitation, which generally emanates from some enterprising bookseller, who has an enterprising rival, and wishes to distinguish himself therefrom by getting (" at great risk and trouble ") Mrs. Fanny Kemble down to read for the edification of the inhabitants and neighbouring gentry, by which speculation he pockets some pounds, and gives his rival a poke in the ribs.

I am hers and yours very affectionately,

FANNY KEMBLE.

[I gave **several** readings in New York for the benefit of the St. George's Society, a benevolent institution, founded and maintained by Englishmen for the assistance of their fellow-countrymen in America, **whose** circumstances rendered them proper objects of **charity or help of other kind.**

On the occasion of my first reading, I observed
that the committee of management (all leading
members of the society) wore on the left breast of
their coats a very handsome badge in silver of the
St. George and the Dragon, familiar to all English
eyes on the current coin of the realm. The well-
known symbol touched a cord of patriotism in my
heart, and I was greatly tempted to ask one of the
gentlemen to lend me his badge for the evening, while
I gave my reading. I withstood the sentimental
impertinence of my impulse, however, and contented
myself merely with the wish.

The readings were very profitable to the charity,
and some time after I had given them a number of
the members called on me and told me that, in
recognition of the service which, they were good
enough to say, I had rendered them, and in which I
had so much pleasure, they had intended and hoped
to make me an honorary member of their society, but
had found it impossible to do so, the terms of their
charter referring to male individuals only, as ("this
English*man*," etc., and "for this English*man*," etc.),
which difficulty they had not known how to obviate.
They therefore gave me a gold badge, similar to the
silver one they wore, and which, as I then told them,
I had so much wished to wear, if only for two hours.

Their present to me was a beautiful jewel, with a
splendid gold chain, to which it was suspended by
a cross of rubies. I had lost nothing by waiting, and
always afterwards wore the noble ornament whenever
I read one of Shakespeare's Historical Plays.

It's very peculiar character has made me reluctant

to wear it in private, **when** it is apt to challenge observation. On **one** occasion **the** eager and close curiosity it excited in one of **my** fellow-guest's (a lady in a great country house), made **me** hasten to **place it** in her hand, lest she should be quicker than myself in taking it **from** my neck. My friend Henry Greville told me that once **in** going **out** from my reading he had heard a **comical** discussion between two gentlemen on the subject **of** the ornament I wore, attached to **a** broad blue **ribbon** across my dress, one of them maintaining that it was a foreign order given **me** by some royal **or princely** personage abroad, " **I** tell you it isn't," **was the** rather testy reply ; " **she never** was *ordered* **abroad or at home by** anybody," " which made me think," **said my friend,** " **that the gentleman knew you**."

In the course **of** several **winters I spent** at Rome, I frequently **passed the evening at** the Palazzo Gaetano, **with the Duke and Duchess of** Sermoneta. (She was an Englishwoman, sister **of my** dear friend, Isabella **Knight**). One evening she **asked** me to let the duke *see* **the ornament I was** wearing. The **duke** *was quite* *blind* **and to let** him *see* anything seemed strange enough. **She took my** George, however, and placed it in the palm **of her** husband's left hand, who rapidly and lightly passing the fingers of **his** right hand **over** it exclaimed, " Ah, Pistrucci's St. **George and the** Dragon," and **then** warmly praised **the** elegance, grace and spirit of the **group**.

He was himself a learned connoisseur of ancient ornamental art, **the Etruscan** remains of which have after the lapse **of** centuries resumed their place as exquisite adornments in the jewel caskets of modern beauty.

The duke, before he became blind, furnished himself some admirably graceful original designs for the great jeweller Castellina. Among other of his remarkable devices were the fine figures of the angel and the devil, familiar to our writing and reading-tables as the most poetical of paper knives.

My first acquaintance with the Duke of Sermoneta, was at a dinner-party, where I had the honour and pleasure of sitting by him, and when he entertained me with a most humorous account of his family, which, as a newly arrived stranger in Rome, he took it for granted I was not acquainted with.

"We are called Gaetani," said he, "because we came from Gaeta; whether directly descended from Cicero's nurse I do not know, but my wife, the duchess, paints upon china vases our arms on a shield in the middle of crooked lines, intended to represent the waves, but if they represented them better the arms would probably be all washed out.

"We began our family existence as brigands and bandits, which you know is the beginning of all nobility; then we became much more respectable, soldiers, condottieri, living decently by seizing other people's land, and building castles of our own upon it, and so were great feudal lords and petty tyrants; then followed priests, prelates, popes, princes, and dukes; but, unfortunately, we were always more poor than powerful, and have gone on getting poorer and poorer, so that now we are positive paupers ('qu'a present nous ne sommes que des gueux et pas autre chose')."

—" Well," said I, " that is bad, but has one advantage, you cannot go any lower in the social scale."—" I beg your pardon, madam, we can and have, helas! descended lower, for we have become bores, which you probably perceive (' Pardon, madame, nous sommes, hélas descendus plus bas encore, nous sommes devenus des enuyeux et je crois que vous vous en apercevez ')."

To the distinction of his noble name and high rank, the Duke of Sermoneta added that of political liberality, social affability, great intellectual and artistic cultivation and accomplishment, and a sparkling gift of keenly witty and brilliant conversational powers.]

Villa Correali, Sorrento, Sunday, June 5th, 1853.

MY DEAR ARTHUR,

In sight of Herculaneum and Pompeii I sit down to thank you for the books concerning them which you gave me before I left England, desiring that I would not acknowledge them until I was at Sorrento. Perhaps, from the long tarrying of my acknowledgments, you may have thought I had shared the fate of those engulfed cities and become illustrious by being buried alive, but no such luck. The only apology I can make for the delay of my thanks is very simply to state the fact that, though we have been at Sorrento five days, this is the first in which the bounteous gods have vouchsafed me an inkstand, for Italian palaces, though built of marble, and rising out of orange groves, and commanding from every window, terrace, and balcony, incomparable views of seas, shores, and islands, renowned in history

and poetry, and lovelier than imagination, are nevertheless much devoid of the common necessaries of life;
and when I tell you that the post takes four days in
bringing our letters from Naples to Sorrento (a distance
of about thirty miles), bethink yourself of Corrybrough and Inverness and Scotch postal privileges
and be thankful. I think you will agree with me that,
to have written to you with a black lead pencil and
trusted to the letter reaching you would have been a
clear tempting of Providence.

I have not been at all well since I came to Italy.
We had three nights of wretched storm on the
Mediterranean, from Marseilles to Civita Vecchia, and
I am only now beginning to recover from the manifold
ailments my voyage entailed upon me.

I found Adelaide and Edward and her children
quite well and thriving, and she inquired very
affectionately after you and Mary Anne. They have
taken a house in Rome, and are having it furnished
for next winter; and, unless some most unforeseen
circumstance prevents it, I shall pass my next winter
there too. I shall not be able to make out my
summer excursion to Switzerland, so that must remain
for some other time. Perhaps on my way back from
Italy next summer I may accomplish it, and who
knows but you may be willing to exchange your own
Alps for the Swiss that year.

The place where we now are is enchantingly
beautiful, and I think we have the best situated house
in all Sorrento. Our windows sweep the whole bay,
from Capo di Monte to the little toe of Naples, with
its whole background of mountains and foreground

of islands. From one of the windows of my bedroom I see Capri and the whole coast between it and Sorrento, and from the other the sea, Naples, Vesuvius, Castellamare, and the whole coast on that side to Sorrento. We have terraces that dominate, as the French say, over earth, sea, and sky; and are surrounded with loveliness and grandeur before, behind, and on either hand. Now you will want to know the drawbacks; but as you probably remember the place very well, you no doubt remember them. There is no beach, and the cliffs, being very high and all crowned with the gardens or orchards of private dwelling houses, one is debarred from that familiar intercourse with the sea which its proximity makes one particularily eager for. We, it is true, shall be able to bathe by passing through the orange orchard of an adjoining villa; but though we may get into the sea, we can very hardly get by it, and our conversation with the nymph of these bright waters, the divine Parthenope, must be rather distant or a plunge into her arms. One would desire a medium. Then, too, Sorrento itself is a mere collection of villas and country houses, whose separate extensive enclosures keep the pedestrian in a labyrinth of stone walls.

Your very affectionate
FANNY KEMBLE.

Villa Correali, Sorrento, Monday, August 8th, **1853**.

O Roman! you need not have triumphed so gloriously and furiously from your northern mountains over us of the southern sea-coast. I neither love nor like Italy as I do Scotland, and would give all that my eyes can **see at this** moment (and they command **the sea and shores** most renowned **in** the world **for** beauty, and among the folds of the mountains lie those plains, the "all manner of deliciousness" which conquered Hannibal's army) for the bleakest stretch of the howling wilderness that lies between Moy and Inverness.

In the first place, "**I** do agnize a natural and prompt alacrity I find in hardness," though Heaven forbid **but that** I should perceive beauty wherever it exists **(seeing** that **a** "thing of beauty is a joy for **ever").** The species of loveliness of this part of **the world** is the least **attractive** possible **to** me. That which is sublime, severe, stern, dark, solemn, wild, and even savage is far more to my **taste than this** profusion of shining, glittering, smiling, sparkling, beaming, brilliant prospects and aspects. Green, white, or even black water pleases me better than this uncanny-looking element, which seems to me to **be of** all the colours of the rainbow, except that of any wholesome water, salt **or** fresh, that one ever saw before. And oh! my dear Arthur, the Blue Grotto of Capri, with men swimming like magical silver images in its magical **blue waters, is nothing so lovely to** my mind as that drumlie pool of brown-black, veined with threads of foam, in the Findhorn, by which **I stood in** the pelting **rain, believing** that it contained **a salmon.**

You are perfectly right; Italy is to be eschewed in summer, and I have good reason to say so, for Sorrento disagrees with me extremely, and a fresh breath of the bleakest mountain air would be as welcome to me as that comfortable kiss from the frozen lips of the north wind that poor King John so pathetically implores in his burning agony.

The volcanic atmosphere of the whole region is utterly repugnant to my constitution; and I think that I have never in all my life been in any place which gave me such a general feeling of ill ease, as the French have it.

We return to Rome in October, and though I find the climate of that place heavy and unwholesome to me, I look forward with the greatest expectation of relief to my departure from this feverish, exciting, irritating, debilitating atmosphere.

Now, do you think that you need have flourished that bundle of Highland blossoms under my nose, to excite my envy? (Ah! you left out a sprig of heather and a branch of rowan, but I added them.)

I do not know at all where I shall be next summer. My sister talks of returning to England, and I suppose will do so towards the end of the spring, and I have serious thoughts of coming up to Glen Falloch and striking a bargain with the keeper of that lovely inn, and trying how a whole year of the Highlands would suit me, and whether it would not be a good antidote to the pernicious poison of these ausonian skies.

I mean to go up to Monte St. Angelo before I leave these parts. I have done but little in the sight-seeing line hitherto, for the extreme heat has made even short excursions very laborious.

I did clamber down that — infernal — Calata at Scariatoyo the other day, under a broiling sun, and have not been *as* right in my mind ever since. Oh! Heavens, what a descent! and how could it have agreed even with a haggis?* Once down on the blazing beach we did not proceed to Amalfi, but falling, boiled, broiled, baked, and utterly extenuated, into the bottom of a boat, we bade the men by all their saints to row us into some shade; and behold, after lying for ten minutes on water, the sight of which seared the *back* of one's eyeballs, we shot under a huge shadowy vault, where a mass of dark rocks rose from the dark-blue water, under the dark canopy of the overhanging cliffs, and up here we clambered and lay and sat and ate figs and oranges and fresh almonds, and saw the syrens across a reach of dazzling smooth sea, but didn't hear them sing because—we were singing ourselves, and a great deal better than ever they did.

Amalfi, Paestum, Pompeii, Vesuvius, etc., expect us at the end of the dog-days; and not having been to any of these famous places, what can I tell you in return for your welcome and pleasant account of Corrybrough and all its belongings. By-the-bye, Arthur, you never said one word about the Cochin-China hens; have they got backs to their bodies yet, or are they still strutting indecently forth, mere fronts of fowls, without even the behinds that may be had at any milliners? They really appear to me very offensive, and if they were mine I should insist upon their wearing false tails, or, at any rate, never turning round.

Your account of your mother is no more sad than of necessity it must be. I wish, if you can think of it, you would send her my very affectionate respects.

* "For a haggis, God bless it! can charge down-hill."
WALTER SCOTT.

Adelaide and I were speaking of her the other day, and Adelaide said that once when she was saying to Edward Fitzgerald how charming your mother appeared to her, he replied with a perfect outburst of affectionate enthusiasm, "Oh! you can never know how charming she was; you never were a schoolboy under her care!" I think that is very nice, and it ought to please you, too, I think.

I was glad that you thought my father looking well, when you saw him. We have both of us written to him since my arrival in Rome, but have heard nothing whatever from him in reply, so that the report of his good looks and good spirits is good news, for which we are very thankful. . . .

I have no idea at all, my dear Arthur, that the Americans will admit, even to themselves, that their exhibition has been a failure. I think it most probable that at this very moment all persons concerned in that enterprise are congratulating themselves in particular, and their country in general, on their having contrived to "flog all Europe." In a letter I got the other day from the other side of the Atlantic, I was assured that Lord Ellesmere pronounced the New York Crystal Palace a much more beautiful and better-built edifice than ours of Hyde Park glorious memory. I suppose his lordship must have been bent upon making himself desperately popular with the New Yorkians. Certainly his and Lady Ellesmere's letters indicate anything but satisfaction, either with their own mission there, which proves to be a most anomalous one, or anything which it has enabled them to observe of America or Americans. I have had a long letter from her, with a long account of my girls, whom she saw in Philadelphia; and I think, judging by that, S—— must be much the prettiest and pleasantest thing she has seen on the other side of the water.

My dear Arthur, you say not one word about Mary Anne. I presume, however, that that is simply because, being well and contented yourself, you have naturally or unnaturally considered that your conditions were necessarily hers; but you have nothing to do with housekeeping and cooks; housemaids and dairy-women are by no means essential parts of your existence, though they are of hers. I trust the whole establishment has been satisfactory in the less noble regions, and that the lower wheels of the household machinery have wrought smoothly and without too much creaking.

Yours always, and most truly,

FANNY KEMBLE.

Respects to all the canines. What manner of amalgamation has my namesake been guilty of to be bringing niggers into the field? I hope the grouse will be discreet and let themselves be shot, and the salmon let themselves be caught, and may the mushrooms flourish!

33, *Via Delle Mercedi, Rome,*
Thursday, December 22nd, 1853.

Your kind and pleasant letter, dear Arthur, which I have just been reading over to see if it contains anything more especially to be answered, ends with a question about that poor wretched Lady L——d, and a hope that she was not much related either by blood or affection to my dear Harriet St. Leger; and here, close by me, lies a letter I received yesterday from her, full of the most painful details of the catastrophe, which occurred at her home, Ardgillan Castle (luckily she was absent from it at the time), where I was staying last autumn twelvemonths, and made acquaintance with the unfortunate young woman whose death has, of course, given an association of horror to the beautiful place, which it will be long before any of the family will be able to overcome. Maria, my friend Harriet's eldest niece, was on the cliffs, and witnessed her cousin's death without being able to render or procure assistance for her. She received the corpse in her arms, when it was at last rescued from the sea, and has ever since been suffering from a most horrible nervous affection of the eyes, which causes her to see half of every one's face like the livid and swollen half of her drowned cousin's face, as she last saw it. Is not that a wretched penalty to pay for having been the most unwilling witness of such a tragedy?

You ask me if I went up Vesuvius. Yes, indeed, I certainly did; and I think in a very proper manner. We drove from Sorrento in an open carriage, on a magnificent moonlight night, to Resina, and ascended the mountain by torchlight, myself and a female friend being carried in Portantina from the Artrio de Cavalli to the summit, and Edward Sartoris struggling up on his own legs. The effect of this very partially lighted ascent was extremely fine, and not a little frightful,

inasmuch as the torchlight, though sufficient for the
well-trained guides and bearers, was quite inadequate
to give one the remotest idea of the details of the
scene, whose larger features surrounded one with
apparently measureless heights and depths of awful
sublimity. The groups of the men carrying, preceding,
and following us, illumined by vivid, but flashing and
capricious glares of light, formed a most picturesque
addition to the scene, and the terrible angles at which
the chair containing one was pitched now forwards,
now backwards, now to either side, according as the
bearers scrambled or sprang alternately on great
blocks of lava, or fell on their knees as their insecure
footing rolled from beneath them, was an additional
circumstance of peril, which added the excitement of
constant fear to all one's other emotions, and is far
pleasanter to remember than experience. We lay on
the edge of the crater, wrapped in shawls and blankets,
all the rest of the night, and the heat of the burning
soil was sufficient to scorch and discolour my woollen
dress. Here we saw the stars go out and the great
fire of the day kindle in the east, and came down
from the mountain when the white clouds issuing
from its huge abyss were all coloured rosy red with
the sun's rays, and as we descended the mountain,
Guido's and Guercino's auroras floated in the radiant
atmosphere, and we saw them under our feet instead
of craning and corkscrewing our necks to look at
them over our heads on the ceilings of the Rospègliosé
pavilions; and we saw the bay and its beautiful shores
smiling like Paradise beneath us, a wonderful, beautiful sight, much beautified by contrast, for Vesuvius

is undoubtedly a great deal more like hell than any imagination that can be formed of hell can be. Not even the return of the blessed beneficent light of day seemed to me to relieve its horrors. I have never seen anything in nature before that seemed to me absolutely hideous as this did. The black dismal heap of cinders within whose bowels the pent-up fire rages, the hateful discoloration of the interior of the crater, its feruginous and sulphuric inequalities, from which, as from the gangrenous surface of some horrid cancer-disease in the earth's bosom, rise the pestiferous poisonous fumes it incessantly exhales, which I am sure vitiate the atmosphere of that whole region in no inconsiderable degree; the whole thing bore a horrible aspect to me, which impressed me even more than its awfulness or sublimity. The depths of the Atlantic and the chasm of Niagara are awful, but they are beautiful as well as terrible, and there is an unspeakable fascination in the contemplation of the tremendous destruction of being delivered to them; but Vesuvius had no particle of this mysterious charm of the grander revelations of nature, and not even the blessed uprising of the day, which seemed to crown the whole earth with loveliness, gave any beauty to or took away any ugliness from the grimness of that *ugliest* place; to which, in my judgment, the term applies with all the shades of significance English or American folk have ever attached to it; and in the common vocabulary of the United States it means (as it should do) *wicked* as well as unsightly.

Never speak or write or hint anything to me about the Monte St. Angelo, because I did not go up it, and that I did not is an abiding sorrow and disappointment to me; but in order to accommodate friends, with whom I was to make the expedition, it was postponed and postponed until finally it had to be given up, and I feel bitterly about it whenever I think of it. The sides and shoulders of the mountain, however, I made some acquaintance with in going over the bridle-path (if such it can be called) from Castellamare to Amalfi; but the Gulf of Salerno, and all that surrounds it, is by far the finest thing I saw; and I am haunted with a longing desire to see Amalfi again, and to settle (not for a year, but for life), on the highest peak of the mountain range behind it, at a place called Ravello, where an Englishman has bought and furnished a house, built in the time of the Normans and Saracens, with a Saracenic cloister and Norman tower to it, and a vine-covered terrace that overlooks the Mediterranean from Punta di Palinuro to Misenium. That's the place, if you please!

Rome, where you see I now am, seems to me the place in the world where one can best dispense with happiness; and from the bottom of my envious ignorance I cannot help thinking that the pleasure nearest happiness (what a gulf there is between!) must be the enjoyment of a great and fine scholar—like Arnold, for instance—in Rome, present and past,—this Rome of which Poussin in his enthusiasm caught up a handful of the soil, exclaiming, "Ecco la Roma antica!" and that other Rome beneath it, with its unburied and unburiable memories.

The outside of Rome is worth all the inside in my judgment, and every day the charm of the Campagna increases in my eyes. I have just got a nice horse, and think with anticipation of pleasure (amounting almost to happiness) of riding every day over that beautiful desert.

We have not a very agreeable society here this winter, at least, I think not; but then I am hard to please, and perhaps other people might think otherwise. Thackeray is here, and the Brownings, so it is not their fault if we are not both witty and poetical.

Thank you for all the pleasant details of the Highland farm. When this reaches you, you will be far enough south of Corrybrough, smothered in London smoke, which you appreciate and I do not. We have had rain and darkness to-day that would not have disgraced the city, and it promises *foul* to continue.

FANNY KEMBLE.

Genoa, Wednesday, June 9th, 1854.

How often have you said, "I wonder if Fanny Kemble ever got that last letter of mine?" written you know best when, for the only date upon it is the 21*st of Wimpole Street,* and I might, if I chose, pretend that I had only received it three days ago; but in truth it is much nearer three months, and I have nothing to say for myself but that I am ashamed of having left your kind remembrance of me so long unacknowledged and unanswered, and now I am coming towards you, not so rapidly but that this, I should think, would precede me by at least ten days.

I am sitting at a balcony at least eighty feet above the pavement of Genoa; the blue Mediterranean is as black as ink, so is the blue heaven of Italy above it, and my right shoulder, which I dislocated by a fall from my horse three weeks ago in the Roman Campagna, and which ever since, though much less useful than usual as a limb, has found out a new cunning, and become extremely expert as a barometer, is aching with the cold and damp of this delicious climate. I do not feel entitled to complain, however, for when I went out this morning I was broiled half through with the intolerable shining of the sun, so that I flatter myself that I enjoy all the atmospheric disadvantages of England and Italy combined just now, and have every reason to be thankful.

I left Rome ten days ago, spent two days at Florence, and two (unwillingly by accident) at Pisa, and was greatly charmed with the dull beauty of the latter place. You know I like stupidity in everything (I can't help how you may take this, and cannot pull my reasoning straight and tidy with such a very aching arm), and was charmed with the appearance of Pisa, perhaps because all my English friends assured me it was the stupidest place on the face of the earth. The journey from Rome to Siena (which I was also credibly informed was a miracle of ugly dulness) seemed to me beautiful, particularly the passage of the mountain wall of the Campagna above the little lake of Vico, coming down upon Viterbo; indeed, the whole road from Roncilione to Aquapendente (do you know it?) enchanted me, as I slept through the ugly part from Radicofani to Siena. I remain in some wonderment as to what the merits of the road by Arezzo and Perugia can be, which caused polite travellers to turn up their noses in disdain at this.

Each time hitherto that I have approached or left
Rome it has **been** by the shortest route and rapidest
conveyance, the Mediterranean and the steamboat;
but this time I determined not to pass by my privileges
(Heaven knows when I shall be near these particular
ones again!), **and so** I have diligently diligenced and
vetturinoed hither by land, and though there is a railroad down in the street, here under my very nose,
with trains running madly every three **or** four hours
to Turin, in less than half **a** day, **I am** going per
diligence **along the** Riviera to **Nice,** and thus per
diligence again over the **Col de** Tende to Turin, and
so home by the Cenis, Geneva, the Jura, and Dijon **to**
Paris.

You professed wanderers in the Alps scorn the **Mont**
Cenis, I know; but to me, **who** have never **seen** one
of the great passes of the Alps, I dare say it will seem
quite handsome, **as** the Americans say, and I hope to
do things in order and systematically, and so, "Belier
mon ami commençons au commencement." If I **live**
till next winter, **and** can come back to Rome, which
I would most gladly do, why then, I will try **the**
Simplon or the Splügen, a promotion in the picturesque
which comparison will probably enable me **to** value
still more highly.

I left Adelaide still lingering at Rome, whence her
time **of** departure appeared to depend upon when
Edward could make up his mind to say they should
go. He's coming to England some time this summer,
but she and the children **will** remain at the Baths of
Lucca till October, when they will all **return** to winter
in **Rome.** They were all, **I** think, a **little the worse,**

physically, for their two **years** uninterrupted sojourn in this perfidious **climate,** and the beautiful **baby** seems **to me** to require the stimulus **of a more** invigorating **atmosphere, especially** during the summer.

Pray give my respectful and grateful remembrance **to your mother.** How long I recollect her, how many **images of my own** youth and that of my brothers, and **the fellowship of** pleasant contemporaries, and Dr. **Malkin's** good-natured notice of and friendly assistance **and** advice to me, **her** graceful figure and sweet countenance conjure up!

I am very sorry that **Lawrence** is obliged to think **of trying** America **as a residence,** because I fear he **will not** find **it answer to him.** To be sure, if it answers no better than England, he will still, as you **very justly observe,** find it easier **to provide** there for **his** large family. But the life **of** competition of a **foreign** artist in America seems to me the last that he **could** endure, refined as he is by nature and used to **the** companionship of those whom I know to be his friends, **poor fellow!**

I have a sort of notion that your temper, like my **own, is not** incapable of irritation, and that I ought **not** to tempt you too much by crossing this execrable handwriting **of** mine, so **keep** your temper (unless you can part with it to advantage) and I have done. Give **my** kindest regards to James Spedding and **my** best **love** to Mary **Anne;** and believe **me** ever, as ever, yours and hers very sincerely attached,

FANNY KEMBLE.

21, Dover Street, Piccadilly, Sunday, July 9th, 1854.

I wasn't the least aware that I was intolerant of bores in general. You say, if "a bore," and therefore perhaps have some particular bore in your eye to whom, in an unusual frame of mind, I may have taken an objection, but I cannot remember any such exception to my universal rule (which at any rate could only be proved thereby) of liking for stupid things, which expression with me includes stupid people, for whom I have not only liking but great esteem and value in this most wearisomely impertinent age of all but universal and infinite cleverness.

What has become of my scheme for spending twelve months at Glen Falloch, say you? Ah! verily, what indeed! My schemes are much like the charming cherubims who declined the courteous country curate's invitation to seat themselves, "n'ayant pas de quoi." They are beautiful from the *head upwards*, but—" but only to the girdle do the gods inherit"—they are sadly wanting in foundation, and they are extremely apt to keep up a fluttering (like humming-birds, which the children say cannot alight, because they have no feet) over every new charming place they come to, so that perhaps it is as well for me that my schemes do not even set one foot on the ground, or by this time I might have a house on the Lake of Geneva, another in the neighbourhood of Turin, another at Mentone, another at Spezia, another at Sestri, another at Pisa, another at Fiesole, another at Rome, another at Mola di Gaeta, another at La Cava, and another at Amalfi, or rather on the tip-top of the peaked mountain of Ravello, looking from one side to another of the

Gulf of Salerno and almost high enough to see Sicily on a fine day.

Perhaps you had no idea I was so inconstant; but I hardly know indeed how you should have, for whenever I wish to enlighten you at all with regard to the real nature of my qualities and character, you are so offended at finding what an odious person you are fond of, that you directly quarrel with me, so that I cannot help it if you do not know that to "stay here" is my invariable feeling in every pretty or pleasant place I come to, partly perhaps because of the wandering "stay-nowhere" sort of life I have led, and partly too from a villainous propensity I have of living entirely and greedily and with all my might in the present, be it whatever it may, a practice of children and poets, but which a woman, who is neither childish nor, I thank the gods, poetical, has no right to indulge in.

You bid me tell you what I am going to do? As far as I know at present it is this: on the twentieth I shall go down to old Windsor and spend three days with Miss Cottin and Mary Anne Thackeray, and on the 25th I think I shall set off with my friend Harriet St. Leger and M—— to Ireland. I believe I had told you of our plot for visiting the English lakes, all three together, this summer. Miss St. Leger's sister, however, having asked me and M—— to come and visit her at Ardgillan, near Dublin, and advised our finishing up our lake explorations with Killarney, we, upon due debate, have determined to give up the English lakes this summer and do some Irish sight-seeing instead, winding up with our visit to our friends, all which, I suppose, will occupy a month or six weeks, and that is as far as I have looked into the future hitherto.

I think my father, who is looking younger and better, and is, I verily believe, stronger than any of us, rather inclines to going abroad this winter. I hope he will take Henry with him, who is extremely ill, suffering horribly from what I suppose to be inflammatory rheumatism, and looking a great deal more dead than alive. If he, I mean my father, should wish me to go with him, I shall do so, and I believe be glad of it, but if he should not, which is just as likely as not, I shall remain very quietly in King Street, and have the pleasure of seeing you and Mary Anne when you return to London.

You must not curse my poor horse on account of my shoulder. She is a most excellent and sure-footed beast, but the whole country was completely blind, the grass in the Campagna nearly as high as her knees, and I, seeing one deep rut from which I turned her, had not sense enough to reflect that ruts do not run single, but that the one I saw had a fellow in the grass that I didn't see. I was particularly fond of that mare, for she was so discreet and docile that she would let me, while on her back, let down the top bar of a stagionata, one of the high Campagna fences, and then in the tidiest style hop over the lower ones with me. I liked her so well, that I have not sold her, but merely sent her out to grass for the chance of my being in Rome again this winter, when I would most assuredly ride her, ay, a hunting too, as I did before, and as to my enormous weight, about which you and Smut [the Highland pony I used to ride at Corry-

brough] think proper to have had your crack
"thegither," I beg to inform you that, thanks to
incessant dyspepsia and all my various unfavourable
Italian influences, I have come home as thin as a
lathe and as light as a feather; so tell that saucy Smut
some day when you get on him with your gun in
your hand and your game-bag very full.

Give my kind love to Mary Anne, and believe me
always yours and hers most truly,

Fanny Kemble.

I am so glad Mrs. Mitchel has bought Lawrence's
sketch of me. King Street was quite full when I
arrived, so I had to turn in here.

29, King Street, St. James's, October 15th, 1854.

My dear Arthur,

My arithmetic is very apt to be wrong, I am
sorry to say, and I do send you nine thanks for my
grouse, with which I enjoyed the pleasures, both of
greediness and munificence, and the birds were pronounced excellent, alike by me and my friends; but I
think, if I had known that grouse were subject to *tape-
worm* (yah!) I should have been even more generous
and less greedy, and given them all away. Goodness
gracious me! what sophistication on the part of moor
fowl! Worms one might understand—heather-worms,
or bog-worms, or hag-worms—but tape-worms! Seeing
the pre-eminently artificial nature of tape, I am
astonished, I confess, and disgusted.

Snow! oh, snow already! That sounds cruel cold,
and I do not think I wish to be at Corrybrough for
the sake of forcing my winter as it were.

Spedding's gold pen deserves retribution, and doubtless **will** get it. No man ought to be so lucky as he is with impunity. But the misfortune is that I suspect **he has** made **quiet** acquaintance (perhaps even friendly) already with his Nemesis, and she will scare him no more than. height or depth or any other creature can. He is an enviable man, and I suppose **a** very meritorious one, for to be born so wise is surely quite out of the question and out of the power of anybody that **ever was born.**

The invitation I gave him I **do** bestow **most cordially on** you and Mary Anne. I do not suppose **I should** have presumed to suggest any such thing as **your all** or any **of you** taking the trouble to come and pay me evening visits; but Spedding was lamentably deploring **to me** one day that there was no such unceremonious evening visiting among us as on the Continent or even in America, and on that hint I spake, being likely to be much at home, much alone, and very glad to see any of **my friends who will** condescend to visit me.

You bid me not answer your letter, but **I** have certain *organic laws* of correspondence from which nothing short of a miracle causes **me** to depart; as, for instance, I never write till I am written to, I always write **when** I am written to, and I make a point of always returning the same amount of paper I receive, as you **may** convince yourself by observing that I send you two sheets of note-paper and Mary Anne only half one, though **I** have nothing more to say to you, and I have to her; to wit, that I have not seen the E——'s for some little time now, and M—— very seldom writes to me. I went with them to spend a day in Burnham Beeches the day before W—— returned to Harrow, about a month ago, but have not seen any of them since.

My father varies very much, and is some days very ill and others again quite wonderfully well. Donne I see pretty frequently, and we are good neighbours. I am going with him on Wednesday to see a revival of "Pericles, Prince of Tyre." I cannot well imagine how that can be represented, but seeing is believing.

Adieu! My regards and respects to the dogs and Smut, believe me, ever yours most truly,

FANNY KEMBLE.

16, *Saville* **Row, Saturday,** *July 7th*, 1855.

Thank you, my dear Arthur, for your screed of news from Corrybrough. It makes me die with envy to read of the flowers, and the river, and the grouse, and the no people. London is more fast and furious, it seems to me, than ever, and though I am not at all embarked on the mad waters, but stand remote from it all on the shore, the uproar fills me with discomfort and dismay. I think nothing can be more depressing to the spirits than to live in the middle of a tremendous bustle without mixing in it. I shall be very glad when my time comes for being able to go; and as Edward Sartoris is now returned, I hope he will give the necessary attention to my poor brother Henry's affairs to make me feel at liberty to leave England for a couple of months.

I am very much obliged to you for your additional suggestions for my Swiss tour. The first part of my expedition is that which I like **best,** and that (I mean Upper Dauphiné **and the** Valais) I trust we shall accomplish.

I am very glad **that** you endorse my approbation of the lower shore of Lochetive. I thought the drive from Dalmally to Thagivilt round these shores one of the loveliest things I ever saw.

I **will give** your message about the grouse to Adelaide the first time I see her, but London avocations interfere not a little with family as well as friendly relations, and I could have chimed in very well with **Mrs.** Procter's lamentation to me this morning, **who said,** "Oh! I was so glad to think that Adelaide had come back from Rome. **She has been** here nearly three weeks and I have seen her once."

Thank you for your kind inquiry after my dear friend, Harriet St. Leger. I escorted her yesterday half way down to York, in the neighbourhood of which city she is going to stay with some friends for change of air and quiet. She is wonderfully recovered already, considering the severity of her attack.

I should like a young Wasp extremely, if you find that **you can** spare me one, and though I shall lie in an hourly agony for fear of losing him, nevertheless I think I should like to have the chance of doing so or the contrary.

I gave your message to our friend the librarian,* who declared that if the thing could be compassed by men, he surely would go up to that "abomination of desolation" of a **country** of yours and pay you **a** small visit.

---

* **Mr.** Donne, Librarian of the **London Library.**

I met Monsieur Jem * at the Romilly's last week. He replied to my asking him if he was going up to Corrybrough, that I must ask Edward Romilly, in whose department of State business he has now accepted some share, and evidently expects to have plenty to do.

FANNY KEMBLE.

Boston, Monday, April 6th, 1857.

MY DEAR ARTHUR,

Your letter was very welcome. I think often and affectionately of you among my other friends, and wondered a little that I had not heard from you. I am, however, a reasonable woman in one respect, I seldom call my friends to account in my own mind. What they give me seems always of pure grace, and my friends have been very liberal in constancy and kindness to me, and therefore when I am inclined to desire other or more demonstration of regard than I receive from them, I always blame myself for a sort of presumptuous trespassing on the liberty of love which should, I think, be unquestioned.

I have often thought with great regret of my declining to take the dog you offered me, and feared more than once that I had offended you and Mary Anne by rejecting your kindness; but I really was afraid of the trouble of the dog on board ship, where I knew I should be quite incapable of looking after him, and then I thought that in my meeting with S—— I should utterly forget and neglect the poor thing, at

* Mr. James Spedding.

least I fancied this, for after all I could very well have cared for him after I landed, for S—— did not join me for two days, and I should have gained his affection and established my authority in some degree in that time. It was not want of regard for either of you that made me refuse him, though, according to the old canine proverb, you may have thought so.

I carried your letter with your account of your Swiss climbing to the house of Agassiz, who is now a Professor of Cambridge (Massachusetts) College, with whom I was invited to spend the evening. His bright face brightened as I read him of your exploits, and he told me some of his own. He showed me, hanging in his library, a magnificent photograph of the glacier of the Aar, and I forget what incredible number of nights and days he told me he had lived and lain there on the ice. I was very much struck with his saying that he never suffered the least distress in climbing the mountains, but had breath to spare for smoking a pipe all the way up the Jungfrau. He is an immense man, but well proportioned, so that I suppose his weight is not too much for his strength. Oh! what would I not give to see those snow-peaks again!

I have been to the great West this winter, to St. Louis, beyond the Mississippi, across the prairies, and to the further shore of Lake Michigan, and very thankful indeed I am to be once more back in New England, which is more like Old England than any other part of this huge and most wonderful country.

The hurry of life in the Western part of this country, the rapidity, energy, and enterprise with

which civilization is there being carried forward
baffles all description, and, I think, can hardly be
believed but by those who have seen it. Cities of
magnificent streets and houses, with wharves, and
quays, and warehouses, and storehouses, and shops full
of Paris luxuries, and railroads from and to them in
every direction, and land worth its weight in gold by
the foot, and populations of fifty and hundreds of
thousands, where, within the memory of men, no trace
of civilization existed, but the forest grew and the
savage wandered.

I was at a place called Milwaukee, on Lake
Michigan, a flourishing town where they invited me
to go and read Shakespeare to them, which I mention
as an indication of advanced civilization, and one of
the residents, a man not fifty years old, told me that
he remembered the spot on which stood the hotel
where I was lodging a tangled wilderness through
which ran an Indian trail. Does not all that sound
wonderful ? You and Mary Anne ought to come out
and see this country ; you have no encumbrances, and
are both good travellers.

My dear Arthur, I have just received a letter from
Mr. Donne, in which he gives me news of you and
Mary Anne, or rather of her, that I am very sorry
indeed to receive, that she is suffering from her eyes
and hindered in all her usual employments and enjoy-
ments by their condition. This is very grievous, and
I am very sorry for it. Pray give my affectionate
remembrance to her. I do not know, after all, but
what I was saying to you that you ought to come to
America might really be of use to her. The sea voyage

does wonders sometimes for all sorts of ill conditions, and might prove salutary to her eyes.

Farewell, my dear Arthur. Give my affectionate respects to your dear mother, and believe me always yours most truly,

FANNY KEMBLE.

I have been working hard all the winter and half believe I shall die a rich woman.

Revere House, Boston, Thursday, November 10th, 1857.

MY DEAR ARTHUR,

Your kind note comes to me through Donne, after I have been near three weeks on the wrong side of the Atlantic, and have not yet got over my sea illness, which is the proper term to apply to my maritime experiences, a usual form of sickness not being among them, which is the reason, I suppose, why I suffer so miserably, both during and after the voyage.

You will have heard, no doubt, from that convenient liar, "somebody," of our obtaining from Sir Samuel Cunard the captain's state room in the steamer of the 8th of October, the date at which I had originally intended to sail.

I wish I had been at Corrybrough when Mr. Wills was there. He must be next best thing to *an Alp*, and I have read of his climbings with envious delight. I do wish with all my heart I could ever have made a Swiss expedition with you and Mary Anne. I shall be too old (and am too fat) three years hence, when, please God, I will see the Alps again.

On my arrival here, my eldest daughter met me

with her new husband. **They stayed** here two days
with me, and then departed for Philadelphia, taking
F——— with them, and now I am alone, settled for the
winter at the Revere House, Boston, Massachusetts,
whither, **if you should direct a** letter or letters, they
would **reach** me.

On my arrival here **I** was greeted with news of
a slave insurrection, a duel between two senators, and
a murder between two **Boston men of** business; and
should have guessed whither **I** had **come, if** I had
not known it.

I do not love to see the "chips fly," **or** to hear that
saddest of all sounds, the slow unwilling crashing
down of a great live tree, which I have heard here in
a lovely wilderness, which looked as if man had never
set foot in it, to a whistled accompaniment by the
woodsman from the Trovatore, a good sample in its
way of the savageness and civilization combined,
which meet one here at every step.

Yours very affectionately,

FANNY KEMBLE.

I direct this to Wimpole Street, knowing no better.

New York, Sunday, November 29th, 1857.

MY DEAR ARTHUR.

The news **of the fall of** Delhi has only this
instant reached me, first with the horrible addition
that our people had massacred all the inhabitants,
which, I thank God, has been contradicted by the
second report, the tenor of which is that the wretched
women and children were spared. The first horror,
however, of hearing that Christian Englishmen had

perpetrated such an atrocity, gave me such a shock that, in spite of **the** blessed later news, I feel **as** if half the bones in my body had been broken. We have, of course, as yet no details, and cannot have till the next mail **comes in ;** but I have lived now so long on the terrible story of all our people have been suffering, that it will be a blessed expectation to look forward to numbers of **the** *Times* newspaper, without fresh horrors and atrocities inflicted on our people by those miserable Eastern savages, or *vice-versâ.*

Thank you for your kind long letter, and thank Mary Anne for her kind short addition to it. I have heard from time to time through Donne, how it was faring with you both, and have sympathized most sincerely in your anxiety about her eyes and her privation of her use of them. I think the German doctor who has restored her, even partially, without the nervous distress **of** an operation, deserves infinite credit.

The best part of my year **is over, the** summer with S——, who returns to Philadelphia for the winter months on the 1st of December ; after that, I shall resume my readings, and work hard, probably the whole time, till the summer months come round again, bringing for me the one blossom of my year.

I find living in America very, very irksome to me in many respects, and I am often sadder than I ought to be, when I think that my home for the rest of my life must certainly be here, even if I should revisit my own country, of which at present I see not the remotest chance. My **child** does not appear to wish to visit Europe, and all idea of her doing so is strongly opposed.

I think you and Mary Anne, who travel so easily
and well, and without encumbrances, ought to "step
over here" and see Niagara; that would perhaps repay
you for the sea voyage, though, if that did not, I
hardly know what would.

You read and hear of course of the sort of financial
and commercial tornado which has swept over this
country. It is impossible to conceive anything so
curious to one on the spot, to whom the real positive
wealth and prosperity of the country is as obvious as
any of its natural features, and who sees in the crashing ruin falling on all sides the most extraordinary
illustration of the fact that moral foundations are the
only stable ones even for material prosperity, and that
a man's faith in his neighbour is a more absolutely
valuable thing than any amount of money they may
either of them possess. The selfish cowardice which
has caused the greater part of all this fearful smash is
the most disgusting exhibition of the meanness of
human nature that can be conceived. Half the people
who have been ruined have been so because they and
their neighbours were afraid they should be ruined,
and for no other earthly reason. I do not believe the
lesson they have received, severe as it has been, will
affect their future proceedings in the least. Gambling
is the only industry the majority of those, so called
"in business," are capable of, and if they were minded
to pursue fortune in a soberer and safer way, they
have not the requisite qualities for so doing.

I spent an evening with Agassiz a short time ago,
and told him of the ascent of the Schreckhorn, which
was chronicled in the *Times*. He says it is a mistake

to say **that it** was never ascended **before,** though it may not have **been climbed by the route** Mr. Anderson took. He himself and certain others, whom he mentioned to me, have ascended certain peaks of the Schreckhorn; **but he** says the crest of the mountain consists **of a** number of peaks, I think he said as many as six or eight, and it is very possible that some may never have been ascended, and some only once. He is thinking of visiting his native country next summer, and will **go to his old** field **of** observation, the **Aar** glacier, to **see what has** become **of** various landmarks he left in the ice, among others a well upwards of a hundred **feet deep, that he** sank **in** the **ice and** filled with gravel and wood and that he expects **to** find in certain conditions of alteration, such **as he** calculates ten years working of the glacier must exhibit on such an experiment. **I** think you ought **to go** and meet **him.** Oh, dear! what would I not give to be able to **be** as near that same trysting-place as my infirm years, size, and sex would allow!

It is not likely, **my dear Arthur,** let me live as **I** will, that **I shall ever be a rich** woman, if I am to live in America; the cost of one's existence here is something fabulous, and the amount of *dis*comfort one obtains for money, that purchases a liberal allowance of luxury as well **as comfort in Europe, is** by no means a small item **of** annoyance in one's daily **life.** For instance, I have just arrived **in** New **York, where I shall** probably spend **the greater** part of the winter at **a** hotel, and have **been making** inquiry **as** to prices of rooms, etc. I have a very **lofty, airy,** cheerful, good-sized drawing-room, with three large looking-glasses set in superb frames, green-and-gold satin curtains and furniture, and carpet and rug of all the splendidest colours in the rainbow. The bedroom, which goes with this magnificent trumpery, is a small closet without curtains to the window or bed, no fireplace (and the range of the winter thermometer in New York is from zero to twenty-one degrees below it), a bed pushed against the door, so that the latter cannot open, a washing-stand, which is a fixture, *i.e.* a corner cupboard, containing a waste-pipe and plug in a sunk marble basin, with a turncock above it, because that saves the housemaid the trouble of emptying slops, there is not even room or any substitute for a towel-horse. Does not the juxtaposition of such a drawing-room and such a bedroom speak volumes for the love of finery and ignorance of all decent comfort, which are alike semi-barbarous. For this accommodation and a bedroom for Marie I am expected to pay sixteen guineas a week, so that you see, let me work as I will, it is not possible for me to save much where my mere board and lodging are at such rates, and everything else, carriage-hire, clothes, etc., are on the same extravagant scale. I cannot help thinking sometimes of the amount of comfort, enjoyment, and pleasure of all sorts I could command almost anywhere on the continent of Europe for the expense that here cannot procure me what we call the decencies of life, simply because they are not to be procured; and then I think that my children are *dear* to me in the most literal sense of the word.

Dear Arthur, I wish I could see the plantations at Corrybrough, and the red water of the Findhorn and the blue distance of the heather hills. I wish I could shake hands with you and Mary Anne again. Give her my kindest love. May Heaven preserve her eyes! Give my most affectionate respects to your mother. I rejoice to hear of her prolonged health and enjoyment of life. Remember me very kindly to James Spedding and the Romillys, and believe me, ever as ever,

Affectionately yours,
FANNY KEMBLE.

Syracuse, Sunday, April 18th, 1858.

This letter was begun three days ago. I didn't lecture on Sunday.

Don't I know what the three per cents. are without pulling anybody's ear, but only tearing my own hair and gnashing my own teeth for the knowledge? Oh, Arthur! (not King, but Malkin), hadn't I seven thousand pounds invested in New York, paying me seven per cent. (the legal interest in that state) which gave me an income of four hundred and ninety pounds a year, and did not my trustees withdraw those same seven thousand pounds from their American investment and put them into the English funds, whereby they yield me precisely two hundred and ten pounds yearly? If this do not teach a woman the nature of the three per cents., she must be a borner fool than I am. Oh! it is bitter to think of, but needs no explanation; the experience is all sufficient, and by night and day, when I can't sleep and have nothing else to think of (both which conditions occur seldom), my sole cogitation, conjecture, and deliberation is " when those men die, shall I be able to get my money's worth again?"

Don't you wish you were one of my trustees, to be so often and affectionately remembered by me?

Thank you, my dear Arthur, for your pleasant letter, for the tidings of your wife and mother. Give my love to Mary Anne. I rejoice that her precious eyesight is preserved to her, even though it be with some limitation of its use and enjoyment. Give my affectionate respects to your mother. I am grateful to her for her remembrance of me. I wish you and Mary Anne would go to Switzerland next summer, for I am mightily minded to be there myself. In Europe I must be, that is to say, I must come to England to look after Henry's boy and our Chancery-pounded property (for we are still without one farthing of the small inheritance my father left us), and to gather together my scattered property in the shape of books, plate, and pictures, to bring them over here for a final settlement, which, unwilling, most unwilling as I am to make it, must be made on this side the water, if I am to make it on this side the grave; so, my dear friends, I have good hope to see you once more, if I live till June next year.

I am glad you went to the Einfishthal. When I wrote the story, I had no idea that there really was a place so called, and rejoiced extremely when I found it in my Murray. I should like much to go thither, but daily grow less able to carry myself and less fit to be carried by others.

Now I will tell you a comical experience I have gone through to-day. I am spending a week at Syracuse. Don't think of Dionysius or Arethusa or its famous Roman conqueror, whose name I forget just now—oh,

Marcellus; I shall forget my own name presently.
This is Syracuse in the State of New York, whither
I have come from Utica, passing through Rome and
Verona on my way, a bustling, busy, thriving town on
the Onondaga lake, and a few miles from the Oneida
lake. (Pray admire the combination of classical and
savage cognomens that I have gathered together from
this immediate neighbourhood for you.) The Erie
canal runs through the town, and the most abundant
and productive salt springs in the United States lie
just beyond it. It has upwards of twenty thousand
inhabitants, the streets are wide, cheerful, clean,
planted with trees, and well endowed with churches
of all denominations, and those real churches of the
United States, their admirable district schools. The
country round is picturesque, and the soil excellent for
agricultural purposes, and a tailor who made himself
a fortune of twenty thousand pounds has built himself
a castle on a commanding eminence near the town,
and shut it up and gone back to tailoring to make the
means to live in it. So much for the various features
of Syracuse.

I am giving readings here just now, and was
besought extremely by a friend of mine, a worthy and
excellent clergyman of this place, to bestow an hour's
reading this morning on a convention of all the school-
masters and school-mistresses of the county, who are
just now assembled here for purposes of public examinations and other matters connected with the interest
of education.

Some years ago I was requested to do the same
thing in the city of New York, and read to an

audience of seven hundred district school teachers ; so
this morning I went my way to the Town Hall with
my clerical friend, who is much interested and employed
in matters relating to public education here.

I found an assembly of nearly two hundred young
men and women, intelligent, conceited, clever, eager-
looking beings, with sallow cheeks, large heads and
foreheads, narrow chests and shoulders, and all the
curious combination of physical characteristics that
mark this most restless, ambitious, pretentious, and
ignorant people, whose real desire for improvement
and progress seems to me only equalled by the shallow
empiricism of the cultivation they achieve. There is
something at once touching and ludicrous in the
extreme in the desire exhibited at all times by the
people of this country for the fine blossoms and jewels,
so to speak, of civilization and education, and their
neglect and ignorance of the roots and foundation of
education and civilization, and so these country school-
masters and mistresses earnestly desired to hear me
read that they might "catch something of my style"
and will *elocutionize*, as they call it, by the hour out
of Shakespeare and Milton, and in their daily converse
employ such *dog* English with allocutions so vulgarly
ungrammatical, and an accent so vile that Shakespeare
and Milton would not know their own native tongue
in their mouth. My reading (to return to that), was
on this wise—

"I will read you Hamlet's soliloquy and speech to
the players." Having finished them, "The air of
this room is pestiferous. You have here no ventila-
tion, and two rusty sheet-iron stoves all but red hot."

" I will now read you the lament of her brothers over the supposed dead body of Imogen." Having finished it, " You have now thrown open windows at the top and bottom, on opposite sides of the hall, producing violent draughts of cold air. Such of you as are exposed to them will get colds or the rheumatism."

" I will now read to you Mercutio's speech about dreams." Having finished it, " There is a strong escape of gas going on in this room; the screws in the gas-burners are none of them turned square; you are inhaling poison, and I am being choked."

" I will now read you Othello's defence before the Senate of Venice."

This being ended, I shut my book and asked them of what use it was for them to listen to or learn poetical declamation while they were sitting there violating every principle of health and neglecting the most necessary of all elementary knowledge, that which concerns the physical well-being of themselves and their pupils. So much for my first and last public lecture on education. I felt so angry with them for what they *wanted to know,* and so sorry for them for what they *did not know!* But surely they are strange people. The president of the " Educational Convention " had been *mad,* and to judge by his restless eyes and unsettled countenance, white cheeks and over-whelming forehead, may be mad again to-morrow.

Affectionately yours,
FANNY KEMBLE.

Oh! I wish I could show you S——, she is so handsome and so clever.

Boston, Monday, November 15th, 1858.

DEAR ARTHUR,

It gave me great pleasure to receive your letter and hear news of all your belongings, from your mother and wife down to poor little Wappy, and my much-supporting and undergoing faithful friend Smut. I had heard from Adelaide of her visit to you, and of her stay at Kinrarra, and **was** glad **to find** that she participates in my enthusiasm **for** the Highlands. Kinrarra, by her account **(and** that of **the** guidebooks), **must** be a bonny place, but I am afraid, even, if I manage to get to Scotland next summer, I may **not** see it, for I do **not think** Lady Monson took it for more than one season. **I wish** my cousins, the Grants, would go home to Rothiemurcus, and then one might visit them, and explore **their** neighbourhood, which I believe includes Kinrarra.

What do you think the men here—Boston—are doing? and chiefly **at** the instigation of Agassiz— organizing a club to buy up a whole region of wilder-**ness,** still existing unredeemed and unsophisticated in the remoter part **of the** State of New York. It is called familiarly the Adirondaks, because it is traversed by a mountain range rejoicing in that name, and is a huge forest, the **only** path through which is a chain of lovely lakes that join hands throughout its length, **and** down whose shining liquid avenue **you** may float for **a week,** seeing nothing but **panthers,** few—bears, fewer—deer, many, and trout most; **and where** Agassiz says he saw **a** waterfall finer than **the** Handeck, which **is** saying **much.**

Parties of sportsmen have **for some years** past

frequented **this** wilderness, under the convoy of guides and native hunters, but the forest is beginning **to** be pared, and on its huge outer edge, as on **the** shore **of** an unknown sea, huts and shanties of wood-fellers are beginning to anchor, and where the streams flow out from the charmed solitude into **the** daylight **of** civilization, huge steam **saw**-mills **stand** panting **to** catch the prostrate giants of the forest, **as** they float **down** from this wide timber preserve, and convert them from columns that prop **the** clouds into the narrow platitude of planks and shingles. Railroads **are** projected figuratively, and already partly, literally into the bosom of the vast hunting-ground, scarcely left by the **Indians** and found by the whites. And so Agassiz and the **Boston** desk and counter men are combining **to** buy up the whole remaining wilderness and keep it savage for themselves, the deer, **and** the trout. Shall they make you **an** honorary member of the Adirondak Club? and give you the freedom of the forest for a month **or** so? I **wanted to** go there very much this summer, but S—— **is** not **at** all savagely disposed, **and** sleeping on hemlock pine branches, with no pomatum for her hair but the resin thereof, **which** is apt **by** the morning to have made an agglomerate of one's mane, would have had few charms for her, and I **shall never be** young enough again **to go** thither.

By-the-bye, **in our** own little way among the hills and valleys of Berkshire, Massachusetts, we have contrived to be **quite effective and** accidental; for, visiting a very **fine mountain gorge** about five and twenty miles from **Lenox, with a party** of people, who

were staying at my house, what should one of them—
a young New York dandy—contrive to do by way of
a pleasing incident, but tumble down a rocky precipice
fifty feet deep into a mountain torrent, which carried
him like a leaf with its own fall into a pool about
twelve feet deep, out of which he swam and scrambled
wet, but none the worse. Wasn't that clever? And
mustn't a man be compact in body, mind, and soul to
bear turning upside down after such a fashion as that?
I left my rheumatism in that same ravine in consequence of the superhuman efforts I made to make
haste and get brandy, and eau-de-cologne, and towels,
and flesh brushes for this same hero, from our
travelling bags, which were waiting in the carriages
at the entrance of the glen, up which I hobbled, and
down which I flew.

If I live, I hope to see England and my friends in
it at the beginning of the month of June. It is very
impossible to say that I shall never again return thither,
but it is certain that I must look to America henceforward as my abiding place, for I have utterly given
up all hope and expectation of my children ever
settling anywhere else, and it is better so, in spite of
all my wishes, and all my regrets.

Good-bye, dear Arthur, God bless you! Give my
affectionate respects to your mother, my kindest love
to Mary Anne, in whose partial recovery of sight
I rejoice with all my heart, and believe me ever, as
ever, yours sincerely attached,

FANNY KEMBLE.

1113, *Walnut Street*, *Philadelphia*,
Monday, *March 1st*, 1859.

MY DEAR ARTHUR,

Your account of Mary Anne's condition is very sad and very saddening. I pray with all my heart that it may be alleviated ere long, for both your sakes, but chiefly for yours, for indeed I think yours the heavier burden of the two. To be condemned helplessly to watch irremediable suffering in those who are dear to us seems to me the heaviest of human sorrows in which sin has no part.

My dear Arthur, it is a very melancholy consideration to me that an income of seventeen hundred a year should be rendered, by the inordinate cost of living in this country, a very narrow one, not sufficient to enable me to live with a couple of servants in two rooms in a boarding-house in Philadelphia; but such is the case. For this lodging (in many respects exceedingly inconvenient and uncomfortable), and the very simplest food, I pay twenty-eight guineas a week, fourteen hundred and fifty-six pounds a year, leaving me a margin of one hundred and fifty pounds for every other necessary and every other luxury of life. It is really lamentable. However, as I shall certainly, if I live, return again to live in this country, I shall be obliged, in order to do so, to accept the offer which S—— and my son-in-law have made to me, that I should make my home with them. This living with married people and in other people's houses is open to many very serious objections in my opinion, and I regret very much that no other course should be open to me, but at present it appears as if

I had no other alternative, if I am to inhabit the same country with my children. In the mean time, I am coming to England in June, when I hope, with all my heart, to find you more happily circumstanced than you are now. I trust I shall spend the summer in Switzerland, and the winter in Italy, and should I do so, may never live to come back and worry myself about the inadequacy of an income of seventeen hundred pounds to keep a single old woman in this dearest of all the worlds.

God bless you, my dear Arthur, and sustain and comfort you in your trouble.

Always affectionately yours,
FANNY KEMBLE.

29, King Street, St. James's,
Thursday, September 8th, 1859.

MY DEAR ARTHUR,

I owe you many thanks for your kind long letter, which I found waiting for me at my present headquarters in London, 29, King Street, to which hospitable roof I shall repair for shelter whenever I have occasion to be in town now till I sail for the "other world." I have been much tempted to delay my return thither, for the chance of going in the *Great Eastern*, and shall still perhaps do so if I find that she returns to the United States, after her trial trip, which she makes to Boston on the 29th of this month.

I was greatly surprised and pleased to hear of Lawrence's being in England, but am afraid I shall not profit thereby, as he and Monsieur Jem are both at Monckton Milnes', in Yorkshire, and I leave town on Saturday for Hampshire, where I hope to remain quietly with Adelaide, until I depart this English life.

I was, as usual, perfectly enchanted with all I saw of Scotland. We had lovely weather, and our route (though I say who chose it and therefore should not) was beautiful. We railed from Edinburgh to Callander, drove from thence to the Trosachs, where we spent a day, from thence half up Loch Katrine by steamer, then across to Loch Lomond at Inversnaid, up Loch Lomond to Inverarnon, where we spent a day and a half, because we there saw twenty-four trout leap up a waterfall in thirty minutes, thence we drove to Dalmally, where we slept, from thence we drove the next day to Oban, and slept there, after one of the most lovely sunsets over the sea and islands that it is possible to behold. Next morning we steamed to Balachulish ferry and breakfasted there, while the raff of tourists aired Glencoe for us. We then drove from Glencoe to Invernouran and slept there, the next day drove to Killin, where we spent a beautiful sunshiny Sunday, and the next day drove from Killin to Callandar by Loch Earnhead, Lubnaig, and the pass of Leny. Was not that a pretty and well-arranged tour? We stayed a day in Edinburgh going and coming, and I was very sorry to hear that your friends, the Sandfords, have met with such serious loss of property.

On our way south we passed a day at Durham, for which place and cathedral I have an especial admiration. We then visited friends in the neighbourhood of York, and I saw for the first time, what doubtless you are familiar with, the chapter house of the Minster. I had often seen the grand church itself, but never that beautiful adjunct to it. I am now reduced to a shopping machine. F—— went off to Westbury with her cousin Greville for escort yesterday, and I am here ordering all things for her and my final flight.

My luck is greater than I expected. I have just received a note from Spedding, promising to come with Lawrence and dine with me on Friday, and as Donne will come too, I have only to wish that you and Mary Anne were here to meet them. I am very sorry indeed to hear of Mary Anne's being so unwell; I trust her eyes will not be affected by this indisposition, as it always seems to me the most cruel visitation on one who made such good use of those blessed members, and one to which the moderate use of merely drawing and reading did not appear to render her liable.

Our Paris excursion did not answer, the heat was perfectly intolerable, our whole time was passed in running in and out of shops, wasting time, spending money, and losing temper—three bad employments if ever there were.

The city is very fine, and Monsieur Louis (the emperor) has made a good clear avenue for cannon (or other military diversions) from the Place Louis Quinze to the Bastille. I have not much fear of his coming to England. It would not be worth while putting us to great inconvenience (which he assuredly would), for the ultimate result of being himself put to much greater. He is, I take it, much wiser in his generation than any child of light; and yet after all the light that is in him (very powerful gas, though it certainly

seems) may turn out sheer darkness in a little while.
He is an uncommonly clever rascal, of whom I do not
think it becomes a nation of honest men to be afraid
—though certainly much aware. These be my views
of Monsieur Louis, with which I bid you farewell.
Give my love to Mary Anne, and keep a due proportion for yourself.

Affectionately yours,
FANNY KEMBLE.

Westbury House, Thursday, September 15th, 1859.

MY DEAR ARTHUR,

Your " fish story " was much relished by us all.
Perhaps I was the most enthusiastic appreciator of
it, as to catch a seven and a half pound salmon would
certainly seem to me the nearest thing to going to
heaven "on my own hook." Would I had been there !
Poor Mr. Williams must have lamented his heroic
tendon more than ever ; he was the fisher of your party
in my days.

I have eaten here grouse due to your friendly
generosity, and I have thanked you unsentimentally
with all my teeth, for how can one thank with all
one's heart for food—even grouse ?

I went out the other morning to see the first cub-
hunting of the season, and clomb through the bright
dewy morning to a high stubble field crested with
tangled thickets, in one of which the hounds and hunters
(my daughter among the rest), were busy searching for
young foxes, while from a small knot of dwarf oaks
woven together with a perfect tapestry of clematis
and blackberry bushes a pet bull dog, who was not

allowed to join the noble company of foxhounds, started for my solitary delectation, two coveys of partridges and five beautiful pheasants. The destroying angel was strong in me, and I *yearned* for a gun.

I think I **wrote** to you before Monsieur Jem and Lawrence dined with **me**. Mr. Ellis, Frank, and Walter, and Donne, made our party, with M—— and myself I thought Lawrence looking well, and I think he is **probably** more glad than he cares to **say to be** once **more on** this side of the Atlantic. **He** said something of perhaps passing the winter here. **I** am afraid America does not **answer to him** as well as he had at first hoped; but Mrs. Lawrence finds it a congenial residence, and I suppose her girls have **a** better chance of getting married there than here.

I hope Mary Anne's toothache has given up even its **short** nightly visit. **As** for me, I came down hither on Saturday with a pestiferous influenza, with which I have more **or** less endowed every member of this household; **I believe** no malady to be more certainly **infectious. Good-bye,** my dear Arthur. I am very grateful **for** Donne's poetical effusion. We are expecting him and Frederick to come down here soon, mean time **I am** obliged to return to London to find, if possible, means of taking my child back to America. My application, made a fortnight ago at the ship office in the city, **for a** passage for **the 8th** of October, was met by the agreeable information that they had not a single berth vacant **for the** whole month of October. **All** America must be in Europe. Once more, good-bye.

Yours always truly,

Fanny Kemble.

Lenox, Wednesday, May 8th, 1860.

DEAR ARTHUR,

The same post that brought me your letter brought me one from Harriet St. Leger, containing the same **sad news and** nearly the same details of Mr. Ellis's death. I could hardly be as much attached to M—— as I am, and not entertain considerable regard for her father, not only **for** her sake either, but **as a natural** consequence of my friendly intercourse **with** him, **and** the cordiality **and** kindness with which he always treated me. **It is** very painful to me to **have** written to M——, to congratulate her **on her** father's recovery, **a** letter which she will have received after his death. I wrote it **in** consequence of having **heard** from Harriet, that Mr. Ellis had **been ill,** but **had** recovered entirely from the attack.

My dear Arthur, I am sorry for the revival of old griefs that this new grief causes you. I am sorry for the sad **tone** of your letter, and for the gloomy winter you **seem** to have passed **in London.** Good Lord! if **you could see** the place **where I** passed the greater part of mine—quite alone—sometimes as nearly as possible without any **servants, at** another **time** with two in my house who had been convicted thieves, and whom I kept partly because I knew not where to turn for others, and partly **in the** hopes of reforming them as they were young people and young offenders!

Corrybrough **in** winter is not **more** lonely than Lenox, and certainly it cannot be colder, for just at the beginning **of** February, after rather temperate weather, **the** thermometer *in one night* fell forty degrees, and in the morning stood at thirty-two degrees below zero. This did not last, but neither had it need, for if it had, I am of opinion that nothing else would have lasted; certainly nothing of me but what is everlasting would.

I am glad, for your sakes, that Adelaide is coming to London; you will mutually benefit each other. If I live, I will be in London, too, about this time next year, and from thence I mean to go to Switzerland, and I wish you and Mary Anne would go along with me. Donne wrote me word that your Alpine wings were clipped, for that you had acknowledged that you had over-exerted yourself on your last Swiss tour, so that you will probably not be so magnificently contemptuous of the grovelling ascensions of a fat elderly female; de mon espèce.

A French Hamlet—um!—Mr. Fechter's; the best I ever saw was German, Emil Devrient's; but, then, German and English, so far as Hamlet is concerned, are one; but a "parlez-vous!" I may like it prodigiously if I ever see it; but I do not feel as if I should.

The United States schism, my dear Arthur, has become a wide yawning cleft, like your favourite Swiss abysms, with a mad tumult of folly and wickedness, and none but *Vie Male* on either side of it. The whole spirit of the people is gone, it seems to me Slavery has made the Southerners insane egotists, and the pursuit of gain has made the Northerners incapable egotists. Manliness, patriotism, honour, loyalty, appear to have been stifled out of these people by material success and their utter abdication to mere material prosperity. **A grievous civil war,** shattering their **financial and** commercial **idols,** and compelling them to find the connection between public safety and private virtue, may be the salvation **of** the country; a blessed, bitter blast of adversity, checking the insolent forwardness of their national spring, may yet perhaps preserve them from that which really seemed impending over the land—unripe rottenness, decay without duration, **or** exertion to excuse and account **for it,** the most amazing and deplorable unworthiness **of the most glorious** advantages that have ever **yet** belonged to any nation in the world.

[**The** bitter blast fulfilled its benevolent mission, and patriotism, honour, courage, self-devotion, and every national virtue put **forth** fresh powerful shoots under its bleak compelling. I once discussed with Waelcker, the great German scholar, the character of the American nation, to **which he** denied *greatness,* saying **no** people had ever been great who had not had a "great heroic **war."** I pleaded their war for Independence under **Washington;** but **he** would not admit it. Had he lived till the war of secession, I think he would have acknowledged that America **had had its blood** baptism, and **its heroic war** on both sides. I was a witness **to the** struggle, **and** cannot think **of it yet** without **the** deepest emotion **and admiration** for **all** the virtue which it called forth—virtue of the heathen and Christian significance, **for** did not the Army **of** Mercy which **now** follows the steps of War first begin its ministry there.]

A short **time** ago **I** was in New York and Philadelphia, **giving** away, as tokens of female affection, swords and pistols to young volunteers, soldiers, whom I remember boys in round jackets. Up here among the hills the great hubbub that fills the land in its more populous regions comes but faintly. The tap of a drum along the village street at evening, calling the men to drill when they have done work, is our faint echo of the great national stir, and the vivid stars and stripes flying from the scattered farmhouses on the hillsides and valleys, the only visible sign of the strife that is preparing—indeed, that is already begun.

Of course I must be prepared for loss of property, at least, certainly diminution of income; but everybody will have to suffer more or less, and I may be thankful that it will not be in the lives of those who are dear to me that I can be touched.

If I were envious, I would envy Mary Anne her new grand piano. What a grand possession! But I can congratulate her instead, and with kind love to both of you, remain always,

Your affectionate
FANNY KEMBLE.

I grieve to hear of Donne being ill; it is a great shame of one's friends to take such an advantage as that of one's absence.

Lenox, Wednesday, May 15th, 1860.

MY DEAR ARTHUR,

I shall indeed be very sorry if I find on my arrival in London that Mary Anne and yourself have left it, though the prospect you hold out of our meeting in Rome in the winter is consolatory. I have no fancy for lonely travelling; I have done so much of that, and found it, as Madame de Stael truly says, such a "triste plaisir;" so that, unless I can find some congenial company with which or whom to go abroad, I may, after all, not perform the lengthened pilgrimage. I had looked forward to beginning with the Alps, which I do most fervently hope to see again, not indeed probably walking quite as valiantly as I did the last time I saw them, but ingloriously on mule-back or in a chaise à porteurs.

Not only, my dear Arthur, do we barbarian Transatlantics receive *Fraser's Magazine* on its periodical appearance, but there are cheap American reprints published of all the English magazines for the benefit of those who cannot afford the expense of importing the originals; and selections are, moreover, made from all the principal European magazines into an American periodical, expressly dedicated to that process of discriminating reproduction. My daughter S—— is a regular subscriber to the *Quarterly*, the *Edinburgh*, the *Westminster*, and *Fraser*, and from her I shall procure your article on Corrybrough, which I am sure I shall read with great pleasure.

Affectionately yours,
Fanny Kemble.

The recent successes of the Federal arms seem to promise a not remote termination to this cruel civil war. There are those, however, who incline to the opinion that the Southerners will proceed to evacuate place after place, drawing the Northerners on further and further into the interior of the slave states, where they hope the swamp fevers and southern deadly malaria will put an effectual stop to their progress. More sanguine persons think that the struggle is nearly now at an end. God send they may be in the right! In this remote and peaceful northern village, nothing indicates the existence of the huge conflict that is going on, except that whereas our normal male population consists of *three* souls, I think we have now only a man and a boy left to represent the nobler sex in the village; but 'tis an Amazonian region, and gets on well enough with them.

Lenox, Berkshire, Thursday, August 2nd, 1860.

MY DEAR ARTHUR,

Oh, how I do wish I was going over the Col de Liseran with you; but I am not! I am going to the flattest region (figuratively as well as literally) in the whole universe, the immediate neighbourhood of Philadelphia, to see my child S—— and her child, who is a month old, and towards whom I feel a most grandmotherly yearning.

I read with great regret your account of poor Mary Anne's martyrdom. I feel great sympathy for the pain she has suffered, greater still for her loss of sleep, greatest of all for her disappointment in not going to Switzerland.

Though you do not write quite as frequently as I might be glad to hear from you, I am not left to suppose you dead and buried, for Donne, who is most excellent about writing, gives me tidings of those whom he knows that I shall wish to hear about, and what he knows of you he always sends to me.

Your account of your season is "awfu'." The

summer here has been most unusually cold, and the weather capricious and strange in all its behaviours; furious storms of wind and rain, and wonderful meteoric apparitions in the sky. I, who dislike heat, have rejoiced in the cold summer, and as the hay harvest has been fine and the Indian corn will ripen (the two principal crops in these parts of the world), I do not feel inhumanly selfish in not wishing for more heat. The woods and fields, thanks to the superabundant rains, are as green as at home.

I am about to sell my small estate here, upon which I have determined not to build a house, lest it should turn out a madhouse when I come to inhabit it. I have taken a tolerably comfortable house, commanding lovely views, nearer the village of Lenox for the next two years, and if I live till 1862 will come home and go over the Col de Liseran in that year of grace.

God bless you, dear Arthur. Give my affectionate remembrance to Mary Anne, and believe me,

Yours always most truly,

FANNY KEMBLE.

Lenox, Sunday, November 24th, 1860.

MY DEAR ARTHUR,

I quite agree with you in thinking it inexpedient for all manner of reasons to leave one's old friend's letters unanswered for any length of time. This is not only my conviction, but my invariable practice is based upon it, and I cannot accuse myself of ever neglecting or postponing a reply, though I am extremely unwilling ever to make the challenge in a correspondence; so that indeed I can with truth declare that I never *write* letters, though I always *answer* them.

Let me congratulate you and Mary Anne very sincerely on the recovery of her health; it is really delightful, after hearing of her suffering so much, to receive your account of her entire restoration. I trust it will prove permanent, and that you and she will be starting for the Alps in August, 1862, just when I turn my steps thither, which I hope and mean to do then if it should please God to spare my life and health; for, though I am old and fat and rheumatic, and shall then be older, fatter and rheumatiker, I will, nevertheless, go over certain of those Swiss passes, if not on my own legs, why, then on mule's legs; and if not on mule's legs, why, then on man's legs, in a chaise à porteurs, with sixteen men to carry me, as I had going up Vesuvius (in the night, to be sure); eight carried torches (which were light), and eight carried me (which *were* heavy). Oh, my dear Arthur, your letter positively made me sick—which you may think no compliment, but it is—sick to be again on those mountains and in those valleys. I seized my Murray, I seized my maps, I seized Bartlett's Swiss views, I envied you and Herbert, sore feet, sore face, sore eyes, and all. But I am very sorry you did not go over the Col de Liseran. I hope to do so again, for my purpose is to retrace my whole former route, only reversing it, and entering Switzerland by the south-east of France, instead of the Rhine, go up that wonderful road from Grenoble to Briançon by the Col de Lauteret, and through the Protestant valleys of Piedmont, which I failed to see, and chiefly desired to see in my last tour on the Continent.

Here, where I now write **to you**, the prospect before me is not unlike what I suppose the winter aspect of Corrybrough to be, a confusion of low hills and intervening valleys rolling and sinking behind each other, till at the horizon the line rises into something almost approaching the dignity of mountains— four thousand feet, I believe, our highest northern **and** southern summits rise ; **but** the country which the eyes survey between Saddle Mountain, **or** Greylock, and Taconagh is **a mere** succession **of** hilly ridges, seldom rising to more than a thousand **feet.** Small lakes lie in **almost all the valleys; we have** three in view from the hill **on which** the village **of Lenox** stands ; but though mountain brooks abound, the nearest river is four miles off, where the Housatonick winds through the principal valley **of** Berkshire, and jumping sheer down about fifty feet in one place, and running down-hill for more than as many miles from **the** outlet to the hill region of which these are the lowest, and the White Mountains **in New** Hampshire the highest degree.

The winter has come suddenly and severely upon us. **The weather** last week **was so** mild that I was sitting without fire, with the window open ; but **now** snow is upon all the hills, the earth is already as hard **as iron, and the water** froze last night **in my** dressing-room **in a** solid body of ice in all the water vessels, which stood unthawed for a quarter **of an hour** before a blazing fire this morning.

Our Prince of Wales, who has kept the whole land **alive with** interest and excitement, must have reached

home ere this.   I was disappointed of a visit I intended
making to Boston while he was there, by a visit here
from an invalid friend, whom I could not leave, and
so I missed seeing him, which I was very sorry for ;
but F—— danced with him at the New York ball, and
I console myself with that honour and glory, of which,
however, she seems less sensible than I am, for when
I asked her if she had laid up in lavender the satin
shoes in which she danced with such a partner, she
shrugged her shoulders and laughed, though she said
he was a "nice little fellow, and danced very well."
Think, my dear Arthur, of the shock to my rather
superstitious respectful loyalty at hearing my future
sovereign, the future sovereign of England, Scotland,
Ireland, Wales, and India, clapped on the shoulder by
this monkey of a democratic damsel of mine.   I
wonder if the Americans, like the Roman ladies of old,
considered a marriage with a foreigner, even a royal
one, a degradation.   [This letter was written thirty
years ago.   At the present day the fair Americans
appear to have no such prejudice, but will condescend
to marry even English Duke's sons.]

We are in all the distraction and uproar of the
presidential election.   The southern states are loud
in vehement threats of secession, if the republican
candidate is elected ; but their bluster is really lamentably ludicrous, for they are without money, without
credit, without power, without character—in short,
sans everything, but so many millions of slaves, sans
good numbers of whom they would also be the very
moment they cut themselves adrift from the protection
of the North.

Good-bye, dear Arthur. Give my kindest love to Mary Anne, and believe me always,

Yours affectionately,

FANNY KEMBLE.

If you see Donne, will you give my love to him, and tell him I will write to him the moment I hear from Coutts what funds of mine are in their hands?

Lenox, Sunday, September 15th, 1861.

DEAR ARTHUR,

The sight of your handwriting, and the tidings of Corrybrough and all its belongings are very welcome. The present condition of this country is so strange, that it seems to place me at a still greater distance from home and all my old-country associations. Certainly the contrast between the peaceful themes of all the letters I receive from England, and the circumstances by which I am surrounded, seems to add remoteness to that which really exists, or to convert the watery chasm of three thousand miles which separates us into a gulf—passable, thank God! indeed between two worlds.

Our daily talk is of fights and flights, weapons and wounds. The stars and stripes flaunt their gay colours from every farm roof among these peaceful hills, and give a sort of gala effect to the quiet New England villages, embowered in maple and elm trees, that would be pretty and pleasing but for the grievous suggestions they awake of bitter civil war, of the cruel interruption of an unparalleled national prosperity, of impending danger and insecurity, of heavy immediate taxation, of probable loss of property, and all the evils, public and personal, which spring from the general disorganization of the government, and disrupture of the national ties.

How nearly I am affected by all these disturbances you can imagine, when I tell you that Mr. B—— is a state prisoner, that he was arrested a month ago on a charge of high treason, and that my children left me the beginning of last week to visit him in a fortress, at the entrance of the Bay of New York, to which they obtained access only by a special order from the President, and where they were only permitted to see Mr. B—— in the presence of one of the officers of the fort. All this sounds strange enough, does it not? The charge against him is that he acted as an agent for the Southerners in a visit he paid to Georgia this spring, having received large sums of money for the purchase and transmission of arms. Knowing Mr. B——'s Southern sympathies, I think the charge very likely to be true; whether it can be proved or not is quite another question, and I think it probable, that, if it is not proved, Mr. B—— will still be detained till the conclusion of the war, as he is not likely to accept any oath of allegiance tendered to him by this government, being a determined democrat and inimical, both on public and private grounds, to Mr. Lincoln and his ministers.

The state of the country is very sad, and I fear will long continue to grieve and mortify its well wishers; but of the ultimate success of the North, I have not a shadow of a doubt. I hope to God that neither England nor any other power from the other

side of **water will meddle** in the matter—but, above
all, *not* England; and thus, after some bad and good
fighting, and an unlimited amount of brag and bluster
on both sides, the South, in spite of a much better state
of preparation, of better soldiers, better officers, and,
above all, a much more unanimous and *venomous*
spirit of hostility, will be obliged to knock under to
the infinitely greater resources **and** less violent but
much more enduring determination of the North.
With **the clearing away of** this storm, slavery will be
swept from among the acknowledged institutions of
America, and **I trust that republican and not** democratic **principles may** prevail **to** the extent of modify-
ing in some degree the exercise of the **franchise,** and
weighting **the** right **of** suffrage with some qualifications which may prevent an Irish **Roman** Catholic
celt, not two removes from **a** brute, from exercising
the same influence in a public election that **a** New
England Puritan farmer does, who is **probably** the
most intelligent **man of** his class that can **be** found
anywhere in the world.

I have nothing to tell you of myself. **The summer**
is passing rapidly **away,** and as pleasantly as the
many and inevitable discomforts of American housekeeping allow. **My** children are both with me, but
not, **I** am sorry to **say, my** grandchild, S—— having
come up to Lenox to recruit **health** and strength, and
judging it best therefore **to** leave her baby with its
father, who, being a doctor, **is** competent to the charge.
She will probably return to her home, husband, and
child in about **a** fortnight; but Mr. B——'s incarcera-
tion **will be** likely to **throw F——** entirely upon my

charge. Perhaps, if she does not (mis)bestow herself in marriage in the mean time, she will return to Europe with me next year.

I am making huge plans of travel, and live surrounded by maps and Murrays. If I can carry out my projects for next summer, I shall spend the whole month of August in Switzerland, and think you and Mary Anne had better leave Corrybrough, and come with me to Mont Blanc, through the Dauphiny Alps, the Vaudois valleys, and over the Col de Liseran, and the little Saint Bernard. *"Do it,"* as I used emphatically to say in the " Hunchback."

Always affectionately yours,
FANNY KEMBLE.

Boston, Friday, December 27th, 1861.

MY DEAR ARTHUR,

I do not wonder that speculators on American affairs on the other side of the Atlantic should find it difficult to come to any conclusion as to the probable issues of this most deplorable civil war. It is impossible for any one here to comprehend the drift of the government, the purposes of the northern people in pursuing this conflict, or what they purpose to do when it should have come to a close. It is infinitely easier to understand the position and principle of the South; it has but one, and, as far as circumstances have gone, has pursued it with energy and ability.

The news of a probable war between England and the northern states interrupts me. I cannot imagine what can have inspired our Government with a notion that the Americans want a war with England. Certainly Mr. Seward's speeches, when first this administration came into power, and the blackguardly press, talked impudent nonsense enough to outrage everybody of common sense and decent feeling, both here and in England; but the wretched people are perfectly aghast at the idea of having to encounter a war with England, as well as all their own home troubles, and though I suppose they will *try it*, if they are absolutely compelled to do so (for in spite of all bragging and Bull's Runs, they are a brave people and have plenty of fight in them, as unquestionably have the French, who brag too); but nothing can exceed the dismay with which the possibility of such an event is looked upon by every living creature here; and, indeed, such a contest, crippled as they are by their internal difficulties, and placed as they would be between two enemies, could have but one issue—their absolute discomfiture, and nobody here takes any other view of the matter. I understand that Lord Lyndhurst, whose relations and connections are many of them Boston people, has written to them, giving his opinion that the Americans are all wrong in the case, and that unless they deliver up Messrs. Slidel and Mason, a war with England is inevitable. This letter has been forwarded to Mr. Seward, and I sincerely hope that when the people here find that France and Germany agree in thinking our demand perfectly reasonable, they will yield with a good grace, and not complicate their present difficulties with such a nut to crack as a war with England.

I shall not be sorry to leave America just now; it

is very sad and very dismal to be in the midst of such
a state of things.

I am very sorry to hear that Mary Anne declines
the Alps henceforth. Certainly she must be quite as
able for them as I am, and I hope to see them several
times again. One thing I am quite determined on, if
I live, and that is, to see the country of Felix Neff,
that is to say, the pass from Pigneroll to Briançon, of
which I was defeated, and the road from Briançon to
Grenoble by the Col de Lauteret, which I traversed
in the night, and which I then swore I would return
and see by daylight some fine day, and if I live I will
do so next August, whether you will or no.

I have nothing to tell you of myself. My summer
and autumn passed pleasantly, happily enough to be
very thankful for, at Lenox. My youngest daughter
spent four months with me, and S—— one. Her
husband came on to fetch her home, and passed a
week with me, during which time two of his patients
took the opportunity of dying shabbily and disgrace-
fully without his assistance, a circumstance which I
am afraid will prevent his venturing on a holiday
again for a long time.

I have not seen my grandchild for a year, but I
hear he is a very charming child, and am prone to
believe it.

I am going southward in February to stay a fortnight with S——, then pass a couple of months in
Washington, which is just now a place of considerable
interest. In May I return to Lenox to pack up, and
early in July I hope to see England and my friends
again. I do not think I shall be in haste to cross the

Atlantic **again**.   **Till** then, good-bye, dear Arthur—by
which I do **not mean, by** any means, **that you** are not
to write to me again.

Give **my** kindest remembrance to Mary Anne, and
believe me always,

Yours very affectionately,
FANNY KEMBLE.

Interlacken, Sunday, July 31st, 1862.

DEAR ARTHUR,

From our pleasant trysting-place, Interlacken,
to **which our** wanderings **have** brought us back, **I**
ans**wer your** "sassy" letter. **We** were very glad to
hear of your successful descent into the beautiful valley,
and I should have regretted not turning up the ravine
at Stalden to meet you, but that I had been so very
unprofitable **a** companion during our whole stay at
Zermatt and the Riffel, that I am sure you were all
well **rid of me.** The young botanist accompanied us
all the **way to Viege, and** when we drove **off,** down
the **Rhone Valley, leaving** him to take the diligence
towards **Italy, I felt as if I** had finished a sort of post-
script to **our** pleasant Zermatt fellowship.

We travelled all the way to Bâle, where I took up
my original tour, **by** a day and **a half** carriage journey
through the Munster **Thal to** see which had been a
very old longing **of mine.** It is beautiful, quite beautiful, and few things that I have seen this summer have
pleased **me more.** We went to Soleure **and** climbed
the **Weissenstein,** but failed to **find** quarters at the
mountain house, where **we** had wished **to** rest for a
week. We then **went to Lucerne, and** took up our

abode on the Righi, at the Kaltbad, for a week. The
house is fine, the situation beautiful, but the visitors,
almost exclusively Swiss or German, and neither they
nor their mode of life and manners agreeable to
me. We steamed down to Fluelen and Altdorf, and I
felt a pang at taking my feet off the first step up the
St. Gotthard returning to Lucerne. I had contemplated
driving through the Entelbuck Thal, from thence to
Thun, but was prevented by stormy weather, which
indeed has been the only weather we have had, and
our wonderful five days at the Riffel have been the
exception in our whole experience. So, thunder and
lightning and floods of rain compelling, we gave up
the road and took the rail to Thun, and thence
hither, where we arrived on Thursday. On Friday we
made a pilgrimage of affectionate remembrance to
Lauterbrunnen, and yesterday we drove up to Grindel-
wald to look again at F——'s first glaciers.

My eyes were misty with tears as we drove down
between the huge mountain portals, with their lovely
hangings of green forests, back to Interlacken. My
delight in this sublime scenery is a sort of enthusiastic
affection.

F—— bids me give her best love to you, and tell
you that she is true to Zermatt, and that the Riffel
keeps her heart above all other peaks and passes.
We have yet to pay our respects to Chamounix, but I
doubt her altering her mind, though she is threatening
me with an independent expedition to the Jardin,
which may perhaps turn the scale. Next week we
think of resting at the pretty hotel by the Griessbach,
if we can find rooms there. The waterfall was a great

bewitchment to F——, and I shall be very glad to linger by it a few days.

The last week of August will end our pilgrimage, and then we shall probably settle down in Hampshire, for Adelaide writes me word that she has taken the cottage at the gate of her domain for me, and F—— seems well content with a prospect of a very quiet winter there. I hope, my dear Arthur, that you found Mary Anne quite well, when you returned to her. How glad she will have been to get you safe home after your Trifft glacier, and your Mittelhorn, and your Weissthor. I hope you are kindly condescending to the Scotch *hills*, and don't take airs of ten and twelve thousand feet high at them. I hope Campbell, and the dogs, and the grouse are all flourishing and to flourish, and that all Corrybrough is thriving and satisfactory. Give my kindest love to Mary Anne. It was right good of her to let you come to Switzerland, and I heartily wish she had been with us. My lassie greets you both, and I am always your

Affectionate and obliged,

FANNY KEMBLE.

New York, Wednesday, April 29th, 1865.

MY DEAR ARTHUR,

It was a very great pleasure to me to get your kind letter and know something of yourself and Mary Anne, how you had fared through the winter, and what your prospects were for the summer. The Alps I shall not see this year, but if it pleases God to spare my life, I hope I shall do so next summer. I sent your note down to Georgia to F——, not without looking, as you bade me do, **at the** photographs it **contains.** I liked **them all very much,** but particularly **the head of** yourself, and if there had been a whisper of warrant for such a proceeding **in** your desire that I should look at them, I should certainly have retained that, **and sent** the full length to F——, the rather that **I do** not plainly see why she should have a whole and **a half** likeness of you, and I not half **a** one.

You cannot **be** sorrier than I was that F——judged it expedient **to go down to the** plantation and spend **the** winter there. **Her sister** and **all** her friends **advised and** entreated **her not to do so,** but she thought it best to **go, and has been** labouring hard all **the** winter to **induce** their former slaves to work steadily **on** the plantation. The consequence is that, having **newly** signed the contract agreeing to work there for this year, **under her personal** influence, it is quite possible that, when that **is** withdrawn, as it must be when she **comes north next week,** they may altogether disregard the engagement they made with her, **and leave** the crop **to take care of** itself. She has simply deferred the **settlement of the question,** which it is **most important to have** speedily settled, namely, **whether these poor** people can be made to understand **that freedom** means leave **to** labour or leave to starve. **She being** down there **has not** helped to make them realize their new position as labourers, but has simply tended to prolong the dependent feeling of the old relation without **the** possibility of bringing back the former relations **between the** negroes and their employers.

Nothing has been done yet to make it at all certain

that the people on my daughters' plantation will work
when she has left it, and if at the beginning of the
winter they had understood that they must do so or
leave it, it would have been ascertained whether their
southern property was or was not worth anything to
them at present. Of course an estate cannot be made
to depend upon a woman's coaxing or scolding the
cultivators, and hitherto F——'s mission at the South
has been simply one of successful coaxing and scolding. Personal influence is one thing, and the laws of
labour another, and these are what the poor negroes
have yet to learn.

I am inexpressibly shocked at what you tell me
about poor young L——. I saw him three summers
ago with his father at the Bell Alp, full of life and
spirits and energy. Poor young fellow, it is horrible
and most grievous to think of the misery of all those
poor people, whose faces I remember beaming with
happiness and enjoyment—father, mother, sister, they
were all there with him at the glorious Bell Alp.
Dear me, I cannot bear to think of it!

The government of this country presents just now
a not very edifying spectacle; but it is astonishing
how prosperous and thriving the country is, in spite
of its government. The activity, energy, wealth, and
material progress are something amazing. The country
has made a wonderful start forward since I went away
six years ago, and the check which its prosperity
received by the four years' civil war seems only to
have accelerated its vigorous action now that the
people's energies have returned to their accustomed
channels. I perceive, however, an enormous change

in one respect, which was probably operating upon the country before I left it, but which now, after several years' absence, strikes me more than anything else, the country is no longer *English;* New England may be so essentially still, but out of New England the English national element has died out almost entirely. When first I came here, thirty-four years ago, the whole country was like some remote part of England that I had never seen before, the people like English provincial or colonial folk ; in short, they were like *queer* English people. Now there is not a trace of their British origin, except their speech, about them, and they are becoming a real nation, and their nation will be German in its character and intellect more than English. Our language is and will be theirs, and the foundations of their laws will be English law, but the people will be more like the great Teutonic people of the Continent of Europe, and not like us, their Anglo-Saxon ancestors. Even in Philadelphia, the Quaker element, which was really one of English conservatism, has died out, and the whole tone of society and manners changed.

It is difficult to conceive anything more interesting and exciting than the aspect of these extraordinary people in their new world. It is not a pleasant place to live in, however wonderful, for an elderly English woman, and I shall find it hard enough to accept my particular share of the conditions of this very vigorous, half-grown civilization, half-ripe as well as half-grown. But my children are Americans, and the gain to my happiness and peace of mind, in no longer being divided from them by the Atlantic, is indescribable.

I shall, I suppose, **live** here henceforward, that is, consider this **country** my abiding place; but as long as my life lasts, **and my** health and strength are equal to the effort of crossing the ocean, I shall, I trust, make **frequent** returns **to** England, my country, and Switzerland, the country of my dear delight.

Next year **I** hope to be again among the Alps for a **summer, and I** am not **without** hope that then **I** may **be able to** bring S—— **with** me. I am now working again very hard, reading four times a week, and earning **a great deal of** money, which **I** had **need** do, **for the expense of living in** this *simple* republican **country passes** all belief.

Good-bye, my dear friends. God bless you both. Remember **me sometimes,** and always as your very affectionately attached

FANNY KEMBLE.

The Crown Inn, Lyndhurst, Monday, August 13th, 1865.
MY DEAR ARTHUR,

Adelaide, with whom **I am** staying **in** this **very charming** place, gave **me** your kind **note,** for **which I** thank you very heartily. God **knows,** America **is far from** being as pleasant as England at **any** time, **but my** children, being Americans, and America their undoubted future home, it would have been more for **my happiness,** whatever it might have been for my **enjoyment, to have** been able to make my home there. The conditions of the poor country just now are, God knows, awful enough; they are, in my opinion, the most manifest judgment for their national **sins, and I** have good hope that the final result will be an infinitely better and nobler national existence.

I have no doubt whatever that to the Americans, above all other people almost, it will prove to be good to have been afflicted and in trouble.

You ask of my winter plans. I have made none beyond the 1st of December, up to which date I have taken a lodging at No. 5, Park Place, immediately opposite my sister's house. I have very nearly relinquished all idea of going abroad, for if she and her children are to spend the winter in England, I do not think I shall make up my mind to leave it. From what you say about not seeing me if I go on the Continent, I suppose you must have changed your plans, which were, I thought, to spend the winter in Rome. I think to do so would be one's only chance of a summer this year, for anything like the cold and gloom and capricious ungeniality of this pleasant month of August in this southern part of England I never felt. We live with mackintoshes on our arms and umbrellas in our hands. If the crops ripen it can only be from a severe sense of (abstract) vegetable duty, and as in the week we have already spent here we have had no day without rain, so we have had no evening when a fire would not have been quite pleasant. We get the same accounts of the season from London, Ireland, and France; the summer has forgotten the world this year. And yet it is wonderful what we learn to accept and be satisfied with. This morning in my walk, after standing looking dolefully at the grey slate-coloured sky and dark lead-coloured landscape, and wondering if the sun was never going

to shine again, I met a man who cheerily exclaimed
to me as he passed, "A beautiful morning, ma'am."
When I have forgotten what light is, which I learned
in America, I suppose I shall think such mornings
beautiful too. Amen!

Good-bye, dear Arthur. With best love to Mary
Anne, believe me always affectionately yours,

FANNY KEMBLE.

We go from here on the 18th to Bournemouth, and
thence to the Isle of Wight, where I have never been ;
but I expect to return to London by the sixth of next
month. I have seen M—— since her return from
abroad, and thought her greatly changed in appearance, though not looking precisely ill.

Cold Spring, New York State, Friday, June 12th, 1867.

MY DEAR ARTHUR,

I imagine this will not reach you until you
return from my mountains, probably you will get it
in London, on your way up to the Scotch mountains,
which are yours in a properer sense, a good deal more
than the Alps are mine. I hope you will not have
used up all your legs and all your wind this summer
in that blessed earthly Paradise of mine, but that you
will have some left for next year, when, please God, I
will be again in Switzerland, and look up to my
mountains if I cannot climb them. Thank you, very
much, for the two photographs. I think them both very
good and am extremely glad to have them. Give my
very kind regards to Mr. Hintchcliffe. I have often
pleasant visions of him, gathering the beautiful things
by our wayside for us, as we went climbing over the

Wengernalps. I think myself unlucky, never to have met him since.

F—— bids me give you her best love, and tell you that she wrote you ever so long a letter, which she (mis)directed to 18, Wimpole Street, instead of 21; but my confidence in our post-office discretion is great, and I have little doubt that, with a little reasonable delay, it will reach you. I have no doubt she gives you detailed accounts of her Georgia experiences, which is more than I can do, inasmuch as, cousin, I was not there. She has been back with us at the North for nearly a month now, and is busy preparing the old farmhouse, where she and her sister were born,.and where I lived my married life, for her summer residence. The place is lamentably run down at heel, out of order, and out of repair; but she is fixing it, as folks here say, and means to inhabit it until Christmas, after which she contemplates returning to the South. This pendulum sort of life seems not without attractions for the damsel, who finds it in variety and excitement, the indulgence of her unfortunate propensity for what she calls independence, and the exercise of a good many of her better qualities and faculties.

I took leave of her and her sister three days ago, and am now in the highlands of the Hudson, visiting an old gentleman of eighty-four of my father's name, who was one of our first acquaintance and friends when I came a girl to this country. His family must originally have been the same as ours, for they have the same arms and crest, as well as name; and it seems quite strange to hear on all sides the home sounds of Gertrude Kemble, Charles Kemble, Stephen Kemble, **besides** many Richards and Williams, which were not among our christian names, designating the members of a numerous American family, settled in this **country since** the early part of the eighteenth century.

My first visit to this place was made thirty-six **years ago, and in** that time the then almost solitary **dwelling** of **my** friend has become surrounded with **a** populous village, not to say small town, chiefly peopled **with** the men and their families employed in a huge iron foundry, where much cannon is, or used **to** be, cast for the **government,** and which is **a** vast, busy, prosperous establishment, once governed by **my** old host, but now managed by **the** younger men of his family. The place is very lovely, immediately on the brink of the noble Hudson river, and **in the** midst **of** some of its most charming scenery, **the** great Military Academy of West Point is directly opposite, **and** the **whole** neighbourhood is beautiful, but the weather is beyond all precedent, **unsummerlike,** bitterly cold, with dark skies **and** incessant **rain, as** heavy as **thunder** showers, and **as** persistent **as a** drizzle. I never remember such an ungenial June in this country, where the light is generally a brilliant blessing, and the **great** heat a positive curse (for which I find myself almost praying). By-the-by, **one** of **the** young American Kemble girls **was** here **this** morning, exclaiming through her **nose,** "Well, I shall tell **Mr.** Murray [**the clergyman**] to give us the prayer **for fair weather next Sunday;** I am tired of this **wet,**" with which piece of religion and piety, I bid you farewell. Give my kindest love to Mary Anne, and believe me, always, dear Arthur,

Affectionately yours,

FANNY KEMBLE.

Butler Place, Sunday, August 30th, 1868.

Many thanks, my dear Arthur, for your kind letter and for the details of your Alpine trip, and for that fine fellow Melchior's photograph; it looks older than the face I remember seeing for the first time in the charming balcony of the Châlet Seiler at Interlacken; but he is older, so we are all, by three summers, or four, is it, since then? and remembering that I read with astonishment your account of all you were able to do in your short mountain tour. I think the photograph hardens Melchior's face, but still leaves on it that peculiar expression of careworn melancholy which I thought I detected on several of the faces of the men who were pointed out to me as experienced guides. I suppose keeping Miss W—— out of "cracks" on the perilous peaks, where she takes her pastime, is anxious work, and I should think a man of at all sensitive nerves or excitable imagination would find it difficult to forebear pushing her into one, one good time for all, and so relieving his natural anxiety for her safety.

I saw two women (neither of them Miss W——) at Zermatt last summer, who had come up some pass from Orsières, which brought them up to the back of the Matterhorn, and over the Zmutt Glacier, down to Zermatt; they had only one guide, a mere porter, with them, had slept in hay châlets, come over ice and snow, with axe and rope, with all due ceremony, etc.,

were very brick-dusty in complexion, and seemed to
me valiant females of the W—— stamp. One was
middle-aged, and the other young. I do not know
who they were.

Your letter reached me at this place, the home of
my very sad married life, and I am writing to you
now in the room where my children were born—*my
room*, as it is once more called. It is full twenty-six
years since I last inhabited it. When my children
ceased to be among the richest girls in America (which
they once were), and had to leave this place, to which
they were extremely attached, to go and live in a
Philadelphia boarding-house, this place was let for a
term of years, to people who took no care of it, let it
get completely out of order, and neglected even to
keep the pleasure-grounds tidy or house in repair; and
so it remained, getting more and more dilapidated and
desolate, and passing through a succession of equally
careless and dishonest hands until last April, when the
lease of the last tenant who had taken it expired.
This gentleman's wife died here about two years ago,
whereupon he left the place, shut up the house, leaving
it and his furniture to rot together, and when, early in
May, I came hither to look at its condition, it seemed
to me too damp and too dreadfully out of repair, for
F—— to find it possible to inhabit it during the
summer, which I knew to be her purpose. As for the
garden, Hood's description of that which surrounded
his haunted house is the only one that fitted it.

I went to visit some of my friends early in June,
and remained at Lenox, in Massachusetts, for the
benefit of the mountain air, until a week ago, when

upon F——'s invitation I came hither, and am quite amazed at the transformation the little woman has made in the place. The house, a small, and ridiculously inconvenient farmhouse, built by an old Frenchman hard upon a hundred years ago, and close upon the turnpike road, has been patched, and darned, and bolstered, and propped, and well-aired, dried, and warmed, and she has furnished and fitted up the rooms so prettily, that the old barn really looks charming.

The place has no beauty whatever, the whole ground round the house being quite flat, and the only undulating pretty portions of the farm being meadows, which are not seen from it ; but green grass and fine trees are pleasant objects, and though there is no really large timber near the house, there are enough well-sized picturesque trees to make pleasant shade, and a bowery greenness all round that is charming in itself.

I have spent a very peaceful and happy week here in this my former purgatory, and leave it with infinite reluctance to-morrow, to start on a three months' tour in the West, reading as I run, as far as Niagara, the great lakes, and the Mississippi. I hope to be home again, that is, with my children, the last week in November, and to spend the winter and spring quietly in Philadelphia, and I do hope most fervently to see the Alps next summer. I am sure, from what you write me, that you must be good for my Swiss climbing, and I think you would do well to come and meet me at Meiringen, or that pleasant place of rendezvous, Interlacken, though I am not well pleased with Seiler, for he gave me such a very poor room in his new palace last **year, that I left him in** disgust, and went off to the Giessbach for the **week I had** meant to have spent with **him.** The fact **is,** that unless *one* is a *party* of twenty German-Jew Americans, one **is** no longer worth the while of the Swiss innkeepers, and they are quite unceremonious in making one aware of the fact.

No doubt, my dear Arthur, your heat this summer has been sufficient for you, but most things in this comparatively good world are comparative, and eighty-anything degrees of heat does not sound overpowering to people who have had it *one hundred and five in the shade*, and can tell of six men on one farm struck down with sunstroke **in one** day. The great **fury of** the summer **is** passed with **us,** however, **thank God,** and now **we** may look forward to the **lovely and** splendid American autumn, a season as perfect as **the** Italian spring.

Of course, **with hard** work and hard travelling before **me, I** deprecate **the** heat, **and** indeed shall be very thankful when my three months' task **is** over, especially if it answers **as** well as my three months spring labour **did.** A net result of four thousand four hundred pounds (all my expenses paid, three hundred pounds *given* **away,** and eleven **hundred** *read away gratis* for charities) is a good three months' job—don't you think **so?** Nevertheless, **it is** time, if ever, for me to rest, at least I think and feel so.

God bless you, my dear Arthur, give my most affectionate remembrance to Mary Ann, and believe me,

Ever, **as** ever, yours,
FANNY KEMBLE.

1113, *Walnut Street, Philadelphia,*
Tuesday, January 26th, **1869.**

MY DEAR ARTHUR,

I do not think that many, if any of those
who are affectionately attached to you, can sympathize
more **sincerely than** myself with your present sorrow.
I think of the kind, good, excellent woman [his
mother], whose cordial friendliness **to me** has never
failed for so many years, and my heart sinks with the
sad foreboding that I may not see her again, perhaps,
and then I think **of how** very lonely **her** loss or the
loss of her companionship (which prolonged illness
would be) will make **you, my** dear friends, both. I
have **had a heavy** cry **over your** condition, and **can
only pray God to support and comfort** you both under
the dispensations of his Providence.

How I should rejoice to think that I might find
you relieved from anxiety, **and** Mary **Anne** from
suffering, when **I come to** England, as I hope to do in
June.

Dear Arthur, I suppose from what I know of my
own rate of earning, **or** as you say "manufacturing"
*greenbacks** that the amount of Mr. Dickens's earnings
has been probably **as violently** exaggerated as that of
mine was. Of mine **I will** now give you the history.
In six months I have earned seven thousand pounds in
greenbacks (that is, about four thousand **three** hundred
pounds **in gold).** During those six months my expenses
of living amounted **to** twelve hundred pounds in
greenbacks (about nine hundred in *real* money), which

* The paper **money circulated after the** war by the United
States Government.

leaves me in round numbers six thousand pounds in greenbacks, or four thousand in *real* money to invest. I do not know whether that comes up to or exceeds what you supposed my earnings to have amounted to, but it falls most ludicrously short of the sum which popular report has rewarded my exertions with.

Now let me tell you something of the chapter of expenses as they are at present in America. I have just settled myself in Philadelphia in a lodging, which I shall occupy until the end of May; it consists of two rooms, a bedroom and sitting-room, opening with folding doors, and both together making one about the size of my drawing-room at St. Leonards. Here I take my meals, sleep, live, move, and have my being. Ellen and Louis, my two servants, have a room a-piece, and all are furnished with sufficient and sufficiently good food, and for this board and lodging for me and mine I pay twenty-seven guineas a-week, which makes fourteen hundred a-year, for the roof over my head and the bit and sup I live on; now, with all the addition that my late earnings will yield to it, my income amounts to little more than seventeen hundred a-year, so that you will perceive I have just three hundred pounds a-year to pay my servants' wages, my own clothes, my carriage-hire, travelling—in short, every necessary expense but food and lodging, and everything here is at the same exorbitant rate of prices, so that having worked, and worked very hard, to make a sufficient income to enable me to live very uncomfortably here, I have hardly done it, and am not a little saddened by the fact. However, I am coming to Europe for a year, in June, and shall determine during that time the best way of making an income of seventeen hundred a-year, sufficient for a single old woman!

I had a letter from F—— to-day from the plantation, written in rather a depressed state of spirits. The old leaven of personal attachment, which survived for a short while among the negroes after their emancipation, or perhaps the natural timidity of absolute ignorance which possessed and paralyzed them at first, is rapidly passing away, and they are asserting their natural and divine right to cultivate happiness (that is, idleness) instead of cotton and rice at any price ; and F——, who over-estimated the strength of their old superstitions, is beginning to despond very much. For my own part, the result seems to me the only one to have been rationally expected, and I have no hope whatever that as long as one man, once a planter, and one man, once a slave, survives, any successful cultivation of the southern estates will be achieved. Indeed, it seems to me most probable that, like other regions long cursed by the evil deeds of their inhabitants, the plantations will be gradually restored to the wild treasury of nature, and the land " enjoy its sabbaths " as a wilderness, peopled with snakes, for perhaps a good half century yet. I do not know why the roots of slavery should be grubbed out of the soil a day sooner. It is unlucky, no doubt, for the present holders of southern property, but then the world has laws, and I do not know that the planters of the southern states were sufficiently meritorious folk to have earned a miracle, especially a very immoral one for their heirs.

God bless you, my dear old friend, give my most affectionate remembrance to Mary Anne, and believe me,

Ever, as ever, your truly attached,

FANNY KEMBLE.

Widmore, Bromley, Sunday, February 18th, 1872.

MY DEAR ARTHUR,

I am very much grieved and distressed at all the melancholy trouble in which you are involved, and to which, I am afraid, there is not soon likely to be a termination. I sincerely hope your apprehensions, with regard to Miss W——, may prove so far unfounded that she may find in her youth a sufficient power of resistance to the evil that threatens her.

My dear old friend, I am grieved to think of you surrounded with sadness and suffering; but can only remember that it is more blessed to minister to others than to be ministered to.

I got your letter yesterday evening, and had been in town in the morning; but am not certainly likely to be there again for at least a week.

I am sure your not going to Rome is a great disappointment to my child, and I regret extremely for her your change of plans. The Roman winter would have been good for you too, body and soul, and though I am here and not there, and so the gainer, I wish heartily that you were there and not here.

My dear old friend Donne is lecturing on Shakespeare, and I have heard him, these last two times. He is looking ill and feeble, and I should like to carry him off too, out of the reach of his too many and too heavy cares.

I hope you will soon **be able to come** down here again. Walter is **gone; but M——** and L—— always rejoice to see you, **and so, you know,** does yours, very affectionately,

F. A. KEMBLE.

I know you will be glad **to** hear that Adelaide has **been down here to** see me.

Macugnaga, Val Ansasca, **Sunday,** *August 17th.*

DEAR ARTHUR,

I write **to** you from an old mountain haunt **of yours, from** the head of **the Val** Ansasca, which you have often told **me** you thought **the most** beautiful valley you knew, and certainly **it** is wonderfully beautiful, **and** deserves all you **ever said** in its praise; **and** here at the foot of these rocky ramparts of Monte Rosa, I receive your letter from Stoneleigh, telling me, **to my** very great regret, of Mrs. Malkin's indisposition there, and **of her not** being able to walk with you through that lovely deer-park, which **is as** perfect in its own peculiar sylvan beauty as such a place can be. I, **too,** cannot help regretting J——'s **leaving** that beautiful English home of his; **but** people must live their own life, and this experiment **has to be** tried. I **follow** wearily enough **across that** often-traversed **ocean, these my magnets,** who **are** all drawing me **thither; perhaps,** when the L——s return to England, I may **be alive** and come back with them; but two years is **too far** to look forward and speculate about anything, especially a life of sixty-four.

My Switzerland this year has been turned topsy-**turvy by my** poor young man-servant's illness. I have, however, seen Evolena and Macugnaga, and shall now, I think, go to the Eggischhorn for the rest of my time, to look once more at as many of the great mountain tops as I can see at once, and, I suppose, for the last time. I was disappointed rather in Evolena, though it is both picturesque and beautiful; but my journey up the Val d'Erence was not made under happy circumstances. The mule-path of former years is now turned into what they call a road, without any exception the most dangerous (in some places I think frightfully so) I ever saw. It is true it is not finished yet, for the guards and parapets along the sides of the deep precipices and at the turns of the steep zigzags are yet wanting, and in no one place, except the village of Useigne, is the road wide enough to admit of two vehicles of any kind passing each other. Up this steep and narrow way we crawled for nearly seven hours, in a light sort of cart with one horse, whom the driver led every step of the road. The sun poured upon us with the most intense glaring heat, and both my maid and myself were quite ill in consequence of our exposure for so many hours to the broiling temperature reflected from the rocks and stones and blinding white dusty path up which we were dragged. I had intended to remain a week at Evolena, but found the little mountain inn very full and so uncomfortable that I determined to leave it the next day, and did so, stopping to be very unwell two days at Sierre, in consequence of my trip up that valley of my imaginations. As for mountain expeditions, they have come to an end for me, my dear Arthur. I can no longer endure the fatigue of riding, or even being carried all day long up and down steep mountain sides. I have lost all the elasticity and spring which enabled me to carry my own fourteen stone weight comfortably either in the saddle or the chaise à porteurs, and an injury to my right foot, of which I broke one of the small bones in the instep a year ago at Stoneleigh, makes climbing up or down on foot impossible. So my Switzerland is over. I may still drive over the great magnificent mountain passes by the carriage roads, or haunt the lovely shores on the lakes, should I live to see this world again; but the shoulders of the Alps are no more for me, as their summits are no more for you, my dear friend. There is a time for all things, and mine is come for *platitudes.*

God knows how grateful I am for all I have enjoyed in this most wonderful and beautiful country. I am staying here at Lochmatter's. The quarters are rough, but quite comfortable enough, and he and his sister-in-law do everything in their power to make them so. He killed an old cow the other morning that I might have the meat, dear to Britons, and got wet to the skin in a tremendous thunder shower yesterday, trying to catch some trout for me in the lovely brook at his door. I hobbled up the valley the day before yesterday to the Moraine and back, and looked up at the Moro Pass, up which Lochmatter says nothing would be easier than to have me carried (I don't think he would like to take a hand at it himself), but I shall try no more such experiments with the backs of my fellow-creatures. Not many people have come up the valley or over the passes since we have been here One Englishman wanted extremely to go over by the Weissthor, but he had a tail of women, and was obliged to take them over the Moro— so much for impedimenta. An English clergyman is here with his wife, and he prayed and preached to her, me, and Ellen, this morning for whole congregation. He comes from a crowded parish at Croydon, and his wife seems to me to pine for pavements and polite existence. She says she feels as if she was in a trap here, and certainly this magnificent *cul de sac* looks a little like a huge trap for creatures without wings. I enjoy it immensely, and am delighted to have come hither at last, and think it a very fit place from which to greet you, my dear old friend, and send my kindest regards to Mrs. Malkin, and sign myself,

Ever, as ever, affectionately yours,

FANNY KEMBLE.

1812, *Rittenhouse Square, Philadelphia, February 7th*, **1874.**

MY DEAR ARTHUR,

I have no silver paper (which I do not think golden) to write to you upon, and hope your eyes will approve of this, which I trust my three postage stamps will carry to you, "regardless of expense." Your letter coming this morning made me feel rather susperstitious; it is the second communication which has reached me latterly from persons I had not heard from for some time, but of whom I had been vividly thinking just before I did so; and this morning, just before the arrival of the postman with your letter, I was musing upon your long silence, and wondering if your later relations and ties were obliterating the memory of old and absent friends. This rather painful cogitation was very pleasantly dispelled by your letter, for which and all its kind words of affection I thank you very sincerely.

I have heard from my poor sister several times. Her grief is unspeakable, and I sit and cry and lament here over her sorrow, helpless to comfort her, and longing only that I were with her to express my infinite pity for her misery, as no words, written or spoken, can do. Poor soul, I almost doubt if even time will help her. She writes me with amazement herself at the fact that her health has not suffered from this dreadful blow. A—— is engaged to General Grant's only daughter. They made acquaintance on board ship, having crossed from England in the same steamer, since which A——, who is in the Western States (not in Canada), met the young lady, and became more intimate with her, at St. Louis, which is, I believe, the home of her mother's family. I understand General Grant has made it a condition of the marriage that his daughter is not to live out of this country, in which case A—— will have to expatriate himself, a thing oftener done by women for their husbands than by men for their wives.

I grieve for the no grouse, and do not think the affluence of rabbits any compensation, the one being in my judgment the worst, as the other are the best of *feræ naturæ*. To be sure, you may have the advantage of quoting, with a realizing sense of its pertinency, the famous rabbittical grace, "for rabbits hot, for rabbits cold," etc. Perhaps I may see Corrybrough again—who knows? If I live two years, I

expect to return to Europe, and that includes Corrybrough as well as other places, of which, if I live, I
hope to renew my memories.

I have been very unhappy about Donne, and
anxious for news of him. B—— and Edward Fitzgerald both wrote me word how ill he had been; both
also that he was better, and B—— added that he
purposed soon writing to me; but that is now some
time ago, and I have not heard from him, and cannot
help fearing that he is again ill.

The L——s write from the South of a satisfactorily
large rice crop, which (as it is an ill wind that blows
nobody good) will probably be enhanced in value by
this miserable Indian scarcity.

S——, to whom I gave your message, did not
appear to me painfully conscious of not deserving it.
She is remarkably well this winter, in good looks and
good spirits; sees a great deal of Philadelphia society,
and grows fat upon it, which shows, I hope, that it
agrees with her. I am sorry to say I do not think
her husband by any means as flourishing; he suffers
frequently from neuralgia in his eyes, which sounds
as if it ought to be horrible. They and I expect to
become country mice in the spring, when the houses
we expect to inhabit are expected to be ready for use.
The W——s will take up their abode in the house,
which was my married home, where both my children
were born, which calls itself, rather pretentiously,
"Butler Place," and I in a house, known as the York
Farm, on the same property, but divided from them
by a road, across which, however, we can throw stones
at each other's windows, though we may not quite

shake hands. Meantime, I hope to have F—— and her husband here by the beginning of May, which month they will pass here in town with me, and then we shall probably all go to the country together. J—— has some notion of going out to the West some time during the summer, and the winter will, of course, take them back to Georgia to carry out their southern experiment and determine whether any good result is to be obtained there or not.

I have nothing to say about myself, dear Arthur, having told you what concerns me most in telling you of my children. My grandson came home at Christmas, looking well and in high spirits, and went back after six weeks with some small abatement of good looks and spirits, but no more than naturally comported with Christmas diet and return to school. He is very clever indeed, and I think may turn out a remarkable engineer, towards which vocation all his tastes, at present, seem to incline. That he will be a *book* man, I doubt; I think he will never be a hard student of anything but mechanical powers, natural laws of force and motion, and the results to be derived from them as applied to machinery.

I am growing very old very fast, nothing loth, and all the senses and the little sense I ever had diminish daily; but I do not know that any one but myself is the worse for that. I shall not rival Miss Sterling Graham, I am quite sure; but while I remain, shall remains always affectionately yours,

FANNY KEMBLE.

Please thank your wife for her kind remembrance of me, and give her my best love.

York Farm, *Branchtown, Monday,* **July** *27th,* 1874.

Many hearty thanks from all of us, dear Arthur, **for your and your** wife's kind congratulations. We **are more proper** objects than the common run of folk for **such congratulations, under our** circumstances, because **we had** sufficient cause for more than usual anxiety **as to the event.** God be thanked, **all** has **gone most** prosperously. The mother is recovering **admirably, and, I** trust, is henceforth to be a sound **woman ;** and the **child** is a very fine, healthy creature ; **and we are all very happy, and were** touched with **gratitude by the expression of your** cordial sympathy.

I have, of course, no news to give you, for my life **is now nothing but very** peaceful and happy monotony. **S—— and her husband are just across** the **road, and I heard their boy practising on the** piano this morning **before our breakfast, which gives you a measure** of **our near** neighbourhood. **He is at home just now** for **his summer** holidays, taller than his mother, very **clever, and not** otherwise than **a** good and an amiable **lad.**

Your account of your niece's experience with her **doctors,** regular **and** irregular, revived a **very** vivid **disgust** which **I feel whenever I** think **of the** treat-**ment F——** was made to undergo for nearly **two years, some part of which,** I feel well convinced, was **much worse than** useless **to her.**

I have heard since I received your letter from **Donne, who tells me of** his resigning the theatre licencership—a gain of peace and quiet, no doubt ; but **a loss of** pounds, shillings, and pence, which, I fear, he **can ill afford. Does he not** receive some pension upon retiring from office? . . . I am very sorry he cannot have the cheer and refreshment of going up to Corrybrough.

Our summer here has been tolerably temperate *for here.* The thermometer has averaged ninety degrees, sometimes as many as a hundred, but oftener standing about eighty-six. There has been almost continual drought; and living on the very edge of a market high-road, as we do, we are as white with dust as millers, and long incessantly for the beneficent water from the skies, which will not fall upon us for all our entreaties.

I have a large drawing of the lower end of the Lake of Geneva hanging over my writing-table, and, as the "hart pants for the living waters," I look at it, and then *gasp* at the thought of the dear mountains.

Good-bye, and **God bless you,** dear Arthur. I know not how long J—— purposes prolonging his experiment of life in America; I, if I live, shall return to England next year.

With kindest love from all here, believe me, ever yours affectionately,

FANNY KEMBLE.

York Farm, Branchtown, Philadelphia,
Friday, July 30th, 1875.

MY DEAR ARTHUR,

I never reckon with my friends, because I am in the habit of thinking that I receive a great deal more from them all than I am in the least entitled to; but I was beginning to think it a very long time since I had seen your handwriting, and was, therefore, all the better **pleased** when I received your last letter. I am very glad, my dear Arthur, that you went to Warsash and saw Adelaide. I **am** sure it would have been a pleasure to you and a comfort to her, for the old early marks of love and friendship may *subside* under the surface of newer circumstance; but they **only go** deeper in, and join the memories which are those that alone survive and are vivid to the last.

S—— **has** been very far from well lately, and so, I am sorry to say, has her husband, who, nevertheless, has resumed the practice of his profession, and **is working very** hard **just now,** the summer being always the sickly season here. Their boy is at home for his holidays, **a great, tall, broad fellow of** fifteen, amiable **and well disposed,** and extremely clever. I am afraid he will not work; otherwise, I think he would be a remarkable person. **He writes** good verses, and has an extraordinary talent for music, and is altogether unusually well endowed with capacity. My other grandchild, **the little L——** baby, is a very delicate little creature at present, but has *held on* to her life through **its** feeble **and** puny beginning with such a **good** *will*, that I think there is enough **of** that to **make a constitution out of** it.

The summer hitherto here has been the reverse of **yours, dry and** dusty and oppressively hot; a long **two months of** broiling, with hardly a bucketful of rain **to put it out; but we** hear of floods and torrents in every other direction—France, England, Australia. I should think **our** turn must come for a wash and a drink. The winter is terrible here; but the summer **is** awful, and not at all awfully jolly. I wish I was

on the heather mountains at this present writing, or
looking into the salmon pool in the Findhorn at the
Straus.

Good-bye, dear Arthur.   Remember me kindly to
your wife, and keep me always in mind as your
always very affectionately,

FANNY KEMBLE.

What a wonderful old she Claverhouse that Miss
Sterling Graham is ! I should like to send my respects
to her.

York Farm, Branchtown, Philadelphia,
Saturday, November 27th, 1875.

MY DEAR ARTHUR,

I am sixty-six years old to-day. It is my
birthday, and has not been by any means a cheerful
one to me, for it began with the departure of F——
and her husband and baby for the South. Of course
this is rather a doleful event. We lose them for five
months at least, and as F——is expecting her confinement in January, of course her absence will be an
eventful season, and I shall feel very anxious till
I hear all has gone well with her. They have gone
by sea, sailing in a fine new steamer from this port,
and though I think they determined wisely in doing
so, the land journey being long and very fatiguing,
still, in spite of possible railroad accidents, I think one
always feels as if a sea voyage involved more risk.
However, the weather is fine now, with every
appearance of continuing so, and their voyage is only
of two days' duration, so I hope all will go well with
them. Their departure leaves a sad blank in my life.

I miss them all extremely, even to J——'s beautiful dog, of which I am very fond, and which is very much devoted to me.

I read your letter, in family conclave assembled, for you have become my children's friend as well as mine, and we all take part in the success of the grouse shooting, and whatever may be your plans for the winter.

The idea of the Pyrenees is very charming, and I do not wonder Mrs. Malkin inclines thither, though I remember that when I was there, great as was my admiration for them, I felt rather as if I was guilty of infidelity to the Alps all the time, and made haste back to the latter, with something of penitence in my delight at being once more upon *my* mountains.

S—— and her husband *mind* what you say, in the Scotch sense of hearing; whether they do in the English sense of heeding is another matter.

About their going back to Europe, and his having a month or so with you and the grouse at Corrybrough, they would both be the better for leaving this country again, where life, for some reason or other, is more difficult and more exhausting than anywhere else in the world, but their boy's studies cannot be interrupted, and they cannot leave him here and betake themselves abroad, so that I see little chance of their moving for at least a couple of years.

I suppose I shall return to England, if I live, next year, and I believe F—— and her husband intend to do so, and if I do come back, it will probably be to take some sort of residence in London, for little as I have loved that great city of my birth all my life,

I suppose it is the best place upon the whole for a lonely old woman to live in, on account of all the conveniences of civilization, and such social intercourse as I may be still fit for, which indeed is not much now.

The B——s were Adelaide's friends, not mine, though I knew them at her house. I liked Mrs. B—— the best of the two. What an extraordinary mimic he was. His imitation of my brother John was so like, both in matter and manner, that with my eyes shut I could have sworn, had he been alive, that he was himself speaking to me. I think the effect of that sort of wonderful imitation is surprising, but not agreeable; there is something *uncanny* in thus going out of yourself and becoming somebody else.

We have had Lord Houghton here, running about the United States, and being crowned with honour and glory, and garlands, and laurels, and made an enormous lion of. If he writes a book about the country, which I think he will, he is certainly bound to speak well of such fervent admirers as he found here.

FANNY KEMBLE.

York Farm, Branchtown, Philadelphia,
Friday, February 11th, **1876.**

MY DEAR ARTHUR,

I received your kind letter to-day with the friendly enclosure of your congratulation to poor F——. This, however, I have taken upon myself to suppress, with, I felt very sure, your approbation of my doing so. . . .

S—— has gone down to the plantation to cheer and sustain her sister, so that O—— and I remain in a state of rather forlorn forsakenness.

I was a good deal interested in the story of your young neighbour. Poor young widow, it seems to me that of all pathetic plights, that of a woman bearing the child of a dead husband is one of the most pitiful.

In my sister's last letter to me, she told me that they were thinking of taking a house in London, large enough to hold them all—Algernon, Sartoris, and Gordon's, children and children's children. She spoke as if it would be a great effort to her to see any society again, but that she thought she ought to do it for the sake of the young ones. So I dare say you will again have many pleasant hours of your old friendly inter-course with her.

I have seen some of the accounts and critiques of Mr. Irving's acting, and rather elaborate ones of his "Hamlet," which, however, give me no very distinct idea of his performance, and a very hazy one indeed of the part itself, as seen from the point of view of his critics. Edward Fitzgerald wrote me word that he looked like my people, and sent me a photograph of him to prove it, which I thought much more like Young than my father or uncle. I have not seen a play of Shakespeare's acted I do not know when. I think I should find such an exhibition extremely curious as well as entertaining.

Dear Donne writes to me now but seldom. I believe it is something of an effort for him to do so. I get reports of him through Edward Fitzgerald, and fear from them that he must be a great deal broken.

I read his review of Macready's life as well as the book itself, which I found extremely interesting from the strong peculiarity of the man's character. How curious it seems to me that he could care, as he did, for his profession, having none of the feeling of contempt and dislike for it *itself* that I had, and then dislike and despise it because he thought it placed him socially in an inferior position to other professional men, or gentlemen of other professions!—that seems to me an incomprehensible thing. I do not think any of my people ever looked at their calling in this fashion, but Macready was a very honest man, and that and his "curst" temper (Shakespeare, you know) give me great sympathy for him.

I saw a very favourable notice in the *Spectator* of a book called "Throslethwaite," and thought I should like to read it, having no idea whom it was written by. But why does not James Spedding exert his *uncular* authority over the lady to give her books easier names for readers not advanced in spelling or pronunciation?

FANNY KEMBLE.

We have had a wonderful, capricious, mild winter. I have rejoiced in its clemency for the poor, the sick, and the aged, and very young, but—my ice-house has not yet been filled, and I am beginning to quake lest there should not come frost cold and hard enough to fill it. "Point de glace, bon Dieu! dans le fort de l'Été—Au mois de Juin!" will be very bad indeed, which don't rhyme, but don't matter.

York Farm, *Branchtown, Philadelphia,*
Sunday, November 19th, 1876.

MY DEAR ARTHUR,

How the "daughter" deals with her correspondence I do not know, but you probably do ; for
me, I am, I flatter myself, perfectly to be relied upon
to answer, like a well-educated ghost, the moment
I am spoken to, and, like a well-educated ghost, never
a moment before.

I have thought more than once lately, that it was
a long time since I had heard from you, and so was
very glad to get my share of your letter, which, having
read, I carried over to S——. I am glad Mr. Hinch-
cliffe was with you at Corrybrough, making a fernery.
I have been reading *of* a book of his—I wish it had
been the book itself—telling of wonderful vegetables
in South America, and wonderful spiders, to run the
risk of meeting one of which all the flowers and ferns
in creation, much as I love them, would not tempt me,
because, you see, a spider is what the French call " my
black beast," and I dread and hate them.

Your story about your legs sitting or standing for
Mr. Baring's, reminded me of a thing Saunders the
miniature painter once told me. He was painting a
likeness of the beautiful Lady Graham (a disastrous
intrigue with whom was almost Charles Greville's first
step in life) and she informed Saunders that, when he
came to her nose, she should bring her sister *to sit for
that*, because her sister's was much handsomer than
her own, which struck me as very droll.

Lawrence's whole career seems to me an exceedingly sad one, and he is so interesting a person himself,

that I always think of his life's struggle with great sympathy and regret. In spite of a good vein of quiet obstinacy, he is not made of the stuff that *wrestles* well with life, perhaps, indeed, on account of the very obstinacy. If people have to live by bread, they should have as few opinions as possible, even about their own business, because one's neighbours always know it better than one's self, in matters of art quite as much as any other matter.

I had a letter from Adelaide the other day, out of reach of grouse. She was at Madame de L'Aigle's, at Frankfort, on her way to spend the winter in Rome with her husband. I hope to be in England by the beginning of February, which, I suppose, will be *early enough* for the wild flowers at Zermatt. I will be sure to meet you there, if I am alive, dear me! how much I should like it! I suppose, old and toothless as I am, I could still sit on a mule, or in a chair. Legs, I have none left, even to stand, much less go upon, and so you see I shall be rather a dilapidated member of your famous club.

The lady you call "dear little Fan," is no more. She is represented by a portly personable body, little inferior to me in size and weight, and with a comely double chin, which I somehow or other have avoided among my many signs of *elderliness*. She and I are living here together, her husband having gone to the plantation to wind up matters there, and place the property in the charge of competent agents, previous to returning to England.

Affectionately yours,

FANNY KEMBLE.

Warnford Cottage, Sunday, 11th.

Many thanks, dear Arthur, for the grouse which flew hither yesterday evening, which we shall eat to your health and our own gratification. I was almost afraid that you had not received the letter I sent to you from Interlacken, till I found an allusion to it in one of your letters to Adelaide. I should have been sorry if it had not reached you, as I thought coming from that charming starting-point of our summer trip together, it would come like the far-away echoes of the Alpine horn, and be accordingly welcome. Here I am, settled for the present, I and my child, in a tiny tenement, with a tiny lawn and tiny flower-beds before, and a tiny kitchen-garden and shrubbery behind it. It is just one of those sort of places where very world-weary folk long to nestle down, and I am more than content to have found such a perch close to my sister's gate. I have taken it till April, and, as far as I can at present judge, shall be glad to renew my lease at that time without prejudice to my pilgrimage to Switzerland in the summer. We ended our mountain life at Chamounix, and both F—— and I agreed that the Riffle was far finer than anything attainable by us at Chamounix. I went up to the Flegère with her, and crossed the Mer de Glace from the Montanvert to the Chapeau, my first, and certainly last, experiment upon the glacier, as I thought the Mauvais Pas an exceedingly disagreeable place, and myself a great fool for going to it. I had never approached Chamounix from Geneva before—always from Martigny—and was enchanted with the drive from Salanche to Chamounix, and with a place opposite

Salanche, where we slept, called Saint Martin, which I thought lovely, in which opinion I was, of course, much comforted to find that Mr. Ruskin endorsed me. I really think the Alpine Club men **are** becoming a little **too** "sassey," when nothing will serve them for a hobby but a thundering avalanche. F——, after reading Tyndall's letter in the *Times*, said she should like to have been of the party, even if her hair should have turned white with fright. For my part, the watch seems to me to be the only reasonable member of the expedition ; but what a fine thing of that guide to jump into that "crack" as he did.

God bless you, and thank you again for the wild *fowls*.

Your affectionate,
FANNY KEMBLE.

Warnford Cottage, Wednesday, **19th.**

DEAR ARTHUR,

Yesterday morning's post brought yours and **Mary Anne's** welcome letters, and yesterday afternoon brought a delightful **box of bonny** birds from the heather-land. They **were all** wrapped in paper, and so, I suppose, died on **the same day, and** may be all eaten **on the** same day—eh ? I **sent up** two brace to **Adelaide,** thinking **the** supply quite too munificent **to** be **intended for the** cottage ; but told her that, in the event **of your sending any** to the hall, I should expect **precise** repayment. **Was** not that all right ? And pray do not **read this into** a hint to send her grouse, for I thought your present good for two **(and many more besides).**

Oh! that dreadful Matterhorn, **at** whose stony feet those **poor men** were flung down to die, how often the awful figure, with its countenance of undistinguishable blackness and its hood and huge sweeping mantle of snow, rises before the eyes **of** my memory! Stony-hearted, dreadful image, how much more terrible she looks to me now than ever! and yet I hope to see her again if I live till next summer. I **am** going **to** write **to Mary Anne, and** so, with my best courtesy for **the** grouse, remain always affectionately yours,

FANNY KEMBLE.

Banisters, Southampton, Thursday, 22nd.

MY DEAR ARTHUR,

"Please the **pyx**," I will sniff Corrybrough air on the 10th **or 11th of next** month. Would **it not** be possible for Marie to lodge at one of the neighbouring **cottages, so as not to** take **up your** room **or rooms** unnecessarily, as her services to me are all performed at stated hours, and are never required when once I **am** dressed **for dinner?** (I have *undone* myself for many **years past, as most of my** friends know.) **If** this would be in **the least** a lightening of Mary Anne's burden, let it **be thought** of and done. I am distressed to hear of **my** little footpage's indisposition. **As for** the **unfortunate Smut,** has he dreams, I wonder, **of** women **weighing twelve stone four.** His nightmare **will sit, contrary to custom, on his back.** Tell him, **however, for my sake,** that there **are yet** heavier females **in** existence **than** myself. **Adelaide** and I were weighed at **Windsor, and** our united ponderosity amounted to—what do you think?—twenty-seven stone four.

Oh, how Mary Anne must have appreciated those inexpressible oak trees, and how you must have enjoyed riding over the forest turf. I am indeed very sorry that we could not have met at the Grove, for you two would have certainly made my stay there pleasant, whereas it was extremely the reverse, and occasioned me many reflections on the peculiar moral gifts by which the most absolute physical comfort, luxury, and satisfaction might be rendered utterly unavailing to content, and the most fortunate combination of external circumstances neutralized for all purposes of happiness, or even pleasure, by the absence of a few mental graces. More of this when we meet. My love to Mary Anne, respects to the rest of your circle, human and canine.

Always, dear Arthur, yours most truly,

FANNY KEMBLE.

Do the flies that catch fish in the Tweed suit those of the Findhorn? I shall pay a visit on my way up to you near Melrose, and shall get my tackle there. However, they will know there what I ought to take up to you, wherewith to betray tawny-finned fish. Do not fail to write me word if I can bring you anything up from London or Edinburgh. I should be so glad to be useful in any such way. I am tired of being so highly ornamental and nothing else.

30, *Marina, St. Leonards-on-Sea, Friday, 22nd.*

MY DEAR ARTHUR,

If you prefer the proceedings of a woman who won't answer your letters to those of one who will, I can't help it. "Disgustibus" (which you may not recognize as "de gustibus," etc.; therefore I translate it for you; it is my way of reading the Latin proverb, and means whatever disgusting things people may like; there is no telling). As for me, I was godly brought up, and in the faith that I was not to speak till I was spoken to, and when I was spoken to, *I was,* *i.e.* to speak.

Thank you for all the home and personal history of Corrybrough and its doings. I am sorry the Findhorn has drunk two girls, but I am not sorry I waded it over my knees for all that.

I have just come in wringing wet with spray and mist from standing by the sea, which is furiously retreating from the shore, apparently much against its will. The wild west wind is driving the big waves of the Atlantic into the Channel, and cramming and piling them on the shore here, which seems almost too small, as our "sleeve," as the French call it, is too narrow for them. It is a grand sight, and makes one wish that one had the Fribourg organ in one's breast, that one might sing aloud, "Glory to God."

I was as far north as Edinburgh till the 19th of December, and then received tidings that my dearest friend, Harriet St. Leger, had lost her dearest friend and companion, Miss Wilson, and was remaining in desolate affliction at St. Leonards. Hither, therefore, I came, cutting short and renouncing all engagements, public and private, a reading bout at Hull and thereawa, and the Christmas holidays at Warnford, which was a pang. I came immediately hither to comfort and console as far as it was possible the sorrow of my friend. I shall spend the rest of the winter here with her, and only leave this place when she does, which will be in April, when she will join her family in Ireland, and something or other will become of me, it does not much matter what. I hope to get my nephew Harry into the Inland Revenue Office some time this summer, and I hope to get myself into Switzerland about the same time. Oh, how I wish I had heard your mountain talk with your climbing friend! Surely if I had been a man I should have lived on a peak, died in a crevice, and been buried in an avalanche. I wish you would go off to those Dauphiné Alps. You do not know anything about them, and they are stupendous.

Of Adelaide I can tell you the newest news, for I had to go up to London on business yesterday, and dined and spent the evening in town—the day before yesterday, I mean—she having come up to London on pleasure (her children's, of course). She was not looking or feeling ill for a woman who had been to a ball the night before, driving twelve miles for that purpose, and returning to her home at four o'clock in the morning. She reported well of herself, and seemed in good spirits. May and Greville were with her, and were making her go through a course of burlesque at the small theatres, a kind of thing that generally makes me sick, but agrees very well with her. Edward and the younger boy had remained at Warnford, not having any call to Lady Waldegrave's ball. They all returned, my sister and the boy and girl, to Warnford to-day.

My life here is that which I most love—monotony itself, with a person whom I love very dearly. I write infinite letters and sonnets on the American war, practice good music, which I play and sing very vilely, read Kingsley's sermons and Mendelssohn's letters, and harrowing French novels to my friend to cheer and soothe and excite her, and finally, go daily and get a shower-bath of salt sea spray, from which I derive much more benefit than my clothes. So farewell.

Yours affectionately,
FANNY KEMBLE.

Our friend D——'s sons infuriate me with their empty pockets and connubial bliss. I think it such monstrous selfishness. I am doing all I can to compensate him for it, *i.e.* working diligently an armchair in tapestry for him.

[The last few letters, date unknown.]

Queen Anne's Mansions, Saturday, September 6th, 1879.

Your welcome letter, my dear Arthur, was almost the *best* welcome home that could have met me on my return, for it loosened my miserable heartstrings, and gave me a freer flow of tears than I have been comforted by, or relieved by rather, since this blow struck me [the death of my sister]. Oh yes! you knew and loved her very well, and her death will have carried you back in sorrowful memory through how many years of constant friendly affectionate intercourse to the bright days when we were all young together, and now "behold I, I alone am left," of the four children of my father, left behind by them all, two of whom in natural course of human existence should have survived me. My friend, I am so sad that I can hardly bear myself. I got back here yesterday, and am glad to rest and be still; but that I shall see her no more, here, anywhere, on this earth seems to me still *incredible*.

Dear Arthur, F—— has written to me how kind you have been to her, and how much her husband has enjoyed the sport you have afforded him. Thank you for them, I have a long habit of gratitude to you; my children inherit excellent friends from me, I am thankful to think.

My Switzerland has been different from any other I ever experienced, I have gone from one charming *hill-top* to another, always lifting mine eyes to the mountains in loving worship. My last fortnight was spent at Glion, where the Dent du Midi is seen from base to summit, at the entrance of the Rhone valley above the waters of the lake, and on the one day I spent at Geneva the whole mass of Mont Blanc was revealed in more magnificence than I ever saw it before from the city. But my whole summer has passed now under a cloud of sorrow that has darkened it, even in its brightest days.

God bless you, my dear friend. Give my kind remembrance to your wife, I am always

Very affectionately yours,

FANNY KEMBLE.

27, Grosvenor Street, London,
Saturday, February 3rd, 1883.

MY DEAR ARTHUR,

You asked me some questions with regard to the sale of the slaves on our southern property, which I could not immediately **answer**, for with a very **vivid** recollection of much tribulation in my middle life, the details **of a great deal of** sorrow are, thank God, dim in the distance, and from **the** blessed effect **of** many happier years.

The former slaves, for they were all free when my children inherited the estate, may have been some that were not carried to Savanah for sale, or they may have been former slaves of their aunt, Mrs. John Butler, their uncle's widow, who owned part of the property. At the time of the sale of those who had been *my* slaves, the *Times* newspaper devoted two long columns to the account of the circumstance and of their proprietor, supposed to be interesting to English readers, on account of their connection with *me*, and during the war, on its being mentioned that their owner was in trouble in the North for his southern *proclivities*, there was rather a sarcastic article on his having, by that sale, sagaciously taken abolition by the forelock, which was not true. The slaves were sold to pay their owner's debts, his own estimate of which amounted to one hundred thousand pounds, the result of gambling on the Stock Exchange. The sale of his slaves, to which he was compelled, caused him extreme pain and mortification. I do not know how much or how little of this his children know, but the condition of things, liable to such results, can neither be held happy for slaves or slave-holders.

Believe me, always affectionately yours,

FANNY KEMBLE.

THE END.

PRINTED BY WILLIAM CLOWES AND SONS, LIMITED,
LONDON AND BECCLES. *J. D. & Co.*